Gu:

Jade Winters

Guilty Hearts

by Jade Winters

Published by Wicked Winters Books

Copyright © 2014 Jade Winters

www.jade-winters.com

All rights reserved. This book or any portion thereof may not be reproduced or used in any manner whatsoever without the express written permission of the author.

All characters in this publication are fictitious and any resemblance to real persons, living or dead, is purely coincidental.

ISBN: 978-1-494-95869-5

Other titles by Jade Winters

Novels

143
A Walk Into Darkness
Caught By Love

Novellas

Talk Me Down From The Edge

Short Stories

The Makeover
The Love Letter
Love On The Cards
A Story Of You

To Ali
For always making the impossible – possible.

## PROLOGUE

Rachel checked her watch — 11:00 p.m. Relief flooded her. Having made a ten minute dash from Kings Cross tube station, she had arrived at the pub just on time. After a long, stressful day at the office she was in desperate need of some light relief — *and God was she looking forward to it*. As she took a seat at the bar she pushed back loose strands of hair from her face and studied her reflection in the bar's mirror, adjusting her low-cut bodice until it revealed more of her womanly attributes.

She scanned the busy room, looking for her date but her attention was quickly drawn behind her, as two women, engaged in a raging argument, knocked over a table. Beer glasses shattered on the wooden floor, spraying dark liquid in every direction.

"Some people really shouldn't drink," the bartender said to Rachel, shaking her shaven head as she placed a Jack Daniels and Coke in front of her. "Special delivery from the woman at the end," she added as she walked away and called another employee to sort out the mess.

Rachel leaned forward, craning her neck to look past the row of women blocking her view. She caught the eye of the young woman in question and liked what she saw — tall and slender with an edgy pixy haircut and a silver stud piercing the right side of her nose. Barely able to contain her excitement, Rachel raised her glass in the air, then brought it down to her lips, her red lipstick staining the rim as she sipped it slowly. The woman smiled back knowingly and headed in her direction.

"Sadie?" Rachel asked as the woman approached, her gaze leaving her face and falling to the swell of her breasts. The woman's hardened nipples strained against the fabric of the black T-shirt she wore.

Sadie nodded. "And you must be Rachel."

For a few minutes they engaged in small talk, until Rachel leaned in closer, her cheek brushing Sadie's. "Well, shall we go then?"

"Sure," Sadie said, her blue eyes flashing with delight.

With that, Rachel slid off the stool on which she was perched and strode towards the women's toilet, with Sadie in tow. Once in the toilet cubicle, Rachel barely had time to lock the door behind them before Sadie pulled Rachel towards her. She could feel the cotton fabric of her flimsy top being torn apart as Sadie's fingers left livid white prints on her breasts as she squeezed them hard. Rachel gasped in pleasurable pain. She kissed Sadie hungrily, her tongue exploring every inch of the other woman's mouth.

"I want you," Sadie whispered, a fierce urgency in her voice. "Do you want me?" she asked between passionate kisses. "Tell me you want me," she said as she pushed up Rachel's short skirt and dropped to her knees.

Some perverse part of her delighted at seeing Sadie's face burying itself between her legs. "Yes, I want you," Rachel groaned, her voice husky, her knees feeling weak as she gave into the ferocity of the other woman's demand. Minutes later, she let out an uncontrollable scream as she felt a sudden cascading release, her body shuddering uncontrollably.

Sadie stood up smiling, meeting Rachel's eyes with a wolf-like hunger. "Now it's my turn."

\*\*\*

Hours later, in the comfort of her bedroom, Rachel sat behind her desk on a tattered grey swivel chair, surfing her usual website, already searching for her next hook-up. She'd had a crazy night, and she was, as usual, eager to find the next candidate. She scrolled through the names and bio's, not finding anyone who suited her. She passed a few people she recognised as previous 'dates', and a few names she never wanted to see again.

As she continued to trawl through the profiles, the computer chimed with the sound of a new message. Clicking on it, she read the text quickly. *Now this looks interesting.* She clicked the reply button and began typing, a wry smile spreading across her lips.

## CHAPTER 1

Kensington Palace stood a few hundred yards away from a two-bedroom penthouse that spanned the entire length of a handsome period building. Inside the upscale and spacious home, Gareth briefly closed his eyes. "Kathryn, will you *please* tell me what's wrong?" he asked through gritted teeth.

He stood in front of his wife, his tall, broad frame towering over her as she sat reading in their elegant living room. The room was awash with light from the imposing chandelier that dangled from the high ceiling. She had not said anything to imply something was bothering her, but Gareth could read her just as easily as she was reading her magazine.

"What makes you think something's wrong?" Kathryn asked with a prodigious yawn, hardly looking up from the page.

He gave her a narrow stare. "Maybe it has something to do with the fact that you've barely said a word to me all evening," he said, his public school drawl dripping with sarcasm as he spun around and left the room.

Gareth knew his wife was not happy. He had tried everything he could think of to make things better between them. Every move he made, every plan he executed, was a shot in the dark. Not long ago, they had been watching a dramatised screening of a novel on TV called *Tipping the Velvet*. The focus of the story was a lesbian love affair between a male impersonator and a music hall star, set in the 1890s. Halfway through, he had asked Kathryn nonchalantly if they should watch something else, expecting her to say yes. When she failed to respond, he'd glanced over to see her sitting erect at the edge of her seat. The two leading ladies were in the midst of a no-holds-barred sex scene. From the side, he could just about make out the expression on Kathryn's face, her unblinking eyes staring at the TV as though she was looking into another world — one that she wanted desperately to be a part of. He had studied her intently for a long time, when a paralysing moment of insight formed in his mind: could his wife be attracted to women? Gareth knew jumping to conclusions did not always make for happy landings, but he had to find out the truth somehow. As he had lain in bed that night, his dilemma probed and poked at him, keeping sleep at arm's length. His dark inner voice told him that he could never make her happy until he exorcised the demon that lay within her. It was then that it dawned on him. He knew what he needed to do if he had any hope of saving his marriage.

Still feeling aggrieved by Kathryn's indifference, Gareth made his way to his office at the end of the hallway. Flopping down onto his brown leather chair, he switched on his computer. When it came to life, he logged onto the 'Girlz-on-Girlz' website. He had found the site quite accidently when he'd clicked on one of the many annoying sex ads that kept popping up on his screen. What had caught his attention was the fact that the ad was solely for women looking for female partners 'for fun, no strings attached'.

Many of the women in the profiles were attractive by any man's standards. He had registered immediately and it wasn't long before he was emailing a beautiful young woman who promised to be the 'soul of discretion for all those frustrated ladies out there'. She had sounded ideal. *One new message.* He listened closely for Kathryn's footsteps. *I hope it's good.*

As he clicked on the message and began to read, a feeling of jubilation rose within him. *Wonderful! Pandora will go to the bar tonight!* As he clicked 'reply', his fingers took over the function of his brain as he responded with a message that he hoped he wouldn't live to regret. It was his last attempt at trying to salvage his marriage. If Kathryn took the bait, at least he would know what he was up against and could figure out what to do next. *But if she didn't?* He shook his head. He didn't even want to think what that would mean for their relationship.

Stretching his arms out wide, he sighed deeply before standing and making his way back to the living room. "Are you still going out tonight?" he asked as he entered the room. Kathryn was still sitting on the chair, mindlessly thumbing through her magazine.

She glanced up from under her eyelashes. "Yes," she replied, her tone mellifluous and smooth. "Unless you don't want me to. I can always give Jo a call and tell her I can't make it."

"No, no," Gareth said, running his finger around the collar of his pinstriped shirt. "You've seemed out of sorts lately; I think spending time with your friends will do you the world of good."

"You can always come with me," she suggested half-heartedly. "You haven't seen Jo in ages."

He could tell by the way she failed to meet his eyes that it was a gesture made out of pity and she didn't really mean it. "No, it's alright. I think I'll read and watch a bit of telly," he said, turning away from her and busying himself by looking for the TV control.

"Okay, but if you change your mind ...." She glanced down at her watch. "I think I'd better get ready," she said as she rose from her seat. She stopped before leaving the room completely and faced him. "You haven't done anything wrong," she said quietly. "I'm sorry for making it seem as if you had. I've just been feeling frustrated lately."

Gareth's face twisted in confusion. "Frustrated about what?" he asked.

"Just ... life in general. It's nothing you or I could change, it's just —" Kathryn sighed, her piercing blue eyes inscrutable. "It's nothing. Forget I said anything," she said quickly as she turned and disappeared down the hallway.

Gareth slumped onto the sofa and switched on the TV. His manicured thumb tapped the button on the remote control as he absent-mindedly flicked through the channels, quietly dwelling on what his wife had just said to him. His lips twisted into a cynical smile. *She's frustrated? I'm the one who feels more like a father figure than a lover* — the only sex that seemed to takes place in their bedroom was what they watched on TV.

"Did you hear me?"

Kathryn's voice drew him back to the present. With his mind so focused on his troubling thoughts, he hadn't realised how quickly the time had passed. Kathryn had showered, dressed in jeans and a black turtle neck jumper and was standing directly beside him.

"Hmm?"

"I said my cab is here, I'm leaving now. I told you about three times. Are you okay?"

"Yes, sorry. I was in a bit of a daze," he said as he stood up to face her.

"Oh, Gareth, *please* don't dwell on what I said. It didn't mean anything. I'm fine. We're fine."

"Yes, I know. I wasn't dwelling. Go. Have fun," Gareth insisted as he ran his fingers through his silver streaked hair. He had made special plans for tonight, and he didn't want Kathryn to ruin what he had tried so hard to arrange.

## CHAPTER 2

"Her name is Kathryn, and she looks absolutely stunning," Rachel gushed as she applied mascara to her long eyelashes in the minute bathroom mirror.

Dressed in a black waistcoat and black skinny jeans, with her long brunette hair teased up on top of her head, she was excited about the evening ahead. "Look for yourself!" she called out to flat mate, Zoe. "Her photo is still open on my laptop."

"Surely you're not going to go through with it?" Zoe scoffed as she picked the computer up off the floor. She inspected the photo of the woman with thick blonde hair tumbling carelessly past her shoulders, facial bones delicately carved and a tempting curved mouth smiling pleasantly at the camera. Shaking her head, she put it back down.

"You're damn right I am." The determination in Rachel's voice was unmistakeable.

"But she's married, and by the sounds of it, to a right creepy bastard at that," Zoe called back.

"Would you be saying that if it was a woman asking me to meet her husband in a bar to see if he found other women attractive? Besides, I'm only doing it because he sounds as if he really loves her," Rachel said as she entered the cramped living room. She brushed past Zoe, who sat on a faux leather chair, and headed towards a mismatched two-seater sofa. "He just wants to find out if she's attracted to women, that's all," she continued as she sat down, picked up a bottle of wine from the coffee table, and poured a generous amount of the liquid into her empty glass.

"What? He loves her so much he would risk her falling for another woman? Tell me you're not buying that crap. I bet he's using this as an excuse to get his sloppy pecker up." Zoe's features scrunched up as she took a gulp of her bitter-tasting beer. "In fact, it wouldn't surprise me if it's all a set-up, and he's got peepholes in the bedroom wall so he can catch a bit of the action when she brings home unsuspecting victims ... like *you*." She crossed one long, gangly leg over the other and rubbed her hand over her short-cropped hair.

"He doesn't want me to sleep with her, Zoe, he just wants me to flirt a bit," Rachel said. "And anyway he might have got it all wrong. She might not even be gay."

"So what's your plan? How do you intend to snare this poor, unsuspecting woman?"

Rachel shrugged. "I don't know yet. I'll just play it by ear. It will most probably amount to nothing anyway." Rachel fully understood why some married women checked out of intimacy in their relationships. It wasn't that they were having an affair or lusting after the milk man. It all boiled down to feeling like they were being taken for granted.

Yet most long-suffering husbands failed to understand this; they would rather blame an external bogey man for their own failings to make their wives feel special. This wasn't the first time she had heard a husband complain he thought his wife was a lesbian just because she didn't want to jump in the sack with him at every given opportunity.

"If, and I mean *if,* she fails to fall for my charms," Rachel said, fluttering her eyelashes. "I'll just email her husband and tell him either I'm not her type, or she's just isn't attracted to women and the problems they are having are nothing to do with her sexuality."

Zoe took off her gold-rimmed glasses and rubbed her eyes. "And if she does fall for your ploy, are you going to tell her that her own husband went on a hook-up site looking for women to out his wife?"

"Of course I wouldn't. Stop being so pedantic! Why don't we actually wait and see what happens?"

"What is the world coming to?" Zoe asked as she slapped her beer bottle on the coffee table. "I remember the days when, if you wanted some truth from your partner, you just asked them and if you wanted a quick shag you trawled the bars until you got lucky."

"Times have changed since your day, Zoe. Welcome to the age of the Internet. It caters to all sorts, sizes and desires." Rachel smiled. She still found it hard to believe that in all the time she had known Zoe, she'd always been single. She'd not even had a one-night stand, which was surprising given her good looks — tall and slim, with flawless coffee-coloured skin, chiselled features, full lips and a taut body. They had been flatmates for nearly five years, having met when Rachel covered a Gay and Lesbian Pride event. At the time, Zoe was one of the organisers she'd interviewed and having hung out with her for the day, found out that she was looking for a place to live after recently splitting up with her girlfriend. Rachel hadn't hesitated in offering her the spare room in her flat and she'd never regretted doing so. Since then they'd become inseparable, and she now looked at Zoe more like a sister than a friend.

"Hmmm, Internet shagging, sounds like great fun," Zoe said sarcastically.

Rachel grinned at her. "I don't know why you don't have a look at the site yourself. You never know, someone might actually catch your eye!"

"Because I'm not desperate."

"Yet," Rachel said under her breath. She raised her voice slightly. "Anyway, I don't see what the big deal is — married women actually pay people to do this kind of thing all the time. I think it will be fun."

"You call that fun?" Zoe said, pointing to the computer, letting her facial expression elongate her disgust. "Setting a honey-trap for a pervert's wife. Whatever happened to sisterhood?"

Rachel put her glass on the table and reached for her boots, which were laying idly in the centre of the room. "Look, her husband contacted me, not the other way round. I didn't send him a message saying, 'Can I have permission to meet your wife and find out if she's a closet lesbian?' I innocently put an ad on a site for people looking for adult *fun*. I can't help it who responds to my ad."

"What? You want me to believe that there wasn't one woman who was single and fully available on a website of hundreds of women looking for *fun,* as you put it — that you really need to involve yourself with a husband setting a trap for his wife?"

"Jeez, take a chill pill, Zoe!" she said, picking up her black and silver-studded bag from beside the sofa and stuffing her keys and purse into it. "I'm not going to murder the woman." She zipped her bag closed with finality.

Rachel had been taken in by the husband's desperate plea. He just wanted to know where he stood in the grand scheme of things and she didn't blame him — who would want to be married to someone who wasn't a hundred per cent into them? Just thinking of marriage gave her the shivers. She was far from the stage where she wanted to settle down. The mere thought of putting all of her eggs in one basket, with one person, filled her with dread. She had seen too many relationships fall to the way side — especially her parents'.

"You just don't get it, do you?" Zoe asked as she moved forward to the edge of her seat, her expression heated. "It would be different if she contacted you, but she didn't. It's like she doesn't have any say in the whole thing."

Rachel eased herself off the sofa and slid her arms into her jacket. "I'm not going to force her to do anything, Zoe."

"Well ... don't come running to me when it all goes tits up," Zoe said as she replaced the rim of her glasses on the ridge of her nose and took another gulp of beer.

"Don't worry Dr Clemens, I won't have to, because nothing's going to go wrong."

CHAPTER 3

Despite being midweek, *The Grove* bar was busy, with many customers lining the pavement in front of the building, dragging on their cigarettes as if their lives depended on it. Kathryn passed them and stood on the fringe of the crowd at the open doorway. She caught sight of her friend Jo at a square wooden table in a crowded corner and eased her way through the throng, apologising each time she bumped into someone.

"Hey, good to see you, babe," Jo shouted above the commotion of voices. She stood up, opening her arms and pulling Kathryn into a tight embrace. Drawing back, she held her at arm's length. "You're looking good, girl." Jo's shoulder-length black hair hung on either side of her oval face, twisted into fat corkscrew curls.

"Thanks, you too."

"I've got the drinks in," Jo said, laughing as she nodded to the bottle of wine on the table.

"Great," Kathryn replied, taking off her jacket and placing it over the back of a chair. "I need to use the ladies first, I'll be right back."

Having fought her way to the toilet, she pushed open the door to the raucous laughter of two women reapplying their make-up in the mirror. As she looked around, she was relieved to see an empty cubicle. Closing the door behind her, she heard boisterous voices reverberating through the air, then diminishing to barely audible as the women left the room.

Moments later, upon opening the cubicle door, Kathryn was startled at the unexpected sight of a dark-haired woman crouched on the floor near the sink. Kathryn watched her for a few seconds before asking tentatively, "Are you okay?"

The woman turned, then rose to her full height at the sound of her voice. "I'm looking for my earring. Well, trying to. I haven't got my contacts in," she explained, flashing her a grin that could melt ice.

"Would you like me to a have look?" Kathryn asked, having some difficulty averting her gaze from the woman's sensual mouth.

"If you wouldn't mind, that would be great," the woman said as she moved aside so Kathryn could bend down to take her position. "It just has great sentimental value; it belonged to my mother," she continued, seemingly oblivious to the effect she was having on Kathryn.

Kathryn began scanning the floor for the elusive earring, her fingers skating over the tiles. "No luck, I'm afraid."

"Oh well, not to worry. Thanks for looking," she said gratefully, helping Kathryn to her feet and holding onto her hands for longer than was necessary.

"No problem," Kathryn replied. Disturbed by the woman's touch and close proximity, she turned to the sink and ran the tap. Pretending to focus on washing her hands, she discreetly sneaked an admiring look at the woman's profile through the mirror's reflection. Loose strands of hair fell delicately over her shoulders, with the remainder upswept into a cream-embellished rose comb clip. To her surprise, the woman caught her gaze and their eyes connected for a brief moment. Kathryn's cheeks suffused with colour as she quickly turned to the automatic dryer and stuck her hands underneath, praying that the woman hadn't seen her blushing.

Kathryn could sense the woman still standing behind her, but couldn't bring herself to turn around. She didn't trust herself to look into those eyes again — scared what her own eyes would reveal.

The door flung open and a plump, platinum blonde woman staggered in. Her breasts jutted from her ill-fitting, pink Lycra dress and her high-heeled, diamante-encrusted shoes scraped the tiled floor as she stumbled into a cubicle.

Saved by the bell.

Thankful for the much needed distraction, Kathryn swung around with the intention of making a speedy exit. Quickly clearing her throat, she said, "Sorry, I couldn't be of more help." But as she moved to pass her, she noticed something glistening in a loose strand of the woman's hair. She reached out to her. "There it is," she said, retrieving the entangled earring and dropping it into her open hand.

"Oh my God," the woman squealed. "Thank you so much. I'm so dopey sometimes. I didn't even think of looking in my hair."

"It's easily done," Kathryn said, pleased that the woman had her heirloom, but still feeling anxious to escape the small confines of the bathroom.

"Would you mind putting it in for me? The clasp is always slipping out of my hand," the woman said, handing over both the earring and clasp and turning to her side.

"Not at all."

As Kathryn moved closer, she tried to ignore the subtle scent of roses and jasmine emanating from the woman. She fought the sudden urge to trace the outline of her long and graceful neck, as she tried to concentrate on the job at hand. She hoped the woman hadn't noticed the slight tremble of her hands as she inserted the earring and took a step back away from her.

"I'm Rachel, by the way," the woman said. Casually, Rachel turned to face her, looking at Kathryn from under thick black eyelashes, her hazel eyes beckoning.

Impulsively Kathryn reached out her hand. "I'm Kathryn," she said with a calm smile that belied the eruption going on inside her.

"Nice to meet you," she paused for a second, "Kathryn." She took Kathryn's hand and shook it gently. Releasing it slowly, she continued, "Busy in here tonight, isn't it?"

"Yes," Kathryn said, tucking her hair behind her ear and glancing towards the door.

"Well, I s'pose I'd better go and see if my date has turned up yet," Rachel said, touching her ear. "And thanks again."

Kathryn smiled and waited until she was alone. Resting against the basin, her eyes traced up to the ceiling as she waited for her heartbeat to resume to its natural rhythm. *What the hell just happened there? I'm a married woman, not a hormonal teenager.* She had felt attracted to women before but nothing like she had just experienced with ... *Rachel.* She shook her head slightly, unable to stop the small smile that played on her lips.

It was times like this when she felt so unsure about

herself that she regretted getting married before she had taken the time to explore her sexuality. Instead of waiting, she had run straight into the open arms of the first person she thought would provide her with the security and love she so desperately needed. That person just happened to be Gareth.

She had tried her best to be a good wife over the years but just couldn't help but feel that something was missing — that little thing that stops you from giving yourself wholeheartedly to someone, no matter how hard you tried.

She turned to look at her reflection in the mirror — the eyes that looked back at her did not resemble those of a content woman. They were empty and devoid of the sparkle she had seen in so many people's eyes when they were in love.

Letting out a sigh, she straightened her top and forced a smile on her face. *I've come out to enjoy myself tonight. There's no point mourning over something I can never have.* Despite their less than perfect relationship, she couldn't envisage a time when she would leave Gareth — she had said her marriage vows and had meant them at the time. This was the life she had chosen, for better or worse, and she was just going to have to get on with it, a tiny voice in her head reminded her.

Minutes later, Kathryn exited the toilets and made her way back to the table to find Jo frantically shrugging her arms into her jacket.

"What's wrong?" Kathryn asked, concerned.

"I'm so sorry to do this to you, Kath, but the babysitter's just phoned. She can't get Marlon to settle, she thinks he's got a temperature — she's freaking out; I'm gonna have to go home."

"Oh no, I'll come with you."

"No, don't worry, you stay and have a drink. Ben will be home in an hour ... are you going to be okay?"

"Yes, of course, go and be with your son."

"I'll make it up to you — I promise." Jo kissed her cheek and jostled her way to the door.

Kathryn watched the retreating back of her friend. Looking down at the table, she sighed. *No point wasting a good bottle of wine.* She lowered herself into the chair and filled her glass halfway. On the periphery of her vision she saw a woman, clad from head to toe in tight black clothing, laughing whole heartedly at something the ruddy-faced man beside her had said. With great effort she attempted to tune out their loud conversation and laughter, instead focusing on the soft melody that drifted through the air. *Isn't this just great? The first night out in ages and I end up spending it by myself.*

"Are you alone as well?" A honeyed voice sounded above the din of the bar.

Kathryn felt a catch in her throat and her skin prickling as she turned slowly towards the voice, "Rachel?"

"I saw your friend leave ten minutes ago. I thought she'd gone out for a cigarette," she said, jerking her head towards the door. "I take it she's not coming back."

Kathryn looked up at her. "No, she had a family emergency."

"Looks like we're both on our lonesome then. My date failed to materialise," Rachel said nonchalantly. "Do you mind if I join you?"

"Erm, of course not," Kathryn said with a hint of apprehension. It was one thing to have a fleeting attraction to someone you thought you were never going to see again but this was more than she could bear. Despite her misgivings, she motioned towards the empty seat, desperately trying to keep her features neutral. Discreetly, she inhaled deeply, thinking she would treat this moment as if she was having an innocent drink with a new client or at the very least she would try to. "Drink?" she invited, picking up the bottle and holding it in mid-air.

"Sure."

Kathryn gave a tense smile as she passed her a glass. *So far so good.* She watched as Rachel sat down, her stomach tightening as Rachel locked eyes with her. The woman had a powerful aura that was hard to resist. By the way she carried herself, she knew it.

"Cheers," Rachel said, eyeing her over the rim of her glass. "So do you come here often, Kathryn?" she asked, lightly setting her glass down on the table.

Kathryn paused to take a sip of her wine, savouring the way Rachel had said her name as well as the fruity taste of the alcohol. "Not as much as I used to"

Rachel tilted her head to the side and looked at her enquiringly. "Oh, and why's that?"

"Work commitments."

"Sounds like your work commitments don't leave much time for play." A friendly smile played on her lips.

"Well, that's what I get for running my own business," Kathryn replied smoothly, her face expressionless. Work wasn't the only reason — Gareth was not the playful type; he preferred the more serious things in life. The thought of him sitting in a bar, just having a beer and a chat with friends was unthinkable.

"Oh, what line of business are you in?"

"Interior design."

"Sounds like my idea of heaven — spending other

people's money for a living."

"It is." Kathryn let out a half laugh as she took another sip of her wine. She was beginning to feel more relaxed as the effects of the alcohol chipped away at her inhibitions. The nervousness she had felt abated, replaced with a feeling of invigoration — Rachel radiated a warmth that Kathryn couldn't help but bask in.

"What about you? What do you do?"

"I'm a journalist," Rachel replied, toying with her wine glass.

"Really! What type of journalism?"

"Lifestyle, most of the time."

Kathryn was pleasantly surprised. Rachel looked like a model — with her lithe figure and striking facial bone structure she wouldn't have looked out of place on the cover of *Vogue*. "Wow, that must be interesting."

"I've recently started working at a new magazine. You may have heard of it: *Women's lifestyle* — 'don't just experience a woman's lifestyle, become a part of it,'" she said, mimicking its voice-over ad.

Kathryn shook her head and grinned. "It sounds as if its target audience are transvestites."

Rachel gasped and covered her mouth with her hand. "Yes it does, doesn't it!" She burst out laughing. "I'd never thought of it like that! It's a great magazine though. It's got a lot of potential. It's really trying to show women that their lives don't just have to be about having babies and getting married."

Rachel went on to explain her boss's dream for the magazine, finally saying, "Trying to find people to contribute and advertise is turning out to be a lot harder than my boss could have imagined. Because it's new, people are reluctant and would rather go with the large, well-established magazines."

Kathryn listened and nodded at the appropriate intervals, only speaking when Rachel had finished. "That's a shame, but I'm sure things will pick up. It's always difficult in the beginning. So what are you writing now?"

"A piece on successful business women, but it's turning out to be a bit of a nightmare as most of the willing participants bore the pants off me; there's no fire in their belly anymore. They seem to have made it to the top and have lost the will to carry on." Rachel rolled her eyes.

"What exactly are you looking for?"

Rachel barely took a breath. "Someone with passion for what they do, someone inspirational."

"Like someone's whose dream came alive through wanting and believing rather than because of circumstances?" Kathryn's mouth curved into an unconscious smile as she thought about her own dreams of becoming an interior designer.

"Yes, exactly. The norm is: 'I started this business because I was a stay at home mum and needed work to fit in with my timetable', or 'my husband left and I needed the money'. I don't mean any disrespect to those women but it's rare to speak to somebody who hasn't had external circumstances push them in a certain direction."

"Well, I knew I wanted to be an interior designer since I was about four years old. My mum always told the story of when I was barely knee high and re-arranging the furniture at home."

"Cute image."

"Well, it wasn't cute when I started doing it when we visited her friends' homes."

"That would be a great starting point for my article," Rachel said, her voice full of excitement as if she sensed an opportunity.

"I don't know if you'd call my story inspirational."

"I think it is. Too many people lose sight of what they always dreamt of when they get pushed into the real world. We are told to put a hold on our dreams and start slaving away at some soul-destroying nine-to-five. The fact that you achieved your dream and you're still passionate about it sounds very inspirational to me."

"Well, thank you."

Rachel's head tilted slightly as she looked at Kathryn with a confused expression on her face. "Hold on a second ... You're not *the* Kathryn Kassel, who designs for the rich and famous?"

Kathryn felt heat rise to her cheeks. "Guilty as charged." She would never get used to people's reactions to her when they found out who she was. They seemed to think that she had the Midas touch — that putting a room together was a piece of cake. The reality was she had to work long and hard hours for every design she came up with.

Rachel's mouth dropped open and she gasped. "Oh my God, I can't believe this. I thought you looked familiar but I just couldn't place you. I've seen your designs in magazines and I must say they are truly amazing."

"Thank you," Kathryn said, as a part of her couldn't help but revel in Rachel's open admiration of her. She drained the last of her wine and refreshed both their glasses.

"Before I realised who you were, I was going to ask if you would let me interview you for my article so you'd gain a bit of publicity — as if you need publicity! I heard you never give interviews. Why is that, if you don't mind me asking?"

"I like my privacy too much." Rachel had been right — she hadn't given an interview in eight years, due to the excessive intrusion into her private life working with famous people had brought.

Though Kathryn loved every aspect of her work — from the demanding clients to the challenge of finding a different design for individual tastes — she had stopped taking interviews when she realised she was spending more time responding to questions about her famous clients than her actual work. For some reason though, the woman in front of her seemed different — so much so, she was willing to take a chance with her.

"You can still ask me."

Looking puzzled, Rachel prompted her, "Ask you …?"

"If I want to be interviewed for your magazine."

"I wouldn't embarrass myself."

"Ask!" Kathryn encouraged her.

"Okay, would you be interested in letting me interview you for *Women's Lifestyle Magazine*?"

"Yes, I would very much," Kathryn said, laughing at the look of disbelief on Rachel's face.

"I can't believe it!" Rachel said ecstatically, as she jumped up from her chair, skirted around the table and grabbed her in a hug that nearly squeezed the breath out of her lungs. "Thank you so much!"

"Don't mention it." Slightly flustered, Kathryn eased back into her seat as Rachel returned to her chair. Though it was brief, she liked the feel of Rachel's arms around her. She wasn't sure if it was her over-familiarity or the scent and touch of this woman that had her heart beat racing ten to the dozen.

As Rachel sat down, Kathryn took a deep breath and exhaled slowly, hoping it would calm her somewhat jangled nerves. After a few seconds, it seemed to be doing the trick.

"I thought most journalists were like a dog with a bone when they wanted something?" she said, finally regaining her composure.

"I'm not most journalists," Rachel replied, still grinning broadly.

Kathryn turned her face partly away, not wanting to meet Rachel's intense stare for fear of getting lost in it. "I gathered that."

"Before I forget, here's my business card," Rachel said, retrieving a card from her bag. "Just give me a call and we can arrange something when you're free."

"Great, thanks," Kathryn replied as she looked at the card, turning it over in her hand. Glancing back up at Rachel, she smiled.

"Shall we get another bottle?" Rachel asked, waving the empty bottle at her.

Though Kathryn always watched her alcohol intake and couldn't remember the last time she had been drunk, she was enjoying herself too much to let the night come to an end. She leaned forward, slightly intoxicated. "Why not?" Kathryn was certain that if she were to look in the mirror at that moment in time there would be more than a sparkle on show —there would be fireworks.

*** 

The taxi drew up bedside her building as Kathryn dug into her purse for the fare. The prematurely balding young driver twisted around as she slipped a note from her purse and handed it to him.

"Keep the change."

"Thanks," he beamed, taking the twenty-pound note from her.

Kathryn made her way into the building and up to their apartment, letting herself in through the large oak door. The apartment was the first project she had designed, where she was in total control of everything. Gareth, a self-made millionaire, had owned the property prior to their marriage. Initially, he'd been worried when she suggested redesigning his masculine bachelor pad, which was awkwardly stark with dark colours. She wanted something with an equal amount of femininity to it — a bit of yin and yang to suit both of them. Dark colours always seemed to depress her — they reminded her too much of her childhood home. At first, Gareth had not been in favour of her drastic changes, concerned it would be at odds with the architecture and style of the building but once she had shown him her vision, he had finally agreed.

As Kathryn crept along the hallway she was startled by Gareth's voice.

"I'm in here," he called out.

She checked her watch before entering the living room and found him on the same chair he had been in when she'd left earlier that evening. She walked over, swaying slightly as she bent over to kiss him on his forehead.

"You're late. Did you have a good night?" Gareth asked, folding away his newspaper.

"Yes, it was lovely. I didn't expect you still to be up, it's almost midnight," she replied, shrugging off her coat and setting it down on the arm of the sofa.

"I was watching a film. How's Jo? I'm surprised you were out so late, what with the baby."

"Oh, yes she's fine ... Erm, we had a lot to catch up on. Ben was looking after Marlon," she answered, consciously trying not to appear drunk and deliberately omitting that she had not shared one drink with Jo. She felt like a naughty child, trying not to put a foot wrong for fear of upsetting her father. But surely she shouldn't feel like that? She was a grown woman and Gareth was her husband, she shouldn't have to walk on egg shells around him.

He rubbed his jaw slowly, eyeing her intently for a few seconds. "Do you want to watch a little TV before you go to bed?"

She looked down at the floor. "No, I'm beat." She paused briefly. *Why did I lie? I have nothing to hide. Should I tell him about Rachel and the interview? What's the point? He would only try and talk me out of it, and I'm not going to let that happen.*

She smiled inwardly, as her thoughts turned to the upcoming interview. She still didn't know why she had agreed to it — she wasn't normally that impulsive.

"I'll see you when you come to bed."

He turned his attention back to the TV. "I'll try not to wake you."

*Thank God for small mercies.* She made her way to their bedroom, aware that most women would be more than grateful to be married to a man like Gareth. Maybe she would have been if she were older and wiser when they first met but she doubted things would have been any different. Many people thought that being rich made you instantly happy. Whilst money helped in some areas of life, it certainly couldn't make up for love. Though Gareth was an honest, hard-working, intelligent man, there just wasn't any chemistry between them and now that she had just experienced the thrill of it with Rachel, she wanted much more.

## CHAPTER 4

Rachel let herself into her flat, closing the door behind her with her foot. As always, she was struck by the stillness — living on top of a funeral home had its benefits — the main one being that the people below her were dead quiet.

As she walked into the tiny kitchen, she shuddered as she noticed the pile of unwashed dishes and cups resting in the sink. *What I wouldn't do to own a dishwasher.* The kitchen was shabby but clean. It only had room for a cooker, washing machine, a small sink and two cupboards barely clinging to the wall. Zoe always joked that she liked the way their minimalist kitchen looked. In reality, both women were desperate to relocate, but due to financial constraints that didn't look like it was going to happen anytime soon.

Having found one remaining clean mug, she made herself a coffee and walked through to the living room. Setting her cup down on the coffee table, she flopped onto the sofa and retrieved her laptop from the floor. *I'd better get it over with.*

Logging onto the Girlz-on-Girlz website, her heart sank when she saw three messages in her inbox, all from Kathryn's husband. She didn't know what she was going to say to him. How could she tell him that whilst she hadn't managed to seduce his wife she had managed to scoop the biggest interview of her career?

Knowing she couldn't avoid replying to him, she clicked on each of his messages all written with the same desperate urgency: *Did all go according to plan? Has she arranged to see you again? Please update me ASAP!*

She typed back with purpose, telling him he had nothing to worry about and that his wife hadn't taken the bait. Pressing the send button, she prayed that it would be the last she heard from him.

*Now back to Kathryn.* She set the computer on the floor, leaned back in the chair and gazed up at the ceiling. Her encounter with Kathryn had worked out perfectly. She'd been sitting near the entrance of the bar, waiting for her to walk in. When she saw her head to the toilet she'd followed and couldn't believe her luck when the only other people in there, apart from Kathryn, had left as she entered. The next part was easy — it wasn't the first time she'd used the lost earring trick to get talking to someone.

She closed her eyes as she brought up the image of Kathryn in her mind's eye — how alluring she'd looked and so totally oblivious of her sexual appeal. She had met so many women like that, who acted as though they were asexual due to their unfulfilling sex lives.

Rachel instinctively knew Kathryn's passion ran deep — she could see it in the depths of her eyes. It was a pity their relationship would not be going any further than the office. *Stop it, just get the interview over with and move on.*

Drawing herself up, she retrieved the computer and logged back into the site. As a precaution, she went into her details and deleted her account. She didn't want to have to correspond with Kathryn's husband again. She didn't think he would be too happy if he ever found out that she had used their chance meeting to further her own needs.

Not that she would blame him. *Why the hell didn't I listen to Zoe and not take part in this silly game?* She wondered what Kathryn would say if she found out. There was only one solution. *She must never find out.* There was no reason why she had to. If she kept a low profile until she finished the interview, everything would turn out fine. She would have a great story to her credit and it would boost the magazine's sales.

She sat up defiantly. It was too late to back out of the situation now. She couldn't afford to let anything spoil this opportunity, not even the strong attraction she felt towards Kathryn.

\*\*\*

*Women's Lifestyle Magazine* was hidden in a narrow side road, a few hundred yards from the fashionable high street, Angel Road, in north London. The small, dowdy office block was situated next to an unkempt skate park, which consisted of a strip of concrete and three ramps.

"Alright, darlin'?" a gangly youth called out as Rachel made her way past. He halted on his skateboard, confidently kicking it up into his hand by tapping the tip of his foot on the tail of the board. She gave him one of her best smiles and watched as he visibly blushed. His friends gathered around to tease him, which he took good-naturedly, before dropping his board to the ground and mounting it, gathering speed and distance from his friends.

She briefly reminisced about her own childhood — being an only child, she didn't have the luxury of living a carefree, stress-free life. After her father had walked out of their lives when she was nine, her childhood had pretty much ended. She had been responsible for caring for her mother, who had suffered from severe depression. Thankfully, those days were long behind her and she was determined to make up for all she had missed out on.

Rachel strolled the remaining distance to the office to the sound of wolf whistles. Still smiling, she pushed open the glass doors to the reception area, giving a quick wave to Debbie, a petite redhead, who was preoccupied with telling a customer on the phone how to unsubscribe from the magazine.

The next set of white, solid doors she walked through led her into an open-plan room, where twelve desks were crammed into the small office space. Eight of the desks were either being used by journalists tapping away at state-of-the-art computers or sales operatives speaking loudly into their headsets. An exasperated female voice drifted loudly above all the chatter: her boss, Gloria, bellowing at some unfortunate soul in her office at the far corner of the room. Rachel weaved her way through the maze of desks, saying brief hellos to her colleagues before hovering outside the tiny cluttered office, the door wide open.

"Look, if you don't get this article finished on time, you're going to have missed yet another deadline, which means I am going to be fucked, basically ...."

The young woman, Kate, tanned and softly rounded, turned pale under Gloria's onslaught, hanging her head like a child being admonished by a headmistress.
"I'm sorry, Gloria," Kate said in a quiet feeble voice. "I'll work all weekend if it takes me that long and I promise I will have it here first thing Monday morning."

Rachel watched as a look of conflict played on Gloria's face, before seeing a brief melting of hostility.

"Okay, Monday it is, but this is your last chance, Kate.

I can't work with unreliable people." She waved her hand in a gesture of dismissal.

"Thanks, Gloria," Kate said quickly as she backed away to the doorway. "Hi, Rachel," she muttered, not meeting her eyes, before scurrying back to her desk.

Gloria let out a long sigh. "Hi, babe, come in, shut the door behind you." One finger played unconsciously with the ends of her twisted, dark hair. Her chocolate brown eyes followed Rachel as she sat opposite her.

"That was a bit harsh, wasn't it?" Rachel said, a little surprised at her abruptness. Gloria was normally the most laidback of people. She was usually gentle, serenely wise and even tempered. That was one of many reasons why Rachel was thrilled to have her as a boss.

"No, Rach, I've just had it with people taking the piss. Every week she has an excuse — the kids are ill, the fish died," she said, mimicking Kate's voice. "If things carry on the way they are, we'll all be out of a job."

"Are things that bad?" Rachel asked, shrugging off her olive-green leather jacket and hanging it on the back of her chair.

"Worse than bad, I'm afraid. If we don't score something big soon, we're going to go under."

Sadness and defeat filled Gloria's eyes. Rachel knew how much the magazine meant to her. Gloria and her husband had put every last penny they had into the business to keep it afloat. Rachel had known things were bad but she hadn't realised they had hit rock bottom.

"Well, I may have just the thing to cheer you up," Rachel said, leaning forward. "I went out last night."

Gloria grimaced. "Oh yeah, what unlucky soul have you managed put under your spell this time?"

"Now, now, Gloria," Rachel chided playfully, "I think even *you* aren't going to believe me when I tell you who she is."

"Right, and who would that be?" Gloria asked, her tone heavy with sarcasm.

Rachel lowered her voice, being purposely mysterious. "Kathryn Kassel."

"What!"

"Yep," she replied.

"You can't be talking about *the* Kathryn Kassel!"

"The one and only, and she's agreed to be interviewed."

Rachel could see the excitement in Gloria's eyes as she stood and quickly manoeuvred her way around her desk, grabbing Rachel's hands and pulling her up from her seat. "Please tell me you're not having me on; you wouldn't be that mean to me, would you?"

"Nope, it's true; she's agreed to let me interview her."

"Oh sweet Jesus, thank you," Gloria said, wringing her hands together as she looked up. "How? When?"

"I met her in a bar last night."

Gloria's mouth fell open. "You're kidding me … she's … but I thought she was married to some hot shot architect."

"She is, and she isn't gay. I met her in a straight bar."

"Like that means anything," Gloria muttered under her breath.

"Oi, you." Rachel laughed.

"So what's the plan?"

"Well, she's going to call me to arrange a time to go over to her office."

Gloria began to prowl the floor of the small room.

"Listen," she said quickly, taking Rachel by the shoulders, "if we play this right, this could be the exact catalyst we need to put this magazine into the big league. No one, and I mean no one, has managed to get an interview with her in years."

"I know," Rachel agreed, nodding her head. "So what are you thinking?"

"Do you think she would let you do a bigger story than just an interview?"

"What did you have in mind?"

"Well," Gloria said, rubbing her hands together, a sheen of perspiration suddenly evident on her dusky brown skin. "What if you asked her if you could spend some time with her whilst she worked on one of her projects? You know, give the reader a real sense of what being an interior design entails."

"Hmmm." Rachel pushed her hair away from her face. "I s'pose that would be a good idea."

"No, it's a brilliant idea. No one has ever gotten this close to seeing how she works or how she comes up with her designs. Nothing, zilch. Come on, Rachel, let's see some enthusiasm here!"

"I am." As much as she wanted to celebrate their good fortune, she didn't want to tempt fate. Kathryn had only agreed to a bog standard interview. She didn't know what she would say about having Rachel hanging around, watching her every move. From what she could tell from meeting Kathryn the night before, she was a very private person and Rachel didn't want to overstep the mark.

"Yes, well, all she can say is no, and I doubt she would say it to you, what with all your charm and all." Gloria smiled sweetly at her. "Even I wouldn't mind having you to look at all day and I'm happily married, for God's sake."

Rachel laughed. "I don't think Tony would appreciate hearing you say that."

"Oh, Tony's just an insecure drama queen," Gloria said affectionately, taking a few seconds to look at the large framed photograph of him on her desk. "We've been together for ten years and he still thinks I'm going to leave him, for who, I don't know. If I'm not working here, I'm at home."

"Well, you are a catch, Gloria," Rachel said, speaking directly to her boss's ego.

"Why thank —"

Gloria was cut short by the sound of Rachel's mobile phone ringing — she held up her hand, motioning her to be quiet. "It's an unknown number," she said, smiling, "I think this might be her."

"Eager much?" Gloria grinned.

Rachel ignored her and flipped open her mobile phone. "Rachel speaking," she answered in a professional voice.

"Hi, Rachel, it's Kathryn."

"Hi, Kathryn," Rachel said, looking at Gloria, who was staring back, her eyes wide in anticipation. "How're you feeling today?"

"Not too bad considering the amount we drank last night. How about you?"

"Good, thanks." Rachel had found a way to beat hangovers years ago — a litre of water and two aspirin before she went to bed normally did the trick.

There was a brief silence.

"So I was calling to see if you were still interested in interviewing me?"

"Are you kidding? Of course I am," she said, nodding her head vigorously even though Kathryn couldn't see her. "Just let me know when it's best for you and I'll be there."

Gloria looked as if she was going to burst a blood vessel. She thrust her face toward Rachel and hissed impatiently, "Ask her."

"Actually, um I wondered if ... you, um, would be willing to let me do a longer piece on you?" Rachel held her breath, waiting for her response.

"What did you have in mind?"

"Well, my boss, Gloria, thought ..." The request stuttered on her lips. "It would be a good idea if I spent some time with you on one of the projects you're working on. You know, to give our readers a real insight into the design process, maybe a before and after piece."

When Kathryn didn't immediately respond, Rachel hastily added, "I mean you don't have to, it was just a suggestion," she said, sounding uncertain. It irked her to think she had put her foot in it by being overly familiar.

"No, that sounds like a great idea. I was just thinking. I'm about to start a new project tomorrow that will last a few weeks, so if you're interested ... you could cover that?"

"That would be brilliant," Rachel said, trying to contain her excitement. "Thank you so much, Kathryn."

"No problem. I'll text you my work address and if tomorrow suits you, we could begin then."

"Tomorrow's not a problem."

"Great, I'll give my client a call and make sure it's okay for you to tag along."

"Brilliant! I look forward to it," Rachel said, unable to mask the excitement in her voice.

"Me too," Kathryn replied, "see you then."

"Okay, bye, and thanks again."

Rachel closed the mobile and stared at it. "I think that went pretty well," she said, looking up at Gloria.

"Go on, tell me," Gloria asked.

"As you may have gathered, she said yes."

Gloria punched the air. "Yes!"

"She's starting with a new client tomorrow. It's going to last a few weeks. Is that alright?"

"Is that alright? Rachel, it could take a year for all I care. We have just scooped the golden egg and she is firmly in our basket. Oh, wait until I tell Tony — he's not going to believe it. Damn *I* can't believe it," Gloria said, proudly beaming at her. "Who would have believed this morning that we would be featuring Kathryn Kassel in our very own magazine?"

"Yes indeed," Rachel said, suddenly feeling weary.

Gloria's smile faded and her face suddenly became serious as she looked down at Rachel. She gave her a stern look. "Do you promise to behave yourself?"

Rachel looked up at her with an expression of disbelief. "Yes, Gloria. I can't believe you even had to ask."

Gloria's laughed affectionately at her. "Just so long as we're both on the same page. Now let me think ...." she said as she returned to her seat, still speaking her thoughts aloud.

Rachel tuned out Gloria's voice as she thought of the problem that she now faced — it was fantastic that Kathryn still wanted to do the interview. What was even better was the fact that she was going to get an insight in to the life of a woman whose work she had long admired. *But what am I going to do about my feelings towards her?*

This was the first time that she had found herself in this position of being attracted to someone she couldn't have. There was no way on this earth that she would try and instigate something between them now given that Gloria would have her head on a plate if she messed up this deal. If she stepped out of line, Kathryn might retract her generous offer of the interview and the magazine would most likely fold. *Can I do it? Can I really keep myself in check?*

She tried to work out the practicalities of the situation in her mind. She was going to be working in close proximity with Kathryn and unless, God forbid, she lost her sight, how was she going to fight the strong attraction she felt to her? For some, it might be a straightforward case of restraint but Rachel didn't know the meaning of the word when it came to things she wanted — and she wanted Kathryn, despite the deafening warning bells ringing in her ears.

Shit, shit, shit, why did I agree to this?

Looking at the excitement on Gloria's face, she knew why and she also knew she was going to have to put her feelings aside, as the consequences of her actions could lead her to breaking the 'golden egg' as Gloria had so delicately put it.

## CHAPTER 5

Rachel had set her alarm for quarter to six the next morning. She needed at least two hours to get through her routine of showering, breakfast, make-up, and hair. Opening her wardrobe, she decided to wear a two-piece business suit — black jacket and matching skirt, which ended inches above her knees, and a white low-cut figure-hugging top.

After dressing, she put on her black-leather high heels and looked at herself in the full-length mirror. Pleased with her appearance, she went out into the living room where Zoe was hunched over her cornflakes, still in her stripy pyjamas bottoms and a white vest. Zoe spluttered the flakes out of her mouth as she looked at her friend in abject disbelief.

Zoe cleared her throat. "Where are you going like that!?"

"What do you mean?" Rachel asked innocently as Zoe stood up. Her six feet tall, slender frame towered over Rachel.

"Don't play the fool with me, Rachel, you know exactly what I mean."

She was hardly surprised by Zoe's reaction — they had spent most of night talking about her chance meeting with Kathryn. Though she had played down her attraction to her, Zoe was no fool and had reprimanded her, telling her in no uncertain terms to leave Kathryn be. Zoe thought she was playing with fire even thinking of involving herself with a married client. But Rachel had been honest with Zoe when she had told her she had no intention being the third wheel in Kathryn's marriage.

Looking directly up at Zoe she said, "I'm going to meet Kathryn."

"Rachel, you can't go to her office, or worse still, to her client's house, dressed like that!"

"Why?"

"You want the truth?"

"I'm not gonna like this, am I?"

"There's no easy way to say this, but you look like a high class hooker."

Rachel was almost rendered speechless. "Tell it like it is, why don't you?" she snorted. "It's a good thing I'm not easily offended."

"You can't be offended by the truth."

"I thought I looked quite nice," she said, twirling on the spot.

"Rachel, you look more than nice, you look stunning — if your intention is to go and pick someone up in a hotel lobby, but you're not, you're meeting with a professional woman whose clients expect a little … shall we say … decorum."

"You're such a bloody spoilsport!"

"No, a life saver."

"You're no fun," Rachel said, pouting like a child.

"Rach, babe," Zoe sat back down, "you told me last night that meeting Kathryn was a life saver for the magazine

— don't do anything to sabotage it."

"I'm not going to," Rachel protested. Even though it was going to be nothing but a business relationship, it didn't mean she had to dress like a nun.

Zoe smiled. "I believe you — not!"

"I know I said I wasn't interested in her, but I still want to look attractive."

"You couldn't be unattractive if you wore a black bag over your head, sweetheart."

"As much as I love you, Zoe, you can be a bloody pain in the arse."

"I know; only because I care about you."

"I know you do," Rachel said, playfully pinching Zoe's cheek until she yelped.

\*\*\*

Rachel arrived at Kathryn's office ten minutes early, dressed demurely in a grey trouser suit. *Kathryn Kassel's Designs* was an office suite situated above a fashionable shop in a prominent position on the Kings Road, Chelsea. She found the entrance to the office, a frosted glass door with the inscription KK elegantly entwined in large letters, next door to an exclusive designer clothes shop. She pressed the bell and waited patiently. Within a few seconds, the door was swung open by a heavy-set fair-haired woman in her late thirties, wearing a long, grey, pleated skirt with a black cardigan over a grey shirt.

"You must be Rachel," she said warmly, holding out her hand.

"Yes," Rachel replied, shaking it.

"I'm Carol, we've been expecting you. Follow me, we're up here." She led her up a flight of wooden stairs and through one of the many doors that led off a narrow corridor. The large welcoming room had a mixture of warm-coloured leather sofas facing each other and bright prints scattered on the pale yellow walls. A bulky coffee table housed catalogues of fabrics, wallpaper designs and interior design magazines. Rachel smiled when she saw a copy of *Women's Lifestyle Magazine*.

"Can I get you something to drink — tea, coffee?" Carol asked.

"No, thank you. I'm fine," Rachel said politely.

"Okay, take a seat and make yourself comfortable," Carol said, her arm outstretched towards the sofas, "Kathryn won't be long, she's just sorting out a few things."

"Okay," Rachel said, sitting down on a plush fabric sofa. *We could do with these in our office*. Although the room was quiet, she could faintly hear the ceaseless hum of traffic from the street below.

She looked towards the door as it opened. Kathryn stepped into the room, holding a pile of folders against her chest. Dressed casually in jeans and a grey-ribbed jumper, she smiled fervently at Rachel. In a blink of an eye, something passed between them and then it was gone. Rachel wondered if she had imagined it.

"Did you find the office okay?" Kathryn asked.

"Yes, the cab driver knew exactly where it was."

"Good." Kathryn dropped the files onto the coffee table and began sorting them into piles, briefly looking up at her. "I bought a copy of your magazine yesterday, I must say I was very impressed with your articles. In fact, I thought the whole magazine was really informative."

"Thanks, I'll let my boss know — she'll be chuffed to hear that coming from you." For no apparent reason, Rachel felt the strange reversal of their roles, Kathryn's energy was different than it had been the night before when Rachel had felt fully in control.

Kathryn smiled. "It's the truth — anyway, the others will be here in a minute, then we can get started."

"Great," Rachel said as her gaze lingered on Kathryn's mouth. She thought the touch of red lipstick seemed remarkably seductive. Only when the other staff members started to enter the room and occupy the empty spaces on the sofas was Rachel able to take her eyes off her.

The air filled with chatter until Kathryn stood and a cloak of silence descended on the room, all eyes focusing on her. "I'd like to introduce you all to Rachel," she said, gesturing toward her.

"Hi, Rachel," they all said in unison, turning to look at her.

"Hello," she said, feeling strangely shy. She was relieved when Kathryn carried on talking.

"Rachel will be following me around for a few weeks for a cover piece in *Women's Lifestyle Magazine*." She smiled at Rachel, warmth echoing in her voice. She continued for several minutes, introducing her staff before coming to the last two members of the team.

"Rob here is our architect."

An easy grin played at the corner of Rob's mouth as he nodded his head towards her.

"And lastly Cody, who is our buyer, here and overseas."

The long-legged, slim woman with short spiky blonde hair stood up and walked the short distance to Rachel, thrusting her hand in front of her. "Nice to meet you." Her emerald green eyes engaged Rachel's with frank interest.

Amused, Rachel placed her hand in hers. "Nice to

meet you too, Cody," she said before the woman flashed her a smile and returned to her seat.

"Kathryn," Carol gently interrupted her before she could go on.

Kathryn looked towards her.

Gesturing to her watch, Carol said, "You'd better get a move on, you don't want to get caught in the rush hour."

"Okay. Rachel, I'll fill you in with more details in the car," Kathryn said, as she moved towards the door and held it open.

"Nice to have met you all," Rachel said, standing up, addressing them all at once. She noticed Cody unabashedly giving her the once over and couldn't help but smile at her — she knew a player when she saw one. She wondered if Kathryn had ever been on the receiving end of her attention.

"The pleasure was all ours," Cody replied, moistening her lips.

***

Kathryn eased her convertible Jaguar into the oncoming traffic — the inside of the car was immaculate and had the potent smell of new leather. A police car whizzed past them in the next lane, its siren undulating down the street ahead of them.

"That's why I don't drive in London," Rachel said, shaking her head, "people drive like maniacs, even the police."

"I totally agree but I'd be lost without my car. I seem to spend eighty percent of my life in it."

Rachel settled back into her seat. "I thought you would have a driver with the amount of travelling you must do."

"Oh God no." Kathryn laughed easily. "I like to have my own space."

"Oh," Rachel said, feigning offence with a smile.

"No, I wasn't talking about you," Kathryn said apologetically, placing her hand on Rachel's leg for a split second.

Rachel's nerve endings tingled at Kathryn's touch, her blood coursing through her veins like an awakened river. For the second time that morning, she felt out of her comfort zone, the confident in-charge Rachel relegated to the back seat.

"So you do have a driving licence?" Kathryn asked, as she calmly swerved the car away from hitting a cyclist who had appeared from nowhere.

"Yes, I passed my test the first time when I was seventeen," Rachel answered quickly, slightly shaken by the near miss and the warm glow that was taking over her body.

"What was your first car?"

Rachel tucked her hair behind her ears. "A mini, what was yours?"

"A Mercedes," Kathryn replied flatly.

"You didn't like it?" Rachel asked, tilting her head to the side. There weren't many people she knew who would be disappointed with owning such a car.

"Oh no, it wasn't the car itself — that was great; it's just that I wanted a Beetle but my husband bought me a Mercedes as a birthday present."

"Some husband you have there; does he have any siblings?" Rachel joked.

"Yes, he has a brother but I don't think he'd be your type."

"Why's that?" Rachel asked, her eyebrows raised.

"You don't strike me as the homey, kiddie type."

Rachel arched her eyebrows. "Definitely not." She lived by the motto *no kids, no ties*. But she was interested to know what sort of impression she had made on Kathryn. "So what type do I strike you as?"

Kathryn slowed the car down to stop at traffic lights and turned to look at her. Rachel looked into her eyes, searching. Something in the way Kathryn looked back terrified her, yet held her.

"I think," Kathryn began slowly, "you're a free spirit ... no man could tie you down."

"Actually I'm —" Rachel began, caught up in the sudden intensity of the moment.

The sound of a horn bleeping from behind them broke the spell. Kathryn put the car into gear and edged forward.

*That was a bit ... intense?* Feeling a little overheated, Rachel depressed the small button on the door and the window effortlessly slid down. An awkward pause hung between them as Rachel prepared herself for what she would say next. The moment where she had been about to set Kathryn straight about her sexuality had been lost. Rachel always found it amusing when people just assumed she was straight because she was feminine. She didn't mind much, it was only when she got hassled by guys that it became a problem. She had lost count of the amount of men who had tried to convince her that she just needed the right man. Fat chance — like that was ever going to ever happen in this lifetime.

Rachel found herself studying Kathryn's profile as she stared straight ahead, concentrating on her driving while she wove her way in and out of the traffic. *She is so Goddamn beautiful.*

Rachel shifted in her seat as she felt an urgent desire to reach over and touch Kathryn, to feel what was forbidden. She tried to imagine what it would be like to be given a free rein over Kathryn's body. Had Kathryn felt the chemistry that had passed between them. If she had, she didn't seem to be that affected by it. For Rachel, it had been a new experience. She had never felt such an intense emotion just by looking into another woman's eyes. She chided herself for getting ahead of herself. What was she thinking? She should know better than to lose herself in childish romantic fantasies. *Stick to reality — Kathryn is married, Gloria needs this interview to go without a hitch and I made a promise to keep away from Kathryn.*

Minutes passed, both women seemingly lost in their own private worlds, when they suddenly both started talking at the same time. They laughed at the synchronicity, breaking the ice.

"After you," Kathryn said.

"I was just going to say what a great team you have working for you," Rachel said, trying to steer the conversation towards neutral ground.

"Yes, they are." Kathryn smiled. "They're like family."

"Do you have any family living nearby?"

"No, my mother died when I was fourteen," Kathryn said with sadness.

"I'm sorry. And your father?" Rachel probed.

"My father ..." Kathryn paused. "No, he doesn't live nearby." Rachel could tell by Kathryn's tone it was best not to try and coax any more information on what was obviously a sore subject but she remained intrigued as to what could have caused a breakdown in their relationship.

Kathryn didn't strike her as the sort of person who fell out with people.

"What about you?" Kathryn asked as she followed the road sign for Knightsbridge.

"I'm an only child, Dad left when I was nine, and my mum …" Rachel cleared her throat. She could feel her eyes starting to moisten, but quickly blinked away the tears; her sense of loss was beyond tears. "My mum has Alzheimer's."

"Oh God, Rachel, I'm so sorry, it must be tough for you."

Rachel crossed her arms protectively around her waist. "It is. The worst part was having to put her in a care home when I couldn't cope looking after her." The misery of that day still haunted her but there was nothing more she could do for her. Her mum had reached the stage where she needed care around the clock and Rachel just didn't have the energy anymore. After six years of caring for her mum by herself, she had been worn down to the point that she dreaded waking up in the morning and that just filled her with more guilt.

"Has she settled in okay?"

"She seems oblivious to the place, to be honest." Rachel let out a heavy sigh. "It's me who's got the problem with it."

"Why, what's wrong with it?"

"What's right with it, you mean? Well, the staff are great — in fact they are bloody fantastic. It's just the building itself … it's so depressing and run down." Rachel could only bring herself to visit her mother once a month — it took her another month just to gather the strength to go back there again. The feelings of guilt always tore at her heart when she saw her mother sitting in the drab colourless room staring out of a window that overlooked a concrete block of flats.

"Can't you get her moved somewhere else?"

"If only it were that easy. Believe it or not, I was actually lucky to get her placed where she is. Anyway, enough of my depressing problems," Rachel said, changing the subject. "Where're we heading?"

"We're nearly there," Kathryn said, as she turned into the road adjacent to Harrods.

Rachel whistled as Kathryn stopped outside a sizable, period white-fronted house.

"Jesus, your client must have money to be living only minutes away from Harrods."

"Yes, she does." Kathryn smiled, turning off the engine and reaching to the back seat to get her bag.

Rachel followed Kathryn up to the house. The door was opened by a man with a full head of thick grey hair, wearing tan khaki trousers and a T-shirt with the wording *I've got one foot in the grave*.

"Kathryn, darling," he said, planting two kisses on each of her cheeks.

"Hello, Theo, may I introduce Rachel, she's the journalist from *Women's Lifestyle Magazine* I told Ellie I was bringing along."

"Rachel, lovely to meet you," he said, stretching out his hand. "I don't understand why you young ladies are not walking the catwalks in Milan. What a waste, total waste. Your beauty should be shared with the world." He spoke with perfect pronunciation. He led them down a long spacious hall, into a large living room furnished in impeccable good taste with antiques and paintings that looked like they belonged in an art museum.

This place has Kathryn's signature touch.

"Oh, do stop rambling, Theo," a well-groomed woman in her seventies dressed in tweeds, called out as she came into view from the kitchen.

Rachel couldn't believe it. Kathryn's client turned out to be Ellie Thorne — a well-known actress, who was enjoying a recent boost to her success with a new crime series, similar to that of Agatha Christie's Miss Marple.

"Well, it's true," Theo continued. "Look at them both, blonde and brunette; this is more than a man can take at my age."

"Go and read your paper, you silly old bugger," Ellie berated him as she took Kathryn by the hands. "Kathryn, my sweet angel, I cannot thank you enough for making this job a priority for me."

"Hello, Ellie," Kathryn said, squeezing her hands gently, "this is Rachel."

"Hello, dear."

"It's such an honour to meet you ..." Rachel stuttered, not knowing how to address her.

"Ellie."

"Ellie, as a kid I absolutely loved you in *Crime at Night*," Rachel said, still stunned by the fact that the woman she had grown up watching on TV was standing in front of her.

"Thank you, dear, you're making me feel quite old."

"No way, you look amazing."

"Thank you, flattery will get you everywhere," Ellie said, before turning back to Kathryn. "Now come, dear, let us discuss what needs to be done. Time is of the essence, you know. I have merely six weeks to get this room prepared before my darlings come home," she said with an air of drama, as she led them into another room. "Do you promise me that it will be done?"

"Yes, Ellie," Kathryn replied as if talking to a child. "Have I ever let you down before?"

"No, dear, never. You're the only one who hasn't."

"So I never make a promise I can't keep."

Ellie smiled as she cupped her arthritis-ridden hand over Kathryn's cheek. "Thank you, darling."

Rachel felt an irrational stab of jealously at the way the old woman touched Kathryn. She shook her head in self-disgust.

"I want them to be so happy here," Ellie continued. "I want them to feel straight at home the moment they arrive. So make it special for them, Kathryn. I would only trust you to create a home for my babies."

Rachel was confused. *Who is the old woman talking about? Whose babies is she referring to?* She would have to wait until they got back to the car before she could ask Kathryn.

"I will, I promise. I have the plans here," Kathryn said as she removed several papers from her bag and handed them to Ellie. Pointing at one particular sheet, she continued, "As you can see, I have also included a 3D design so you can see exactly what it will look like. It has everything we discussed."

"Oh, Kathryn. It's wonderful, wonderful. You are a genius." Ellie beamed, as she put the papers down on a table and clasped her bony hands together. "You must both come to their welcome home party," she insisted, as she happily walked them to the front door.

\*\*\*

Once seated back in the car, Rachel's mind was still on the mystery of who the room was being prepared for. She waited patiently while Kathryn settled into the driver's seat and started the engine. "Is Ellie getting the room ready for her grandchildren?"

"Nope," Kathryn answered, pulling the seatbelt across her chest.

"Please don't keep me in suspense. Who is the room for then?"

"A pair of Bengalese kittens."

"What!" Rachel shook her head. *Are these people crazy?*

"Kittens, very beautiful ones at that."

She scrutinised Kathryn's face with disbelief. "Please tell me you're joking."

"I'm not, I swear," Kathryn said, laughing.

"You're telling me that room in there," Rachel said, shifting in her seat to face Kathryn, "the one that's bigger than my flat, is going to be used to house two cats?"

Tears of laughter formed in Kathryn's eyes. "Yes, Rachel. I am designing a very exclusive luxury penthouse-type pad for two kittens." She giggled.

"This is too much. I mean, get them a little scratching post by all means, but a whole room!" Rachel blew out her lips, making a hissing sound.

"It's not going to be just any old room — it's going to be an adventure playground for them."

"I just can't believe it — can I be nosey and ask how much she is paying for this cat house?"

"Thirty grand."

Rachel put her head in her hands. "Oh my God. My flat mate is not going to believe it when I tell her about this. In her line of work Zoe's convinced she's heard it all."

As Kathryn laid her hand briefly on her shoulder, Rachel experienced a feeling of excitement mixed with exhilaration and fear — Kathryn's touch made her feel as though she were looking down from a high cliff.

"What line of work is she in?"

"She's a therapist." Rachel shook her head. "I just can't believe anyone would pay that much to house cats."

"Don't worry. If it makes you feel any better, once the expenses have been paid for, the remaining money is going to a cat charity."

"Oh, well that makes me feel a lot better," Rachel replied, still feeling the heat emanating from where Kathryn's hand had been.

"Would you like to come back to the office for a coffee?"

"Sure, I think I'm going to need something to help get over the shock," Rachel said as Kathryn manoeuvred the car around the one in front and headed back to the King's road.

Twenty minutes later, Kathryn led Rachel straight to her office, a spacious room with floor-to-ceiling windows along the length of one wall. The pastel colours used in the room had a soothing effect on Rachel as soon as she entered. She noticed a large whiteboard covered with design ideas. Walking over to it, she peered at a picture of Bengalese cats pinned in the centre, with an assortment of cat products surrounding it.

"That looks enormous," Rachel said, pointing at a photo of what looked like a scratching post with platforms.

"That," Kathryn replied as she walked to stand beside her, "is a cat tree house and it's ten feet tall."

"Are you kidding me? Where on earth do they sell them that size?"

"It's being custom made in Denmark."

"I see," Rachel said, peering at it more closely before

turning back to look at Kathryn. "So can I have a look at the designs? I didn't manage to get a good look when you gave them to Ellie."

"Yes, of course." Kathryn went over to her glass desk, signalling Rachel to join her. Sitting down, she clicked the mouse with her perfectly manicured fingers. Opening up a file on her computer, she motioned to Rachel to take a closer look.

"Ellie wants the cats to have full access to the rest of the house from their play room."

"Obviously," Rachel said sweetly, enjoying the closeness of the moment as Kathryn ran her through the design.

Kathryn smiled. "So as you can see here," she said, pointing to the screen, "there'll be cat steps that will lead up to open air cat walks. Rob will be making nooks throughout the house for cat hideouts, as well as an enclosed deck area and special fences to prevent the cats escaping. There'll be cat flaps in every door, and lastly they will have their very own bathroom."

"Well, that goes without saying."

"The walls will be white, the floor tiled with under-floor heating for the little ones during the winter and air conditioning for the summer." Kathryn finished by closing the file.

"Will they be having their own butler and cook as well?" Rachel asked, trying to keep a straight face.

"I think Ellie will draw the line at that." Kathryn laughed.

Kathryn looked so sexy when she laughed that Rachel couldn't help but feel stirrings of desire. Pushing her thoughts aside she straightened up. "Seriously though, your design looks fantastic," Rachel said genuinely. "If I come back after I've died, I want to be a cat, but not just any cat — Ellie's cat."

"Me too."

"I find that hard to believe. Is there anything else you want in your life that you don't already have?"

"Yes."

"Like?" Rachel inquired.

The beginning of a smile tipped the corner of Kathryn's mouth. A look of mischief in her eyes. "Is that a personal or professional question?"

*Is it my imagination or is Kathryn flirting with me?* Rachel badly wanted to say personal, to find out what was lacking in Kathryn's life, but she thought better of it. "Professional."

"Oh, lots: more staff to handle the crazy demands of clients, more time to complete jobs, more time off —"

There was a gentle tap at the door and Carol walked in, carrying two cups of coffee. Both women thanked her as she laid them on the desk and left the room. An easy companionable silence ensued as they drank.

"So," Kathryn said, putting her cup down, "do you get invaluable advice from your flat mate?"

"Hmm, mostly unwanted advice."

"Oh why's that?"

"Because she thinks I should settle down with a nice woman."

Kathryn looked at her, visibly shocked.

"Yes, I'm gay," Rachel said to the questioning look in Kathryn's eyes.

When Kathryn spoke, her voice wavered slightly. "I'm sorry, I didn't mean anything ... it's just that —" She stirred uneasily in her chair.

"It's okay, I get it all the time. People still have preconceived ideas about what a lesbian looks like. Maybe if I cut my hair?"

Kathryn seemed hesitant, choosing her words carefully. "I really am sorry, I didn't mean to come across as stereotyping. It's just you said you had been stood up ... and I met you in a straight bar."

"We do get about, you know, we don't only meet in seedy bars down back alleys," Rachel said with mock seriousness. "Most of the lesbians I know frequent straight bars. We lipstick lesbians are all the rage nowadays. You never know where you'll find us."

Kathryn stood up. "I feel like I've offended you."

"Don't be silly. Sit down. I'm just teasing you."

Kathryn sat down, smiling uneasily. The phone on her desk suddenly started to ring. Obviously grateful for the distraction, she picked it up. "Speaking," she said into the mouthpiece.

Rachel watched as an expression of concern shadowed Kathryn's face as she asked, "Which hospital?"

## CHAPTER 6

"Don't fuss, Kathryn. It's only a bump," Gareth said as she tried to put an ice pack on his forehead.

"You could have really been hurt."

"Well, I wasn't. Honestly, this is all a big fuss over nothing."

"I don't think bricks crashing down on your head is nothing," she said, recalling the story he'd told her at the hospital.

"Ouch," he said as he tried to stand up.

"Sit back down," she scolded, holding him by his arm and gently helping him back into the chair. "The doctor said to rest and that's what you're going to do. I think we should cancel dinner with your brother on Sunday."

"No, no, I'll be fine. It's really not that bad, and we haven't seen him in an age."

"Ok, if you are sure. Now I think I'll go and make us something to eat."

"Aren't you going back to work?"

"And leave you here by yourself? No, I know exactly what you'll be up to, as soon as I walk out the door — work. For one day you can just give it a rest," she said, concern etched on her face.

"Okay, boss," he replied. "I'm sorry you had to leave

work early."

"Don't worry about it," she said. "I didn't have much to do today." She couldn't even begin to tell him how grateful she was for his intervention.

"Why don't you sit down with me?" he asked, placing his hand on her arm.

Kathryn gently pulled her arm away and turned to leave the room. "I can't, I need to make your dinner."

"It can wait."

She stopped and looked back at him. "It can't. I'm starving. I haven't eaten all day."

"Okay," he said, with a look of resignation.

"What do you fancy? I could make pasta and a salad."

"That'll be fine," he said, glancing away.

She noticed the hurt look in his eyes and with all her might she wished she could go to him. He was her husband, after all, but she couldn't, she needed to keep her mind busy. She didn't know which had shocked her the most this afternoon — the phone call from the hospital from Gareth or finding out Rachel was gay.

She made her way to the kitchen and began chopping the red onion and cucumber. Kathryn thought back to earlier that day, remembering how hard it had been to hide her feelings behind a professional mask. *But why did I react that way when she told me? Did I make a complete idiot of myself?* It wasn't as if Rachel was the first lesbian she had ever met; she'd known about Cody but she'd never felt threatened by her in any way — so why did Rachel feel like such a threat to her? The realisation hit her like a bolt of lightning — what she saw as a silly crush before was now actually obtainable.

She absent-mindedly pushed the chopped food into a

salad bowl and took out the ingredients to make a vinaigrette.

"Oh shit," she said aloud as she realised that she had ruined the dressing by using vegetable oil instead of extra virgin oil.

"Is everything alright?" Gareth called from the living room.

"Yes, it's fine," she called back, pouring the oil down the sink, knowing in her heart that everything was far from fine.

## CHAPTER 7

Thick grey clouds cast a gloomy and lifeless atmosphere over Hyde Park. Two men, one tall and the other slightly shorter, dressed in matching black puffer jackets with fur trimmed hoods, walked past Rachel and Zoe in silence, heads bowed with their hands stuffed deep into their pockets.

"Whoa, let's start from the beginning. A once famous actress now turned crazy cat woman is spending thirty grand — three-O, on a glorified cat house?" Zoe asked. Though she hugged herself tightly, the gesture did little to improve her body heat.

"Yep, you've got it in one." Zoe moved to the edge of the park bench, shaking her head in amazement.

"The worst thing is the room is bigger than our flat," Rachel continued, biting into the chocolate flake on her ice cream.

"Man, we must have done something really bad in our last life if cats are getting better treatment than we are."

"Tell me about it," Rachel said, offering her ice cream to Zoe, who declined it with a small shake of her head.

"Apart from cat woman, anything else happen at your meeting today?" Zoe asked, raising her eyebrow.

"Not what you're thinking," Rachel said. She paused

for a second as she watched a small grey squirrel expertly scale the trunk of a grand oak tree and effortlessly jump onto its bare branch. "But I did tell her I was gay."

"I bet that went down well — not."

"She did seem a bit taken aback, but she didn't run out of the office screaming, so that's something, I suppose." Rachel had actually felt sorry for Kathryn. She'd looked like a deer in front of an oncoming vehicle. She'd wanted to laugh at her reaction but didn't think it would have been appreciated. What was it with women who thought because you were a lesbian you were going to find *them* irresistible? Though she had to admit in this case it was actually true.

"Do you think it was smart telling her? If I remember rightly, you said you weren't going to be crossing any boundaries," Zoe said with a wry smile.

Rachel laughed. "You know me, my mouth speaks before my brain engages sometimes." The truth was she was relieved to have it out in the open so they both knew where they stood. If she wanted Kathryn to bare her soul to her in an interview, the least she could do was be honest about who she was.

Zoe turned to look at her. "So what did she say after you told her?"

"Not much. She looked embarrassed and then she got a call from the hospital about her husband and that sort of put an end to our conversation."

"Why what happened?"

"I didn't get the full story, just that something had fallen on his head."

"Oh no — is he ok?"

"I don't think it was serious. She had to rush off though so I don't know much."

"Let's hope it knocked some sense into him."

A sudden vicious gust of wind swept past them, sending a shiver through Zoe's body.

"Let's go and get a coffee, I'm freezing," Zoe said, standing and pulling her multi-coloured scarf closer to her neck. "Why did I agree to meet you here? It's crazy and I don't know how you can eat ice cream in this weather."

Rachel rose to her feet, oblivious to the cold, as her jacket flapped open, revealing just a thin fabric underneath. "Why not? Did you know people consume more ice cream in the winter than they do in the summer?" She quickened her pace to keep up with Zoe's long strides.

"Really? And where did you hear that?" Zoe asked, looking down at her in disbelief.

"On the Internet."

"Oh right, 'cause everything that's written on the Internet has to be true."

"Well, it does make sense. If you think about it, most people comfort eat more in the winter," Rachel said, polishing off the cone.

"Is that what you're doing?"

Rachel stared thoughtfully ahead of her. "Zoe, we both know where my comfort comes from," she said with an exaggerated wink.

Zoe winced. "Don't remind me."

"Oh, you're so frigid, honestly." Sometimes Rachel thought Zoe was born in the wrong era — that she would have been happier living in Victorian times where sex was hidden and not spoken about. She often wished she would just loosen up and live a little.

"I'm not frigid, I just don't understand your behaviour, that's all. It's so out of odds with the rest of your character."

"You're thinking too much — as usual."

"Studies have shown —"

"Oh stop it with your mumbo jumbo nonsense! And stop trying to analyse me, if I wanted a therapist I'd go and see one," Rachel said, blowing out a noisy breath.

"I'm sorry."

"There's no need to apologise," Rachel said with a fixed stare, "just get off my back. You're always probing and prodding, hoping to uncover some dark dirty secret. Well, there isn't one. I'm the way I am because I just am."

Zoe met the rebuke with a sheepish grin. "Ok I'll let it drop. From now on I promise to leave my other persona at the office."

"Good."

"Friends?" Zoe asked, holding out her little finger.

"Always." Rachel entwined her finger with Zoe's. At times, Zoe made her feel crazy — everything in her world was black or white, no room for grey, whereas that's all there was in Rachel's world.

They made their way past the Princess Diana Memorial fountain and headed towards an outdoor coffee stand that was situated by the Albert Memorial. The server's bulky body was wrapped in a dark-brown sheepskin jacket and a cream woolly hat covered his head; his bare hands were red from the cold air, matching the tip of his bulbous nose.

"A large coffee, please," Zoe said as she turned to Rachel. "Do you want something?"

Rachel shook her head from side to side as the wind blew fiercely across her face. She scanned the vastness of the 350-acre park. She closed them briefly and drew in a deep breath to totally absorb the freshness of the air.

"This is what I want one day," Rachel said to Zoe, who now appeared beside her, happier that she had something hot to drink. "A space where I can breathe. That's the thing with London, there's too many people and not enough open spaces."

"You can say that again." Zoe took a sip of the coffee, then wrapped both hands around it to keep them warm.

A man dressed in a black overcoat walked briskly by them, his eyes lingering on Rachel's face a few seconds longer than human protocol allowed.

"Me thinks you've got an admirer," Zoe said, her eyes following the stranger as he kept looking backwards at Rachel every few seconds.

"Wrong sex."

"Talking of sex, have you got any plans for this evening?"

Rachel rolled her eyes. "Nope."

"Friday night and you're staying in?" Zoe opened her eyes wide. "This has got to be a first, not that I'm judging," she said, laughing.

"I'm knackered, besides there's not much action going on in the bars when the weather's this cold," Rachel said, putting her hand over her mouth as she stifled a yawn. The truth was the thought of meeting someone else didn't appeal to her. For whatever reason, she seemed to be getting all the thrills she needed from Kathryn.

"Do you fancy Chinese and a DVD?"

"Could do."

"Great, I think we should start making our way home," Zoe said, looking up to the sky, as the grey clouds darkened and rain drops began to fall.

CHAPTER 8

Although Kathryn would have preferred to skip the meal, Gareth had insisted they attend. Meeting Gareth's brother and his wife for dinner was a monthly ritual. On any other given day, she wouldn't have minded, but she was still feeling anxious about her last meeting with Rachel. Until she actually saw her again, she wouldn't know if her reaction had offended her. She prayed it hadn't.

Nobody at the table could have ever been aware of the turmoil she was going through as she sat placidly, looking like the picture-perfect wife. Her plate was the only one that still had food remaining on it — she had barely touched the steamed sea bass and assortment of vegetables, such were the butterflies in her stomach she didn't think she'd be able to keep anything down.

"Nice choice of restaurant, Gareth," Bill said, reaching over and slapping his brother on his back with a thud. "Isn't it, Porsche?" he asked, planting a kiss on the cheek of his bleach-blonde wife, who sat beside him in a blue sparkling sequin dress, her hair wild and untamed.

"It sure is. Thanks for a lovely meal," Porsche said, fluttering her false eye lashes at Gareth, before turning to Kathryn and smiling as she eyed the silver and cream print dress she wore.

"It's our pleasure," Gareth replied, taking hold of Kathryn's hand and squeezing it gently.

"So, Gareth tells me you're working on some sort of cat project?" Bill said as he turned his strong and powerful-looking body in her direction. Ten years younger than Gareth, he had his brother's good looks but personality wise, they couldn't have been more different.

"Oh God, cats, yuck," Porsche interrupted, before Kathryn could respond.

Kathryn forced a smile, trying to hide her annoyance before turning her attention to Bill. "Yes, a client of mine has a pair of Bengalese kittens arriving soon, she wanted —"

"Some people have more money than sense!" Porsche interjected, as Bill used his napkin to dab at the beads of sweat forming on his tanned forehead, his dark blue eyes looking intensely at her.

"Oh I don't know, just because they're cats doesn't mean they don't deserve to live in stimulating surroundings. The whole idea of the design is to emulate their natural living conditions as closely as possible," Kathryn continued despite Porsche scowling face.

"Cats should be kept outside, that's the only natural place for them," Porsche said, breaking eye contact with Kathryn as she glanced around the elegant Michelin-starred restaurant and its well-dressed patrons. She tapped the tips of her long finger nails on the stark white cotton table cloth.

"I think it would be too dangerous for them, seeing as the property is close to a main road." Kathryn didn't know why she let herself get dragged into confrontations with Porsche each time they met. It had always been the same from the first time they were introduced. Back when she had first met Gareth, she had found her sister-in-law very intimidating, now she saw her for what she was — a woman who was unhappy with her lot in life and felt everyone else should be just as miserable.

Had they been friends, Porsche would have realised they had more in common than she could ever imagine. But as things stood, it seemed as if her mission in life was to state the opposite to whatever Kathryn said. If Kathryn said the sky was blue, Porsche would try to convince her it was black — she could never win with her.

Porsche returned her gaze to Kathryn before snapping, "Then people shouldn't have them."

"So what do you suggest? Have the animals put down rather than keep them in a safe environment?" Kathryn felt like screaming — this woman infuriated her and by the way she stared at her, she knew it.

Porsche leaned towards her with a look of superiority, propping her elbows on the table. "I'm not saying that, what I —"

"Porsche," Gareth said firmly, "what people decide to do their animals has nothing to do with anyone but themselves."

"But —"

"Perhaps you'd like some bubbly?" Bill said quickly, clearly attempting to break the building tension.

Porsche's face brightened, her eyes wrinkling with amusement. "Go on then," she said, relaxing back into her chair and flashing a devastating smile at Bill's disapproving face.

Gareth caught the attention of a young, well-groomed, dark-haired waiter and ordered a bottle of champagne.

"I'd like to see pictures of the cats," Bill whispered to

Kathryn as Porsche's attention focused on the waiter pouring the fizzy liquid into her champagne flute moments later.

Kathryn heard Gareth groan as he caught the comment, and noting her husband's body language, quickly changed the subject.

"So how's Mercedes coming along with her studies?" Kathryn asked Bill, who she was very fond of and always enjoyed seeing on a night out. *If only he didn't have to bring his wife.*

Bill's face broke into a wide smile. "Oh really good, isn't she, Porsche? Her teachers are very impressed with her. She thought maybe she could come and work for you during the summer to earn a bit of pin money," he said, looking hopefully at Kathryn.

"Sure, I'd like that."

Bill responded by smiling warmly at her.

"I don't like the sound of that one bit," Porsche said.

"Oh, and why not?" Kathryn asked, raising her eyebrows. It was just another thing Porsche could have a disagreement about — Kathryn never understood people who constantly wanted to bring misery wherever they went.

"I don't want my daughter wasting her time with that flowery nonsense; she's going to be a doctor."

"What flowery nonsense?" Kathryn asked, pressing her hand against her chest. If she didn't get away from this woman soon, she wouldn't be held responsible for her actions.

"You know — what you do. Glorified painter and decorator, if you ask me. My Mercedes is destined for better things than that." "Porsche!" Bill said, his cheeks reddening.

Her nostrils flared, an animalistic growl rising from

her throat. "I only say it how it is."

Kathryn's mouth fell open. She was unable to find the words to respond. *A glorified ...*

"I'm sorry for her rudeness," Bill said, obviously embarrassed, as Kathryn's face contorted with anger. "Porsche, come on now, you've had too much to drink."

"Don't apologise for me."

"I think we've heard enough of this now. I'm going to get the bill," Gareth said.

"Good idea," Kathryn agreed, nodding. *And it's about time you found a voice to shut her up.* She glanced at Gareth with a little resentment. Sometimes he was just too passive for his own good.

As Bill got up to put on his coat, he leant over to Kathryn and whispered, "I'm so sorry, Kath. She'll hate herself in the morning when she remembers how she's behaved tonight."

*I very much doubt it.* Kathryn smiled at him, grateful the night was over.

\*\*\*

"That woman bloody infuriates me, the things she comes out with," Kathryn called out from the bathroom to Gareth, who sat on the bed, taking his shoes off.

"Which part?"

"Are you kidding me?" She poked her head out the door, holding her toothbrush in her hand. "How about all of it. Sometimes I can't believe Bill would have married someone like her."

"It was his choice."

"You should have said something to her." She was still angry that he had let Porsche speak to her the way she did — it was getting beyond a joke now. His unwillingness to defend her was definitely not one of Gareth's best features.

"What did you want me to say?" He tugged his tie loose, before unbuttoning his shirt, revealing grey wispy hairs on his chest.

"For starters, she insulted me and you just sat there and said nothing."

"Yes, I did, I told her the evening was over."

"But you didn't defend what I do. Is that because you find it meaningless too?" she said, walking into the bedroom and standing before him, her hand resting on her hip.

"No, of course not. You are blowing this out of proportion," he replied, splaying his hands out on the bed and leaning back on to them.

"You always say that. Why can't you just admit when you're in the wrong?" She tilted her head to one side, carefully scrutinising his features. Trying to get him to talk about anything to do with his emotions was like trying to get blood out of a stone. She didn't know if it was because of the fifteen year age gap between them but at times like this they just seemed miles apart from each other.

When she thought about how easy it was to be with Rachel, it only served to remind her of all the things she was missing out on in life and it saddened her deeply. If she felt this way, how on earth did Gareth feel? There would be no point asking him, he'd just repeat the same old mantra *I'm happy if you're happy*. But that was the problem, she wasn't.

"Look, I think we've had enough discord for one evening, let's just get some sleep," he said wearily as he brought his hands up to his head.

"Are you feeling okay?" Kathryn asked, going to his

side, suddenly feeling guilty for having a go at him. It wasn't his fault he didn't like confrontation, it was just the way he was, he couldn't help it — just as she couldn't help the way she felt.

He shook his head. "No, my head is still a bit sore."

"Get into bed, I'll go and get you some aspirin," she said as she drew back the quilt and puffed up the pillows. "Can I get you anything else?"

"No thanks, just a painkiller will do."

She stopped with the door ajar a few inches and turned to him as he finished undressing. "Are you sure you are alright?"

"I'm positive," he said with a faint smile before she left the room.

## CHAPTER 9

Gareth patted the space next to him several times before he realised Kathryn wasn't there. He lay still before turning onto his back and glancing at the digital clock on the bedside table. *Just after eight.* He sank his head back into the softness of the pillow and tentatively felt the swelling on his forehead. It still throbbed — the pain killers he had taken the night before had little or no effect on the pain. He felt like a bumbling idiot when he recalled how his mind had been so distracted thinking about Kathryn that he had missed the enormous sign stating 'falling objects'.

He had been lucky that only one of the many bricks that had been hurtling towards him made contact with his head — if he hadn't reacted so quickly and darted underneath the protection of the scaffolding, his injuries would have been a lot worse.

Swinging his legs off the bed, he walked gingerly to the en-suite bathroom. Running the shower cold, he stood underneath the spray, letting it soothe his aching lump, his thoughts once again lost in Kathryn. It had been three days since he had received the brief reply from Pandora, stating that his wife had not fallen for her advances. So there was only one other possibility to consider now — Kathryn just wasn't attracted to him either.

The realisation depressed him more than he could have imagined. He had really believed that his relationship with Kathryn was a strong one, that it could weather any storm but he was finding out fast that just wasn't the case. *Is she going to leave me?* The fear of being alone enveloped him. Though he knew he still looked good for his age, the thought of being on the dating scene scared him beyond belief. But that wasn't the main reason — he just so happened to love his wife and didn't want to live his life without her.

Gareth stepped out of the shower and dried himself down before dressing quickly in a dark blue suit, yellow tie and black leather shoes before making his way downstairs.

Hearing the sound of clattering plates as he neared the kitchen door, he pushed it open, holding it slightly ajar, taking the time to watch his wife, who was dressed simply in a white embroidered blouse and faded blue jeans, as she prepared the table for breakfast.

Not for the first time, he wondered what was going on in her mind. What could he do to make her happy? Obviously setting her up with a woman wasn't the answer. Did she want to have a baby? Was that it? When they had broached the subject in the past, he hadn't been that enthusiastic about it, but if it meant seeing her smile again he would do it. He would do anything to save his marriage.

Kathryn jumped when she turned and saw him through the gap of the door. "Peeping Tom," she teased.

"No," he said, pushing the door open, "just a humble man looking at his beautiful wife."

He walked over to her, encircling her waist and nuzzling her neck. He felt the familiar tensing of her body and let go, then took his usual chair at the breakfast table.

Yet again the rejection had gone straight to his heart. *How long can this go on for?* She brought his coffee to the table and placed it in front of him and, as if an afterthought, she kissed him on the top of his head.

"What are your plans today?" he asked

"Oh, the usual," she replied, pouring cream into her coffee, before taking a seat opposite him.

"How's the cat project coming along?" he said.

"Good." She smiled. "In fact, I met a journalist on my night out with Jo and their magazine is covering it."

"Really?" he said, his eyes widening, "you didn't mention it before." He snapped the paper open, pretending to scan the front page. *Was this what it was all about? Had she met a man on her night out with Jo?*

"I know, I was so overwhelmed with work. I'd sort of put it to the back of my mind."

No wonder she didn't take the bait. She'd already met someone.

"Which magazine are they from?"

"A newish one called *Women's Lifestyle*."

"Hmm, never heard of it. Seems funny, a man writing for a women's magazine."

"The reporter isn't a man, it's a woman," she replied.

"Really!" he replied a little too quickly.

"Yes."

The pieces of the puzzle were starting to fit together. Was this reporter his Pandora? But why had she lied and said nothing happened? "You don't normally do interviews." His mind was reeling. He hadn't been able to get in touch with Pandora since she sent her last message. When he'd tried he find her profile again it was no longer there. He felt conflicted. Wasn't this what he wanted?

Hadn't that been the whole point of setting the meeting up? Half of him wanted to free his wife and let her walk her own path. But the other half wanted their relationship to be how it was in the beginning.

"Are you ready for your breakfast?" she asked as she stood up.

"Yes, please. I think I'll just have muesli and fruit this morning."

She opened the fridge, her back to him. "I liked the vision of the magazine. I think it's a good fit for me."

"Really?" he replied, as he tried his best to remain casual.

"Yes, I can't even remember how the conversation came about if I'm honest, but there was something about the way she spoke of the magazine that made me think it was about time I put myself out there a bit more."

"You hardly need the publicity, darling, or the work."

"I know," she said, tipping the dry textured cereal into a bowl and topping it with pieces of fruit. "But I just thought it would be nice to speak to a new audience."

"You mean a younger audience."

"Well, it wouldn't hurt, would it?" she asked. "I wouldn't mind creating designs for less money."

"You mean you want to start designing for commoners, just like *The House Doctor*?"

"Oh don't be such a bloody snob, Gareth." She sighed with exasperation. "Honestly, sometimes you can be such a ...." She stopped.

Gareth quickly realised he had overstepped the mark. He rose from his chair. "I'm sorry," he said, going to her and placing his hand gently on her shoulder. "I just didn't think before I opened my big mouth."

"But you thought it though, didn't you?" she said, pushing his hand away and shoving his breakfast bowl to him. "I'll grab a bite to eat at work, suddenly my appetite has gone."

Within minutes, he heard the front door slam shut.

Why the bloody hell do I do that? No wonder she's unhappy. He emptied the contents of his bowl into the bin. Maybe it's time to let her go. If she loves me, she will come back and if she doesn't, do I want to spend the rest of my life with someone who doesn't want to be with me?

CHAPTER 10

Kathryn could hear Rachel's gentle laughter rippling through the air as she neared Cody's office. Although the door was ajar, she couldn't quite make out what was being said.

"Ah, Kathryn, you're here," Carol said, loud enough that the laughter stopped abruptly.

Kathryn spun towards Carol with a start. "Jesus, you scared me, I didn't hear you."

"Sorry, sweetheart, your mind must be elsewhere. I think they can hear my elephant feet in the next building," Carol said with humour. "I've put your mail on your desk."

"Thank you."

"And Rachel is here. Cody is keeping her amused by the sound of it," Carol said, jerking her thumb towards her office, just as the door opened fully and Rachel stepped out into the corridor wearing a charcoal top, distressed skinny jeans and black knee-high boots.

Her close proximity brought with it the aroma of jasmine. Immediately, Kathryn's mind flashed back to their first meeting and its intensity. She suddenly felt caged in between Rachel and the narrowness of the walls.

"Good morning," Rachel said, her eyes dancing.

"Morning," Kathryn replied, glancing at Rachel and

then at Cody, who smirked back at her. They seemed to be very pally with each other. She knew from the office gossip that Cody was single, she couldn't remember a time when she was anything but — it seemed she was always dating someone new, but never for very long. Watching them both goad each other playfully, she could sense the similarity between them — their carefree attitude. In a way, she felt jealous of the freedom they had to do whatever they wanted — they answered to nobody. That was something she had never experienced.

"So what's on the agenda today?" Rachel asked, drawing Kathryn's attention back to her.

"My morning is free so we can start the interview now, if you like," Kathryn replied, trying her best to sound light and cheerful. "Shall we?" she said, signalling for Rachel to follow her into her office.

"Great."

"I'll see you later," Cody called out as the door to Kathryn's office closed behind them.

Rachel took a seat opposite Kathryn's desk and dropped her black leather handbag to the floor. "So I take it your husband's injuries were not life threatening?" she asked as Kathryn busied herself opening the mail.

Kathryn looked up briefly. "No, just a rather nasty lump on his head, he'll live." She flicked through the rest of the letters and, deciding they could wait, sat down, feeling safer behind her desk.

The mere mention of Gareth caused anger to rise within her. She was still reeling from the comment he had made earlier. She had to work for everything she'd achieved in life and was also a 'commoner'. So for him to look down on people because they didn't live in a swanky house or drive flashy cars was an insult not just to her but to every hard-working person out there.

"Do you want something to drink before we start?" Kathryn asked, remembering her manners and pushing thoughts of Gareth to the back of her mind.

"No thanks." Rachel withdrew a pen and pad from her bag, clicked her phone onto record and crossed one leg over the other.

"Okay, go ahead," Kathryn said, trying to relax. If there was one saving grace of the day it was that Rachel was being open and friendly, so she was pretty certain that she had not offended her. She was relieved, as she had spent most of the night worrying and wondering how she was going to face her today.

"So tell me, what tips can you offer the lay person who can't afford to hire someone like you?" Rachel began.

"Good question. I think the most important is to go for quality over quantity. I know it can be difficult when you don't have much to spend, but there is no point having a room full of junk when you could have one or two very nice pieces of furniture." She paused, resting her chin on her hand. "I would also emphasise how important it is to decorate one room at a time. Trying to decorate a whole house at once leads to a loss of focus and usually ends in a half-hearted attempt when it all becomes too much."

Rachel nodded and began scribbling on her pad. Kathryn watched her delicate fingers as they clutched the pen and roamed effortlessly across the page. A silver ring entwined with abstract branches adorned her middle finger and a second thick band, her thumb.

Noticing the pause, Rachel looked up, prompting Kathryn to continue.

"I always decide on the colour of fabrics before I choose paint colours and keep bright colours for small items and more neutral colours for large spaces. I also only use the least prominent colour in the room to accessorise and group the accessories so that the room is balanced."

For the next hour, Rachel grilled her like she was interviewing a politician, and Kathryn answered the questions honestly and candidly. Finally Rachel switched off her recorder and closed her pad.

"You'd give Jeremy Paxman a run for his money if you ever decide to get into investigative journalism," Kathryn said, feeling pleased but mentally exhausted. It was the first time she had opened up to someone about her work in that depth. She wondered how she'd feel when she interviewed her next about her private life.

"That was really interesting and I can say, hand on heart, I enjoyed every moment of it." Rachel smiled.

"I'm glad, I like your style of interviewing."

"Well," Rachel said, putting her things away. "I think I have enough to get started."

"Good."

Rachel stood up to go.

"So will you be going straight back to your office?"

"Later. Cody asked me to join her for lunch, apparently there's a fantastic noodle bar nearby."

"Oh, erm, yes there is — Cultural Revolution, they do very tasty dumplings." Kathryn's muscles tightened. She silently prayed that lunch was the only thing that they intended having together. The thought of Rachel and Cody as a couple would be too much to bear.

"I'll give them a go, you're more than welcome to join us."

"No, no, you go, I have a few things I need to be getting on with."

"Okay. When would be a good time for me to come back for another interview?"

"Huh?" Kathryn said, her mind a million miles away. "Oh, erm, let me just check my diary," she said, picking up the thick book from her desk. "Thursday would be okay, if that's alright with you?"

"That's perfect."

\*\*\*

The noodle bar was situated over two floors — stacks of bare wooden tables were placed only inches apart, an ingenious idea thought up by the owner, who wanted to cram in as many people as possible.

"Thankfully we're here before the rest of the office crowd," Cody said as she took off her blue suit jacket, hanging it on the back of her chair before they took their seats.

Rachel eyed the interior, admiring the simplicity of the decor. It was just the way she liked life — uncluttered.

"The smells are making my mouth water," Rachel said, inhaling the garlic aroma. She picked up the menu and began flicking through the pages.

"The food tastes even better," Cody replied, as she sat back in her chair.

After scanning the menu for a few moments, Rachel came across the mixed dumplings Kathryn had recommended and decided to have those.

"I'll have the same," Cody said to the petite young waitress, who wore a black skirt and white shirt, "and a glass of house red, please."

"And I think I'll have ..." Rachel paused whilst she read

over the drinks list. "The carrot juice, please."

"Not a day drinker, huh?"

"No, if I drink during the day, the alcohol seems to have a funny effect on my body."

"How did your interview go?" Cody asked.

"Good, Kathryn's an interesting person, as you must know."

"Yes, she is."

"How long have you been working for her?"

"Oh God, it seems like forever, but in reality only about five years."

"Do you like it?"

"Do I ever. What's there not to like? The hours are long but I get to travel and the boss is hot, which I'm sure you've noticed," Cody said as if sharing a dirty secret.

Rachel smiled sweetly without answering. The less anyone knew about her the better, especially Kathryn's employee.

"I see the way you look at her, I know you like her," Cody said, her eyes boring into Rachel's.

The waitress brought their drinks and placed them on the table without interrupting.

"Really?" Rachel asked, neither confirming nor denying her claim.

Cody took a mouthful of wine. "Yes, and if you want a little bit of friendly advice — one sister to another, I wouldn't even think about it. She's as straight as they come ... I am right in thinking that you are in the club?"

Rachel nodded as she sipped on the fresh juice, enjoying the sweet taste. One thing she would never do is deny her sexuality — it was a part of who she was.

"Phew, for a minute I thought the old gaydar had

broken down again."

"What do you mean *again*? Did you hit on someone who didn't appreciate it?"

Cody laughed. "Well, yes." Her cheeks slightly reddened. "Kathryn."

A good-looking person like Cody wouldn't normally have a problem attracting any woman, so she wasn't surprised that she had set her sights on Kathryn.

"When I first met her, I swear I thought I was going to die, she literally took my breath away."

The waitress brought their steaming hot food to the table.

"I was young and naive," Cody said, expertly plucking a dumpling with her chopsticks and taking a bite. "I stupidly believed that if you felt that strongly for someone they would automatically feel the same way." She shook her head. "Boy, was I in for a shock." She laughed at the memory. "Let's just say that was a hard lesson to learn, not to mention a shock to my ego."

"So you actually told her you liked her?" Rachel asked as she chased a dumpling around her plate.

"No, but she's not stupid. She just let me down very gently without me making an idiot of myself." She placed her chopsticks down and looked at Rachel earnestly. "So take it from a seasoned fool, if you have any notions about Kathryn, don't bother."

"My intentions are purely business," Rachel said as she stabbed a dumpling with one chopstick and triumphantly popped it into her mouth.

Cody grinned. "Yeah, of course they are. Do you want me to get you a fork?"

"No, no, it's fine. I think I've got the hang of it."

Easing back in her chair, Cody eyed Rachel up and down slowly as she finished her meal. As Rachel speared her last dumpling, Cody leaned forward and propped both elbows on the table. Lowering her eyes she said, "Look — if you're not busy this weekend maybe we can hang out together?"

"Maybe."

\*\*\*

"Girl, you had better watch yourself," Zoe said, opening a puzzle box and spreading the pieces over the coffee table in their living room. "Working on two women in the same office, tut tut."

"It was only lunch, Zoe." Rachel sat on the armchair beside her, watching as she arranged the pieces.

"For now!"

"No, not just for now. Nothing's going to happen — now or ever — with either of them."

Zoe stopped what she was doing and looked up, her eyebrows raised. "I've known you too long to not put anything past you."

Rachel knew she had a reputation but she did draw the line somewhere. She may not have any control over who she was attracted to but she could *try* and control what she did about it. She congratulated herself on having stuck by the cast iron rule she had put in place for herself — absolutely no flirting.

The first part of the interview had gone smoothly and there was no reason to think the second part wouldn't go the same way. Then it was goodbye to temptation.

Both women jumped when they heard a loud knock on the door.

"Are we expecting somebody?" Zoe asked in surprise.

"Not anyone for me," Rachel said as Zoe got up to answer it. "It's most probably the plumber, the kitchen tap burst again yesterday whilst you were at work."

"Who is it?" Zoe shouted from behind the front door.

Rachel heard the front door opening and the brief sound of a male voice. When Zoe returned, she had a man in tow.

"Someone for you. I'll be in my room if you need me," she said before leaving the room.

Rachel's posture stiffened as she looked up at the middle-aged man, dressed casually in jeans, T-shirt and a black fleece jacket.

"Alright, Rach?" he said.

She did a quick retake as she noted he was the spitting image of her father — rich blondish-brown hair, wide shoulders and a strong, square jaw line.

Rachel stood up. "How did you find me?" Her voice was as cold as ice.

"Is that how you greet your own uncle after all this time?"

"I asked how you found me?" she said again, crossing her arms tightly against her chest.

"Your cousin saw your face in some magazine you write for. Right impressed she was, to be related to a fancy writer. Once we found the name you hide under, tracking you down was easy."

"What do you want, Dean?" Like a statue, she stood motionless.

"Oh, it's like that, is it? First names, no uncle."

She let out a bark of bitter laughter. "You lost that privilege years ago when you abandoned us. As far as I'm concerned, the only family I have is my mother. Now can you tell me what you want?"

He stepped towards her, extending his hand. She shuffled backwards, steadying herself before nearly falling onto the sofa.

"Don't put your hands anywhere near me." Rachel raised her voice, her face turning crimson.

"Hold your horses, young lady. What do you think I'm going to do?" he said, lifting his hand up and backing away. "I don't have to be here, you know, I'm just doing your old man a favour."

Rachel's jaw tightened. "I'm not the slightest bit interested in anything that man has to say."

A grave expression settled on his face. "Yeah, well that's why I'm here. He isn't going to be saying much from where he is. He pegged it a few weeks ago."

"He's ... dead?" The words caught in her throat as she raised her hand to her mouth. The room around her seemed to be closing in on her as she used the back of the chair to steady herself.

Dean's shoulders dropped. "I'm sorry I had to tell you like this," he said in a monotone voice. "He was ill for some time. He'd been looking for you, wanted to set the record straight and all. You know, about him disappearing when you was a girl."

"I'm glad he didn't find me, I did fine without him."

"Yeah, looks that way," he said, looking her up and down. "You've turned into a right stunner, girl. You got your dad's looks, all right."

"Well, you've told me now. If there isn't anything else ...."

"Just need to give you this." He tugged a large folded envelope out from his back pocket and held it out to her.

"This is from your dad." He bent over and laid it on the coffee table when she made no attempt to take it from him. "And this," he said, drawing a smaller envelope from his front pocket. "Is from the solicitor who dealt with your dad's estate."

He tossed it down on the table.

"Right then, I'll be off," he said, rubbing the back of his neck, but making no attempt to move.

There was a moment of silence as they both looked at each other.

"Why did you do it? Why did you abandon us when we needed you most?" Rachel spoke first.

He averted his gaze to his feet, before looking up to meet her eyes. "Everything you need to know is in that," he said, pointing to the letter. "It's not my place to tell you. In there's your dad's words, only he can tell you the truth."

"It's like that, is it? Denial sure runs through your family, doesn't it?"

"You don't know the half of it, Rach. Before you start making judgements, you need to know the facts."

"I know the facts — my mum told me all about him and his wandering eye."

"Look, my number's on the back if you want to talk," he said as he turned on his heel.

"Don't hold your breath," she called out to him as the front door slammed shut.

Zoe stepped into the living room and was quickly beside her. Rachel's body shuddered as she sobbed into her hands.

"What's the matter? What did the bastard say?" Zoe asked, rubbing her back.

"My ... my dad's ... dead," Rachel murmured, as Zoe

coaxed her onto the sofa. She would never have believed she'd react this way — it felt as though someone had ripped her heart out with their bare hands. *But he left me.*

"Oh, Rach, babe, I'm sorry," Zoe said, grabbing a tissue from the box on the coffee table and handing it to her.

"Don't be." Rachel blew her nose. After a few seconds, she continued, her voice getting stronger, "It was just a bit of a shock seeing him again. It just brought back a flood of feelings I don't understand."

"Like what?"

"I don't know, something unnerving."

"Maybe it's just the shock of hearing your dad's passed away."

"How can I mourn a father I haven't seen in years?" It was true, she hadn't seen him in over fifteen years, but regardless, unwanted emotions enveloped her being.

"Hello! Remember the Princess Diana fiasco? Jeez, the country mourned her death like she was the second coming. At least you actually were blood related to him." Zoe let out a deep sigh. "Unfortunately, this means you're never going to get closure now."

"I don't need closure," Rachel said. Eyes now dry, she picked up the large envelope, noticing for the first time it was addressed to 'my darling daughter'. She snorted, hardening her heart against the man who had once broken it. "What a bloody joke," she said as she threw it in the bin.

She travelled back in her mind to a time that belonged to someone else, a child who loved her father more than anything in the world. She still remembered how he always tucked her in for her bedtime story and the smell of fresh lemon soap as she clung to his neck, begging him for just one more story. To which he always relented. He had promised to take her to Disneyland, where she would meet all of her favourite cartoon characters, but that had never come to pass. One day, he had just ceased to exist.

Her memory of this time was blurred. When she tried to recall their final encounter, she was filled with a feeling of terror and dread. Her mum told her it was the trauma of seeing him leaving with his tart. And now he was dead and all he had to say to her was in a pathetic letter.

"What's that one?" Zoe asked, pointing to the remaining letter.

"From his solicitor," she said, toying with a small tear on the flap.

"Are you going to open it?"

"Yeah, why not?"

Rachel tore it open, taking a few seconds to read its contents. Looking up at Zoe, she said in surprise, "Seems like he has left me something in his will."

"Really, what?"

"Doesn't say, just that I should call to make an appointment."

"Are you going to?"

"Might as well, you never know I might be a millionaire." Rachel forced a smile.

"Don't you think you should read his letter? It might have an explanation."

"What use is it now? He's not here to answer for himself. Seriously, what type of man walks out on his family? There could never be a plausible explanation for that."

"Sometimes people —"

Rachel held up her hand. "Please, Zoe, I don't want to

hear 'maybe he had his reasons'. Maybe he did, but that doesn't make it right, what he did to us."

"I know," Zoe muttered.

"Anyway," Rachel said, fishing her phone from her bag next to her, "let's see what all this is about."

## CHAPTER 11

"Porsche really said all that?" Jo called from the open-plan kitchen, as she checked the temperature of the baby's bottle by splashing some milk on her arm.

"Yes, she did," Kathryn replied.

"And Gareth just sat there and said nothing? He definitely wins 'prick of the day'," she said, wiping a speck of milk off her grey draped tank top.

"It's not his fault, I think he just wants an easy life," Kathryn said as she bounced Jo's son Marlon on her lap. "Who's a beautiful boy?" she said as he gurgled happily.

Jo crossed the spacious living room, strewn with baby toys and furniture, and stood in front of Kathryn, bottle in hand. "At your wedding, she looked like a right bimbo, putting on airs and graces. I don't know how you put up with her."

"I have to, for Gareth's sake."

"How are things between you two, any better?"

"No, not really." Jo was the only person Kathryn could talk to about how she truly felt about Gareth. Everybody thought he was Mr Wonderful and said she was lucky to have him. Maybe if she wasn't … She couldn't bring herself to finish the sentence. It was an area of her life that she just wasn't ready to bring out into the open. But now that she had met Rachel, how long could she go on denying it? It felt like the beginning of a new identity was emerging from her, whether she wanted it to or not.

Jo looked at her thoughtfully. "That answer's a bit ambiguous."

Kathryn took a deep breath. "I don't know, it's not him, it's me. I just don't know how I feel anymore."

"Do you want to feed Marlon?" Jo asked, holding the bottle out to her.

"No, he'll most probably end up choking or something," Kathryn said, kissing him on the top of his head before handing him to Jo.

"I think you'll make a good mother," Jo said, heaving the child into her arms and then sitting down on the arm chair.

"Not in this life time, I won't. Not if it means having a baby with Gareth."

"You must have wanted a baby with him at some point?"

"If I'm honest, no, I didn't. I don't know whether that's because I just don't want children, or more to do with him. There just isn't a spark there."

"Was there ever?" Jo asked, as the baby sucked greedily on the teat.

"Not really, but I thought it would grow. I mean, what do any of us know at eighteen?"

"Hmmm, I think I told you at the time that marrying a man fifteen years older wasn't going to be a great idea." She held the baby against her chest and began rubbing his back gently until he let out a loud burp, followed by a smile. "You liked that, didn't you. Yes you did," Jo teased him lovingly, before putting the teat back in his mouth.

Kathryn looked down to the floor. "When I met him, he was so worldly, fascinating even."

"Are we talking about the same Gareth here?"

Kathryn let out a small laugh and looked up at her. "Yes, I know, you found him boring from the word go but to me — his passion for his work, for life even, kind of blindsided me."

"So do you regret it now?"

Kathryn nodded her head slowly. "But is there any point in regretting something I can't change?"

Jo pulled the teat from the baby's mouth and sat stock still, as the realisation of Kathryn's situation dawned on her.

"Kathryn! If I didn't know better, I'd say you've met someone else."

"What! No, of course I haven't," Kathryn said, inclining her head as she felt the blood rushing to her cheeks.

The baby began to cry, his wailing drawing Jo's attention back to his needs. Repositioning the bottle Jo continued, "Are you sure? You can tell me, who is he?"

"Of course I'm sure. There isn't anybody," Kathryn said as a quick mental image of Rachel flashed through her mind. She felt like an infatuated teenager — her mind was consumed with thoughts about Rachel from the time she awoke until last thing at night.

Aware that Jo was still waiting for an answer, she spoke in what she hoped was a matter-of-fact tone. "What makes you think that there's anybody else?"

"Well, for starters, you're blushing like crazy."

Kathryn's eyes darted across the room, desperately trying to avoid Jo's stare. "It's just warm in here and I swear to you, I have not met another man," she said truthfully.

Jo frowned. "So what's brought all this on now then? Something must have kick started it. I know you've had your problems over the years but this feels different somehow."

"Maybe I'm having a midlife crisis, who knows," Kathryn replied, gently biting her lip.

"I think you're a little too young for that," Jo said, standing up. "Let me just put this little man down for his nap. Why don't we have a drink? Maybe the booze will loosen your tongue."

As Jo left the room, Kathryn retrieved a bottle of wine as she flipped back mentally to her interview with Rachel. She had felt so comfortable discussing her life with her even though she had only known her for a short amount of time. She replayed the interview in her mind — remembering the way Rachel played with her pen as she spoke, the way her hand brushed her hair from her face as she wrote, the way she... *Pull yourself together, this is just a silly crush and if Jo has notices something's amiss how long do you think it will be before Gareth begins to get suspicious?*

"So as you were saying?" Jo said, as she returned to her seat picking up the wine glass Kathryn had filled for her.

"I wasn't saying anything. It was you that was letting your imagination run away with you."

"Come on, Kath, I've known you since we were tiny. Gosh, that seems so long ago now."

Kathryn sighed. "Yes, it does."

"So there's nothing you want to tell me?" Jo took a sip of wine and replaced it on the table.

"No, nothing," Kathryn replied, gazing down at the floor.

"And how's work?"

Kathryn sagged in her chair and crossed her legs. "Good, I'm doing an interview for a new women's magazine."

"Really? Which one?"

"I don't think you would have heard of it, *Women's Lifestyle*."

"Hello!" Jo said, reaching under the coffee table and bringing a magazine out. "Every woman should have a copy," she said, handing it to Kathryn. "It's really fresh and quite inspiring, if the truth be told."

Kathryn opened the magazine. On the first page was list of the contributors as well as their pictures. Rachel was near the top, placed under the editor Gloria. Kathryn stared at the image. *She is so beautiful*.

"They've been going for few months now and unlike other magazines their copy seems to be getting stronger — are you listening to me?"

"What? Oh yes, stronger, yes."

"So who was the lucky journalist who managed to bag an interview with you?"

"Um, Rachel."

"Let me see," Jo said, taking the magazine from her hands. "Wow, she's hot."

"I met her the other day at the Grove bar, when you had to leave."

"Wow, that's a bit of a coincidence for you and a lorra lorra luck for her," she said, using her impersonation of Cilla Black.

Kathryn laughed. "Yeah."

"So what's she like? Someone that gorgeous has to have some flaws."

"From what I've seen of her, none are glaringly

obvious but I have only met her a few times."

"I bet she's got a string of boyfriends behind her," Jo said, putting the magazine back under the table.

"Actually, she's, um gay."

"Are you kidding me?!"

Kathryn laughed.

"No way is that woman gay," Jo said, scooping up the magazine again and finding her picture.

"I swear she is."

"Oh my God, Ben had better watch out, with women like this on the loose —"

"With women like who on the loose?" Ben called out from the hallway. As he entered the room he strode over to Kathryn and bent down to kiss her cheek. "What trouble are you two getting up to now?" he teased.

"Nothing for you to worry about," Jo said, returning his kiss.

Tall, with well-defined muscles, thick black hair and blue eyes, Ben was very attractive. Not only was he good to look at, but his personality was one of warmth and humour. Though Kathryn had never been attracted to him personally, she totally understood why Jo had fought tooth and nail to get him.

"This woman's a lesbian," Jo said, thrusting the magazine into his hand.

He took the magazine from her and whistled as he eyed the picture of Rachel. "Mmm, very nice."

"Oi, you," Jo said, slapping him playfully on the arm. "Don't start getting any ideas, if anyone's got a chance with her, it's me," she said, joking.

"I wouldn't mind, only if I could watch," he said, winking at Kathryn. "Now, wench, what's for dinner? I'm starving."

"You know where the kitchen is."

"Oh come on, Jo, I've been at work all day."

"And what do you think I've been doing? Twiddling my thumbs?"

He stared at the wine bottle.

"That was my doing, I'm afraid," Kathryn said, standing up and putting her jacket on.

"Don't go yet, we haven't finished talking."

"Yes," she said leaning down to draw Jo in for a quick hug, "we have. Now go and feed your husband. I'll call you tomorrow."

"Okay and make sure you do, this discussion isn't over yet."

She closed the front door to the sound of their laughter. That was what she wanted — an easy going kind of relationship where she could just be herself and not Gareth's wife or Kathryn Kassel the interior designer. It had been a long time since she had just been plain and simple Kathryn — though when she really thought about it, she wasn't sure if there ever had been such a time.

## CHAPTER 12

The tempo at *Women's Lifestyle Magazine* was at fever pitch as all members of staff worked towards the deadline with renewed enthusiasm. Having Kathryn as their lead story meant the magazine was getting more attention than it ever had. There was a buzz in the air that hadn't been there before.

"I hope you're behaving yourself?" Gloria said, sitting at the vacant seat next to Rachel's desk.

Rachel stopped typing up her interview notes. "The police haven't been round to press charges against me for sexual harassment again, have they?" she asked with mock seriousness.

"Don't be funny."

"Well, you're the one insinuating I'm a nymphomaniac."

"Now you know I didn't mean that."

"I know, Gloria." Rachel smiled and turned towards her, pulling her draped striped cardigan together at the front. "And yes I've been good, in fact I'm being so good, I haven't tried it on with Kathryn and I haven't hit the bars for gosh — what is it? Nearly a week now."

"Really? Are you having me on?"

"Nope," Rachel said, her attention returning to her computer screen.

"Well, that's good to hear." Like Zoe, Gloria worried incessantly about her and the women she met on the Internet.

"I thought you'd say that."

Rachel wondered what Gloria would say if she told her how she felt about Kathryn. *She'd go berserk is what she'd do.* If she thought for one minute that Rachel could do anything to mess up the one thing that could save her magazine, Gloria would not be happy and she didn't blame her.

"So does that mean you're looking for like, a one-to-one relationship?" Gloria said hopefully.

"Let's not go that far, Gloria — I only meant for now."

"At least I can have a few nights of sleeping through, without thinking I'll be printing your eulogy instead of your articles."

"Blimey, Gloria. What type of women do you think I meet?"

"Just because you're mixing with women, that doesn't make them any safer — everyone is a potential harmer," Gloria said quietly.

"Between you and Zoe, soon I'll be too scared to put a foot outside my front door."

"We just care about you," Gloria said softly, putting her hand on Rachel's shoulder.

Rachel looked directly into Gloria's eyes. "I know you do and I appreciate it, but you really have nothing to worry about. I'm very street smart." She smiled, trying to lighten the mood.

"Until you're not. Don't think you're invincible, Rachel, because you're not — none of us are."

"What's gotten into you today? Have you been

watching *Dates from Hell* again? You know that program makes you paranoid."

Gloria threw her hands up into the air. "Okay, take the piss out of me."

"Gloria, are you alright?"

"Yes, I'm fine," Gloria replied, as she pretended to inspect her inch-long, hot-red, acrylic nails.

"What's brought all this on?" Rachel grabbed her hand and held it gently.

"You're like a daughter to me, Rachel. I don't want anything bad happening to you."

"It won't, I promise," Rachel replied, releasing her hand.

"Just be careful."

"Okay, now can the real Gloria step forward? You know, the one who is always screaming about deadlines and copy not being sassy enough, me being — "

"Gloria," one of the sales woman called, "I think you should see this."

Gloria stood up, walked the short distance to the next desk and took the sheets of paper from her hand. As she scanned sheet after sheet, her eyes widened in amazement.

"I can't believe it, I honestly can't believe it," she finished, shaking the papers in her hand.

"What's the matter?" Rachel was by her side in seconds.

"Look at this!" Gloria said, thrusting the papers into Rachel's hands, "from practically begging people to advertise with us, they are throwing themselves at us."

"I take it from these figures, you've been spreading the word that Kathryn is going to be in next month's copy," Rachel said with a wide grin.

"You're damn right I have been," Gloria said, thrusting her chest out. "The first thing I learnt in life was not to look a gift horse in the mouth." She put the papers down and marched into her office. "Stella, Rachel," she hollered, "follow me, please, we're going to up the ante."

Once both women were in the office, Gloria's voice took on a serious tone. "Look, I'm not going to beat around the bush, we are one step away from closing the magazine down. Even with this influx of new advertisers, it's only a plaster on a gaping hole. We need to take full advantage of this and make sure these advertisers stick with us."

"How do we do that?" Rachel asked, caught up in her excitement.

"We're going to throw a party. We'll invite all the advertisers as well as designers; everybody who's anybody in the industry."

"And how are we going to wangle that, or have I missed something? Do you have a fairy Godmother you haven't introduced me to?" Rachel asked, trying to keep the sarcasm out of her voice. *If most of the industry didn't turn up to the launch party a year ago, why would they turn up now?*

"I don't, but you do," Gloria said with a large grin. "Her name is Kathryn Kassel."

## CHAPTER 13

Kathryn looked out of her office window as the crowded street loomed below, seemingly giving careful consideration to what Rachel was asking her.

"Look, I know this is no concern of yours, we hardly know each other, but we are desperate, to the point the magazine may have to fold if we can't make up revenue through advertising."

"I can't see what harm it would do. When is this bash?"

"Four weeks," Rachel said, lowering her eyes. "I know it's terribly short notice, but Gloria has just come up with the idea to make it coincide with the day your interview is out."

"Four weeks," Kathryn said, more to herself than Rachel. "That doesn't give you a lot of time to get the word out." She moved behind her desk and flicked through her organiser. "Okay, I'll come. As well as that, I'll get Carol to draw up a list of my contacts and call in some favours — I'm sure they'd be more than happy to attend a party."

"Are you serious?" Rachel asked, struck by her kindness to help out her boss, someone she'd never even met.

"Yes, I'm serious, I would have thought by now that

you would've realised I don't say things I don't mean."

"I'll never be able to thank you enough," Rachel said, reaching out and clasping her hand for a brief moment. Rachel looked into her heavy-lidded eyes as she touched her, noticing for the first time the dark blue rim of her iris and golden halo surrounding her enlarged pupils.

"As long as your article shows me in a good light, that will be enough," Kathryn joked, breaking her gaze as she retreated to her chair.

"Well, that's easy."

"We'd better get on with the interview, otherwise you'll have nothing to print."

"Yes, boss," Rachel said, saluting her.

Once settled into her seat, Rachel began, "So, I have enough information about your professional life, now down to the nitty gritty of your personal life. Is it alright to start off with talking a bit about your marriage to —" She looked at her note pad. "— Gareth?"

Kathryn smiled and nodded.

Noticing the smile didn't reach her eyes, Rachel continued, "So you've been married for ten years, any tips on what makes for a happy marriage?"

"Honesty," Kathryn replied.

Rachel told herself to concentrate on the job at hand and not to be thinking about whether Kathryn's marriage was a happy one. She turned back to her task and wrote diligently as Kathryn spoke of the wonderful support she had received from her husband and friends, and the pain that she had gone through growing up without a mother figure, especially when it came to dating. "What a nightmare," she laughed.

"I take it your father wasn't the type to sit you down

and tell you about the birds and the bees?" Rachel asked.

"No, no he wasn't." Kathryn let out a sigh. There was something in her eyes that Rachel couldn't quite read. *Was it sadness? Hatred? Resentment?* She decided to probe a bit deeper.

"So what type of relationship did you have with your father? Were you a daddy's girl?"

"You could say that, well up until my mother died. After that, I was more like a ... a burden," Kathryn finally managed to say.

"I'm sorry."

"It's okay." Kathryn smiled faintly.

"But it must have been tough, not having the support you needed after losing your mother."

Kathryn was silent for several moments. "Yes, it was, but thankfully I had Jo, who was like a sister to me and her mum basically gave me the love my father couldn't."

"Did your dad remarry?"

Kathryn gave a bitter laugh. "He sure did, oh what was it now," she said, pretending to try and remember. "It was six weeks after we buried my mother that he married our neighbour. Who also happened to be my mum's best friend. I think it must have been going on for a while, even when my mum was alive."

"That must have been rough on you."

"It was, but he didn't care what I or anybody else thought, as long as he was alright, that was all that mattered."

"Do you still see him?" Rachel wanted to stop asking her questions but couldn't. It was her job to get answers, but she felt bad getting Kathryn to relive something she had obviously buried in the past.

"No," Kathryn said, shaking her head. "I last saw him about eleven years ago. He didn't even come to my wedding." She stifled a sob that had risen out of nowhere.

*What a bastard, his own daughter, what kind of man would do that?* Rachel's heart went out to Kathryn as she watched her go from the confident business woman to a lost little girl, all alone in an untrusting world. She so desperately wanted to hold her, to banish the look of insecurity from her face and her heart.

Kathryn gave a shrug of her shoulders. "Like I said, that was a long time ago."

Sensing that she had said enough on that subject, Rachel moved on to other generic topics about what the future held for her and what her personal aspirations were.

"I think we're done," Rachel said an hour later, closing her note pad.

"Great," Kathryn said, sounding disappointed.

"So, once I've written everything up and it's been approved, I'll let you see a copy before it goes to print."

"That'll be great."

"How is the project is progressing?"

"Rob's there now with the builders, it's going pretty well at the moment, fingers crossed."

"Brilliant." Rachel felt the need to prolong the conversation. She didn't want to just get up and leave Kathryn, having opened her up emotionally.

There was a knock at the door, and Carol popped her head around the corner.

"Sorry to interrupt, ladies." Carol nodded hello to Rachel. "Kathryn, there are problems with those bloody tree houses. Rob said they sent him an image and outline of what they had started to make and it is different to what he asked for. He's been on the phone to them all morning and has gotten nowhere."

"What does he propose?" Kathryn asked, her business hat back on.

"That you both fly to Denmark and go to the factory to make sure they're are making the ones you ordered."

"Do we have the time?"

"From what Rob says, you're going to have to make time, he's doing his nut. He said the company should have taken his points into account. He doesn't trust that they'll rectify the problem, that's why he wants you both to go there in person."

"Okay," Kathryn said flicking through her diary, "tell him we'll go on Tuesday. And get him to call them again and put a hold on everything until we get there."

"I'll tell him and get everything booked, one night or two?"

"One. See if you can book the earliest flight on both days."

"Will do."

"Thanks, Carol," Kathryn said as her head disappeared behind the door. "Looks like I spoke too soon," she said, pushing a strand of hair behind her ear. "So where were we?"

"I think we were just about done. Do you really have to go all that way for a tree house? I mean isn't there a cheaper way of sorting it out?"

"They are very, very expensive tree houses and are the centre pieces of the design. There are also structural implications to take into account. If they arrive and are wrong, then the project won't be finished on time and Ellie will be furious."

Rachel stood to leave. "Ah, I see. I'll let you get on then, as it seems you've got your hands full. I'll stop by next week when you get back, if that's okay?"

Kathryn looked up. "Yes, that'll be fine, although I am going to have to go to Ellie's tomorrow now, to check a few things before we leave for Denmark. You're welcome to come."

"Yep, tomorrow it is then!" Rachel said, leaving Kathryn flicking through a cat catalogue.

\*\*\*

With the office now to herself, Kathryn sat back in her chair and took a deep breath. Sadness overtook her. Never having talked to anyone in-depth about her past before, not even to Gareth, meant today had taken its toll. She felt as though a gaping wound had been reopened.

She looked out of the window as rain drummed against the window pane. Whenever it rained, in spite of her resolve, inexorably her mind returned to the day her life had drastically changed forever.

She could still remember the panic she felt that day, seeing her mother lying motionless on the kitchen floor. She brushed away the tears that were threatening to spill — she wasn't the only one who had lost someone.

She knew Rachel was suffering in her own way with her mother's mind locked in a prison that she had no access to — maybe emotional suffering was a common bond they both shared. She felt helpless that there wasn't anything she could do to ease her pain — *or was there?* A plan formed in her mind.

Later that evening at home, she stared at the TV, trying her hardest to look engaged, but her mind was on Rachel — her emotions were all over the place. She felt like she was on a roller coaster ride. When she was with Rachel, she was at the peak of the highest ride in the world. When they were apart, everything went speedily downhill. Her phone bleeped signalling a message — flipping it open, her heart sank when she read the text message.

>Sorry I can't make it tomorrow after all.
>I have an appt I can't break.
>Mike will drop by to take photos if that's ok?
>Can I come by Monday?
>R

## CHAPTER 14

"I can't believe I'm here when I should be with Kathryn," Rachel said, standing outside a tall glass-fronted building, stretching high into the sky. She'd received a call from her father's solicitor the previous day, asking to rearrange her appointment due to an emergency. If she hadn't agreed, it would have been weeks before another opening came up.

"There'll be other days, it's not the end of the world," Zoe replied.

"The point is, I really don't want to be here. Even from the grave he's affecting my life in a negative way." She was still reeling from the news, made worse by the fact she couldn't talk to her mother about it.

"Give his memory a break, Rachel, he's gone now. Can't you find it in your heart to forgive him so he can rest in peace?"

"If I could, I would have years ago. You don't know what he put my mum through, all the suffering she endured because he couldn't keep his pants up. Sorry, but if that makes me a class A bitch, so be it."

"I didn't say you were a bitch, I just think at some stage you've got to let go of the anger."

"I'm not angry, Zoe, I just don't want any memories in my life of him — dead or alive."

"Okay, point taken. Shall we go in?"

"In a minute."

"Are you nervous?"

"Yes, I dread to think what he's left me. What if it's a couple of kids?"

Zoe let out a hearty laugh. "You walk straight back out denying he's your real father. That it's all been a dreadful mistake. If, on the other hand, it's a large amount of money ...." Her expression spoke for itself.

Rachel let out a deep sigh. "Let's get this over with."

"It's not going to be as bad as you think," Zoe said as they headed toward the glass door. A young man held it open for them before exiting himself, turning back to ogle Rachel's tanned, bare legs beneath the black pencil skirt she wore.

"We're here to see Bette Willis," Rachel said to the young receptionist behind a mahogany desk.

"One moment please," she replied, picking up the phone and announcing their arrival to the person on the other end. "Miss Willis will see you now."

"Thank you."

"Her office is on the second floor, the lifts are to the right."

Rachel smiled at her as they strode towards the lift, eventually finding themselves on the second floor.

"Rachel Collins?" the solicitor said, opening the door to her plush office. Standing at just over five feet, she was an attractive middle-aged woman with short blonde hair, brown eyes and a pretty smile, which she beamed at them both. "Come in, come in. Sit down," she said, gesturing to two leather swivel chairs in front of her glass panelled desk.

"I hope it's okay, I brought my friend Zoe along,"

Rachel said.

"Of course it is," she said, shaking both their hands. "Nice to meet you."

Both women smiled back at her, before she skirted around her desk and sat down. Her attention on Rachel, she spoke in a soft tone. "Thank you for coming in. As I explained on the phone, it's something I would rather do in person."

Rachel waited for her to continue. Bette picked up a large envelope that lay in front of her and unsealed it, fishing inside for its contents.

"Firstly, I would like to offer you my sincerest condolences, your father was a good man," she said as she brought out a single sheet of A4 paper.

*To who? Not to my mum and definitely not to me.*

Bette continued, "Mr Lexington had one asset, which has been left to you." She perched a pair of rimless glass on her pert nose. "A property in Battersea. There is no mortgage ...." she said, looking at Rachel for a response, to which she gave none.

Rachel sat impassively whilst Bette read out legalities, which took another half an hour. Finally, she stopped talking and Rachel and Zoe stood up to leave.

"Please don't hesitate to get in touch if you need clarification on anything we've discussed here today."

Rachel and Zoe looked at each other and said nothing.

Outside, away from the building the two women screamed, hugging and spinning around in a waltz.

"Oh my God, I can't believe it — a house ... and in Battersea of all places," Zoe said, breathless. "Please pinch me so I know this isn't a dream."

Rachel reached out and pinched her.

"Ouch, I was talking metaphorically," Zoe said, rubbing her arm.

"Sorry," Rachel said ruefully. "Anyway, let's go and see it before we get too excited yet, it might be worse than the place we're living in at the moment." She couldn't believe all these years he had been living somewhere so close — she could have, for all she knew, passed him on the street. That thought depressed her.

"Rachel, you and I both know that would be impossible. A beach hut would be better than where we're living."

Rachel laughed a little, still struggling to comprehend the situation.

"I think I need to sit down," Rachel said as they neared a wooden bench, and collapsed onto it. "I wonder why he did this?"

Zoe chose her words carefully. "Maybe it was just his way of showing you that he still cared."

"He never cared about anyone but himself. I don't think a person can change that much."

"You'd be surprised, Rach. Maybe it took until he was staring death in the face to realise all the hurt and pain he caused you. Your uncle did say he had been looking for you for quite a while."

"And what about my mum? Not one mention of her in his will."

"How do you know what went on between them, Rach? You only heard one side of the story. Perhaps if you would have read the letter, you could have made sense of things — gained some closure."

"This is all too depressing for me," Rachel said, standing up abruptly. "Do you think it's a bit morbid to go and have a celebratory drink?"

"No, isn't that the norm, to hit the pub after someone dies?"

"Yeah, you're right, I know just the place and with who."

"Oh no, what have I let myself in for?" Zoe groaned, as she followed Rachel to the tube station.

***

Millets Bar in Soho was empty, apart from the three women and the members of staff, who were milling around, laughing and joking amongst themselves. This was the quiet before the storm. In a few hours, the place would be swarming with customers. It was one of the busiest gay bars in London.

"So what are we celebrating?" Cody asked, as she raised her glass to meet Rachel and Zoe's.

"We're moving home, we went to view it before we came here. It's an amazing three bedroom house," Rachel said, leaving out how it had come about. The last thing she wanted to do was speak about her father or even think about him — it hurt too much.

"Congratulations!" Cody said, raising her voice, a big grin on her face as she toasted both women. "When you moving in?"

"In a few weeks, we're just sorting out the paperwork."

"I hope I'm going to get an invite to the house warming," Cody said, glancing over at Zoe.

"Of course," Rachel replied, smiling at Cody's obvious attraction to her flatmate.

"So you're a therapist, huh?" Cody asked Zoe, who had sat quietly while the two women had spoken.

"Yes."

"Doesn't it get you down, listening to depressed people all day?"

"No, not really. I enjoy helping people and I always have Rachel to go home to after," she said, looking at her fondly.

"Zoe is very good at what she does," Rachel interjected, gently nudging Zoe's shoulder. She was relieved to see that her idea seemed to be working — on Cody anyway. She just needed to get a few more drinks into Zoe so she could relax.

"And you work for Kathryn Kassel?" Zoe asked.

"I sure do," Cody said. "I take it you know Rachel has a little crush on her? I've told her not to even bother, Kathryn is as straight as a dye."

"And like I told you, our relationship is purely business. I can't help finding her attractive, but that's all there is to it."

"Uh huh," Zoe chimed in. "And Rachel doesn't lie. When she says something, she means it."

"And what about you?" Cody asked. "Have you got your eye on somebody?"

Zoe turned to Rachel. "Um yeah, yeah I do, but it's a long story, I wouldn't want to bore you."

"No, Zoe, I'm sure she'd be interested to hear about ...?" Rachel said, raising her eyebrows.

"Um, Claire, you don't know her. She works at the centre."

"Really? You'll have to bring her over for dinner one night."

"I will," Zoe said through gritted teeth. "Why don't we go and get some more drinks?" She stood up, pulling

Rachel up by her hands. "We won't be a minute," she said to Cody, before edging Rachel towards the bar.

"That wasn't very discreet," Rachel said, glancing around, assuring herself that they were out of Cody's hearing range.

"What are you doing?" Zoe hissed.

"Trying to set you up with a funny, intelligent, hot woman." Rachel glanced over at Cody dressed in light-washed jeans and a black leather jacket.

"Ahh, so you're not denying it?" Zoe asked, wrong-footed by Rachel's honesty.

"No, I'm not, I think she likes you and let's be honest, you could do a lot worse."

"But I'm not looking for a partner. I'm not being funny, but only a few days ago she was trying to get in *your* pants."

"No, she wasn't, it was just a bit of harmless flirting." She looked over at Cody, who was watching them, and gave a little wave. "Look, Zoe," she said, turning back to her, "you can't remain caught in the past. Bloody hell, what is your favourite line to your clients — 'you've got to move on, take the next step'," she mimicked. "I think it's time you took your own advice, don't you?"

After a few seconds, Zoe threw her hands up in the air. "Oh, what the hell," she said, taking a sly look at Cody. "I suppose she is nice and she does have a job."

"Exactly, anyway, I'm going to leave you love birds and head home and get some work done."

"What! You're leaving me alone with her?" Zoe asked, panic in her voice.

"Yes, all that can happen is that you'll have a good time."

"That's what I'm afraid of."

***

Hours later, Rachel was sat on her living room floor, mulling over the sheets of paper spread out before her, desperately trying to keep her mind occupied. Since she had arrived home, she'd gathered generic information from the Internet about Gareth, as she had all the information about Kathryn she needed. She noted he was a handsome man and his youthful looks belied the fact that he was fifteen years older than his wife. *Is that why her father had refused to attend the wedding because her husband-to-be was so much older?* She reflected over what Kathryn had said about her father marrying the neighbour so quickly after her mother's passing. That was in stark contrast to her own mother, who had never recovered from her dad walking out on her — she had never remarried nor even dated again.

She studied a photo of Kathryn and Gareth at a gala event—they looked the perfect couple, holding hands and smiles plastered on their faces. She noted the date the picture was taken — eight years ago. She shook her head sadly — she didn't understand how relationships worked, because she had never had one. Her childhood and most of her adulthood had been spent caring for her mother; first through depression, then when she developed Alzheimer's five years previously. It was why she maintained the philosophy of living in the moment and doing as she pleased. Life was too short, nobody knew what was around the corner.

Rachel heard the front door open and close, then the sound of Zoe's heavy footsteps advancing along the hall, followed by another set. Rachel looked up in amazement when Zoe and Cody appeared.

"Well, this is a surprise," Rachel teased.

"We thought we'd bring the party back here," Zoe said, her voice slurred.

"What have you done to the poor girl?" Rachel asked Cody, who was leaning against the door frame with a bottle of wine in her hand.

"Nothing yet," Cody said with a mischievous glint in her eyes.

"That's right, nothing yet," Zoe said, swaying as she went into the kitchen. "Gonna get some glasses then we're going to my room. It's your first door on your left," she said to an eagerly waiting Cody, whose eyes were bright and glossy. "Go and make yourself comfortable."

"I don't need telling twice," Cody replied, before disappearing behind the door.

Walking over to the kitchen, Rachel stopped Zoe leaving the room. "This is a bit fast, isn't it?"

"This coming from the would-shag-you-in-a-minute woman," Zoe said, letting out a laugh.

"Zoe, I'm not kidding, don't go and do something that you're gonna regret."

"What's to regret? I like her, she likes me, she wants sex, I want sex," Zoe rambled.

"Drunk sex is never a good idea," Rachel said, shaking her head.

"So what? My God, is that what I sound like when I'm going on at you?"

"Well, yes."

"Then I sincerely apologise, because I am a kill joy, I feel great!" Zoe said, undoing her grey zip-up jacket.

Let's hope you feel that way in the morning. Rachel stepped aside.

"Do you want to join us?" A slow smile built on Zoe's face.

"Now that really is disgusting," Rachel said, laughing. "Go on, go and have fun."

"Okay, don't say I didn't ask."

"I promise *I will* remind you that you did ask in the morning."

"Spoil sport," Zoe sang heartedly as she went into her bedroom.

Rachel closed the living room door, hoping that would block out any noises she didn't want to hear. She sat down on the floor to resume her work. Her eyes were drawn back to the photo of Kathryn. She loved looking at her, more than any woman she had ever met. She outlined the shape of her face with her finger, wishing it was the real thing she was touching. With great force, she snapped herself out of her daydream. *The lack of sex is obviously having an adverse effect on me.* She gathered all the papers together and began typing. The sooner she got this interview over with, the sooner she could resume her normal life and the happier she would be — or would she, she begrudging asked herself, fully knowing what the answer would be.

## CHAPTER 15

Kathryn looked up from her paperwork as her office door opened and Rachel poked her head in before entering.

"Rachel, it's good to see you," Kathryn said. Although it had only been three days since their last meeting, it had felt like a lifetime. Kathryn had missed Rachel in a way that felt new for her. She had never missed Gareth, *ever*. Years ago, when he had travelled extensively with his job, she had hardly noticed he was gone, but a few days without seeing Rachel had been like trying to breathe without oxygen.

"Busy?" Rachel enquired.

"Nothing that can't wait ... so what's new?" Kathryn asked, leaning back in her chair, a giddy feeling enveloping her.

"Well," Rachel said, extracting a folder from her bag, "I have a rough copy of the interview. I thought you might want to look at it before I give it to Gloria, if there are things that you'd rather I left out …."

"No, don't be silly, everything I told you was for you to print."

"Okay then, well here you go," Rachel said, handing her it to her, feeling the tips of her fingers brush hers as the folder passed between them.

Kathryn bent her head and studied the papers in front

of her. "Do you want me to read it now?"

Rachel shook her head. "Not this minute but if you could approve it by the end of the week that would be great."

"No problem."

"Oh, and I've got the photos," she said as she retrieved them from her bag. "Mike said what you've accomplished so far looked amazing."

Taking the photos from Rachel, Kathryn smiled. "Good, he's a really nice bloke," she said, flicking through the pictures, "and a fantastic photographer."

"He'll be pleased he did your work justice."

"I might hire him to take my photos if they all turn out this good," she said, handing the photos to Rachel and sitting back down.

"Sorry I couldn't be there on the day, I hadn't realised that I had an appointment booked for that morning."

"No worries you can come at the end of the week."

A knock on the door preceded a frazzled-looking Rob, wearing black jeans and a red and blue chequered shirt.

"I'm sorry to have to do this to you, Kathryn, but I can't come to the meeting tomorrow," he said, pacing up and down the office, unable to settle in one spot.

"Calm down, what's happened?"

"It's Claire, she's been taken to the hospital. They think they're going to have to induce the baby. I can't leave her at a time like this," he said, clenching his hands into fists.

Kathryn stood up and put her hand on his shoulder, forcing him to stop. "I wouldn't expect you to, Rob. You needn't have come in to tell me, you should have just called."

"I wanted to give you this," he said, pulling a sheet of

paper from his pocket and thrusting it towards her. "It's got all the details and dimensions the piece should have — if you explain it and they follow it to the letter, everything should be alright. So we can most probably finish the place next week."

"I really appreciate this, Rob," Kathryn replied, taking the paper, "now go, before Claire comes by to find you, in labour or not." She laughed as he gave her a grateful smile. It wouldn't be the first time Rob's wife had tracked him down at work, when for some reason or another he should have been at home.

"I'm out of here," he said, rushing to the door. "Any problems, call me, I'll have my phone on day and night."

"I will, now go."

He laughed. "Okay, okay, have a safe trip."

"Give my love to Claire," Kathryn called as the door closed behind him.

"Is it his first child?"

"Yes," Kathryn said as she sat back down.

Rachel grinned. "Ah, that will explain his jitters, I thought he was going to hyperventilate."

"My friend's husband was the same. She said his behaviour made her feel worse."

"I can imagine." Rachel's eyes widened. "Ah, that's what I forgot to ask you — about kids?"

"What about them?" Kathryn asked, knowing full well what the question was going to be.

"Are you planning on having any?"

"No, not at the moment anyway."

"Does your husband want children?"

"I suppose so. Believe it or not, it's not something that we've really discussed at length."

All of their friends had thought it would just be a matter of time before she got pregnant after their wedding. Some even thought they had got married for that very reason. But as each year passed and a baby wasn't produced, people stopped asking and she was relieved about that.

"I'd have thought it would have been the icing on the cake for such a successful couple."

"Well, looks can be deceiving," Kathryn said cryptically. "What about you? Any little Rachels planned for the future?"

"Oh God no, I'd most probably leave it somewhere by accident. I couldn't imagine being tied down by a child or relationship when it comes to that."

Though Kathryn laughed, she wondered to herself what had made Rachel such a commitment-phobe. Had she been in a relationship and been hurt?

"Do you want a coffee or are you going somewhere?" Kathryn asked, desperate for her to stay.

"I was going to pop in to see my mum, but I've got time for a coffee. It's not as if she's going to know I'm there."

"I'm sure she does," Kathryn said, rising from her seat and putting her hand over hers and giving a reassuring squeeze. "I won't be a minute, I'll get the coffee and tell Carol to cancel Rob's ticket."

"If you wouldn't mind some company, I'd like to come with you tomorrow," Rachel called, just as she reached the door.

Temporarily flustered, Kathryn eventually managed to respond. "Really?"

"Yes, it will be good to add it to the rest of the piece I'm doing on you. That's if you don't mind."

"Erm, of course not. I'll go and sort the tickets out," Kathryn said, feeling more alive than she had in years.

\*\*\*

Kathryn could feel Gareth watching her from behind his steel-rimmed glasses. There had been a spring in her step since she'd arrived home that evening and she knew Gareth must be wondering why, but she didn't care. Rachel was becoming like an addictive drug and today she had finally had her fix.

"How are things at work?" he enquired from the dining table where he sat, drink in hand.

"Fine," she replied, dropping the spaghetti into a boiling pan of water.

"And your interview?"

"I've got the first draft for my approval." She brought a spoonful of the tomato sauce to her mouth, tasted it then added a little more salt.

"And ..."

"I haven't read it yet." She poured herself a generous amount of red wine and took a sip before replacing it on the worktop.

"I see. I was thinking, would you like to go away for the weekend?"

She froze. "I can't. I've got too much on at the moment. What with going to Denmark tomorrow, I'll be behind with some of my other projects when I get back."

"Are you sure you don't want me to come with you? I could take a couple of days off and we could do some sightseeing."

"That sounds wonderful, but I forgot to mention Rob is going as well and we really need to be back on Wednesday."

"Oh okay, don't worry then."

She knew he would back down as soon as she mentioned Rob. For some reason Gareth didn't like him, despite the fact that he was obviously very much in love with his wife. She couldn't understand why a man who had everything would feel so threatened.

Turning around, spoon in hand, she said, "And I forgot to tell you —"

"My, you are getting forgetful, aren't you?" he replied, taking a long sip of his drink.

She placed the spoon on the kitchen worktop and stepped through into the dining room. Pulling out a grey upholstered chair from underneath the six-foot oak table, which dominated the room, she sat down before she continued, "I'm sorry, I've just got a lot on my mind."

He put his hand on hers. "It's okay, so what else did you forget to tell me?"

She gently broached the idea, knowing that if she wanted to get Gareth to do something he had to be reeled in slowly. "We've been invited to a party being held by the magazine."

"Why's that then?"

"Oh, it might go bust if they can't bring in more advertisers."

"What's that got to do with you?"

"Well, nothing really, but I said I'd go to show my support and invite a few people I know in the business. You know yourself it's all about who you know that impresses advertisers. I just thought we could give them a helping hand."

He smirked. "So first you're the House Doctor, today you're Mother Theresa, whatever will you be next?"

She put her hand to her head. "I could really do without your sarcastic comments, if I'm honest with you. What has gotten into you lately? You keep picking on me, have I done something wrong?"

"I don't know, you tell me — have you?" he said, tilting his head, his eyebrows raised.

She fixed her gaze on him across the dining table. Had he been suspicious all this time about her and she hadn't even realised? The guilt she felt caused her to react defensively to his covert accusation. "Are you being serious? What on earth could I have been doing? Is this all because I went out with Jo a couple of weeks ago? Because if I remember rightly, it's only since then you've been acting strangely."

"I don't know what you're talking about," he said, averting his eyes. "I'm tired, I'm going to have an early night — don't worry, I'm not going to ask you to join me," he said as he jumped out of his chair and made his way out the door.

Kathryn took a deep breath and released it slowly. *What is happening to me? Why did I lie to Gareth about Rob going to Denmark?* She had never outright lied to him before — well, not verbally anyway. But the thought of spending a whole evening with Rachel, uninterrupted by work colleagues or phones or distance, put an end to her feelings of guilt. Nothing was going to happen — she just wanted to have some fun.

## CHAPTER 16

As a loud crack of thunder rolled across the darkened sky, Rachel was wasting no time packing for the next morning. She threw her overnight bag on the bed and began filling it with clothing and toiletries.

"Come in!" she called out in response to the faint knock on her door.

The door creaked as Zoe pushed it open, lingering at the threshold for a few seconds, her deep-set eyes meeting Rachel's amused smile.

"Why didn't you stop me?" Zoe cried out, wearing black track suit bottoms and a pink T-shirt. She entered the bedroom and fell heavily onto Rachel's bed, burying her face deep into the feather pillow.

"And how was I meant to do that? You seemed quite in control last night," Rachel reminded her.

Zoe sprawled out her lanky body, her bare feet dangling over the edge of the bed. "I want to die." Her voice was muffled, barely audible.

"Why? Because you had sex?" Rachel shook her head sympathetically.

"Yes," Zoe groaned. "It wasn't just sex, it was great sex and now I want more. Lots more."

"So what's the problem?"

Zoe dragged her face away from the pillow, opening one blood shot eye to look at her. "No insult intended, but she's like you."

"What the hell is that supposed to mean?" Rachel asked as she moved towards the chest of drawers and began rummaging through them.

"You know what I mean. She's a player, she isn't looking for a one to one relationship." Zoe rolled over onto her back and drew her knees up.

"I really don't see the problem," Rachel said, retrieving the top she was looking for then throwing it in her case. She could never understand why so many people got caught up with feelings of guilt or regret when it came to sex. How did something so intimate and so enjoyable get such a bad rap — for women anyway?

"You don't see the problem?" Zoe asked her incredulously. "In the five years you've known me, how many women have I slept with?"

"Let's see now," Rachel said, pretending to count, "er none."

"Exactly," Zoe pounded the mattress with her fist, "because I'm not that kind of person. I do one on one — not one on many. Now do you see what I mean?" She peered up at Rachel through one eye.

"Yes, Zoe, but if that's what you're looking for, you shouldn't have jumped into bed with her without getting know her first."

"Are you kidding me? You're the bloody one who introduced me to her."

"That I am guilty of but," she held up her hand, "I introduced you in a bar, not in your bed — that was all your doing."

"I knew you wouldn't understand," Zoe said, rolling off the bed and heading for the door.

"I do, but I don't know what you want me to say — you're the therapist, what would you tell your client?"

Zoe turned to her. "To grow the hell up — hey, why are you packing?" she asked, as if only noticing for the first time Rachel was putting clothes in an overnight bag.

"I'm going away tomorrow for the night."

"Where to?"

"Denmark."

"Why on earth would you be going to Denmark?"

"Kathryn has an appointment to do with work. I said I'd tag along."

Zoe's eyes widened. "Are you joking?"

"No, I'm not."

"But I thought ...."

"Zoe, we're going to be sleeping in separate rooms. It's all very innocent. We fly back early Wednesday morning."

"Innocent and you do not appear in the same sentence."

Rachel laughed. "Well, it's true. I thought by now you would have realised that I've been true to my word. I've not made any attempt to go beyond a professional business relationship."

"I s'pose not. Alright, I believe you, now back to my problem."

"Do you want to see Cody again?"

Zoe nodded.

"Does she want to see you again?

"Well, she said she did."

"When?"

"She wants to come back tomorrow."

Thank God I'm not going to be here. The walls are way too thin for another night like last night.

"So what's the problem then?"

"I don't want to be used."

"Oh for God's sake, Zoe, get dressed and get down to a sex shop and show her what you're made of."

"After all your years of seducing women, that's the only piece of advice you can come up with?" Zoe picked up a pillow off the bed and threw it at her. "I'm so not impressed," she said as she burst out laughing.

"I won't even mention your invitation to join you last night."

"Oh God no," Zoe said, covering her ears. "Please don't tell me."

## CHAPTER 17

Just under two hours after leaving Heathrow airport, the British Airways plane touched down on the tarmac in Copenhagen. A short time later, Kathryn and Rachel arrived at Park View Hotel, which was positioned conveniently on the promenade overlooking Copenhagen's southern harbour front. Resembling a postmodern cube, its glassy exterior afforded sweeping views across the harbour from the reception area.

As Kathryn checked in, Rachel looked at her surroundings in awe. Minimalist furniture was positioned with precision around a contemporary angular fireplace. The ceiling height spanned two floors, with the first floor corridors and rooms visible from the ground floor. Guests walked up and down an elegantly lit central staircase, which served as the centrepiece of the reception area.

Having obtained their room keys, the women made their way to the lifts.

"If we just drop our bags off, we can head straight to my appointment," Kathryn said as they stepped out of the lift on the third floor. "Is that alright?"

Rachel nodded. "Yep, maybe I can talk them into taking an ad out in our magazine," she added.

"It's worth a shot," Kathryn replied.

They remained silent as they walked along the corridor, searching for their room numbers.

"Here we are," Rachel said at last. "We're opposite each other."

"Great," Kathryn said, sliding her hotel key card into the silver slot mechanism on the door. "See you in five minutes."

"Okay," Rachel replied, pushing her own door open and then immediately being taken aback by the enormous floor-to-ceiling window that dominated the far wall. Dropping her bag to the floor, she surveyed the rest of the room. A plush cream sofa with an assortment of coloured cushions sat in front of the large seamless window, overseeing an array of boats in the harbour below. She pressed down on the most notable feature of the room with her fingertips — a king-size bed, covered with a crimson duvet and gold runner at the end. "Nice," she said to herself as she walked over to a rosewood cabinet where a crystal decanter set stood on a silver tray. Taking the lid off one, she bent over to sniff the contents. "Ugh, port," she said, wiggling her nose and replacing it. She strode over to a closed door and pushed it open. Peeking inside, she was impressed with the size of the oval-shaped Jacuzzi — she let out a low whistle through her teeth. This was the life, she thought as she heard a gentle tap on the door.

***

The steel-grey factory sat amongst other newly built factories and office blocks in Ørestad, a recently developed area of Copenhagen. As they entered the reception, they were met by Blas, a tall middle-aged man with long red hair, pulled back into a ponytail.

"Mrs Kassel," he said with an outstretched hand.

"Kathryn, please," she smiled, taking his hand, "and this is Rachel, the journalist I told you about."

"Yes, of course. Pleasure to meet you both," he said in stilted English. "Please come this way. I think you'll be pleased with what we've done." He guided them into a brightly lit lobby and through a pair of swing doors leading to a large, noisy workshop. Over a dozen male workers, dressed in dark blue overalls, laboured diligently at metal work stations whilst the local radio station sounded throughout the room. Several of the men looked up as the women entered, then swiftly turned back to what they were doing.

"Just through here," Blas said as he pointed to another door. Inside, the enormous cat tree was clamped in a large vice.

"Wow," Rachel commented.

"Very impressive," Kathryn said as she walked around it, feeling the roughness of the stiff fibre bound to the pole.

"Yes, it is very good quality. We stopped work on it as you asked, but it won't take long to complete once you are satisfied that it is correct."

"Ok, I have the readjustments Rob wants here," Kathryn said, handing him a piece of paper she had taken from her bag.

"Ah, yes. He emailed this over to me as well. They are only minor modifications, I told him you need not come all of this way."

"It's for a very important client so I had to come and see it for myself."

"I understand. Would you like me to show you what we intend to do? Then if you are able, you can come by later today when it is completed."

"That would be great, thanks."

For the next few minutes, Blas detailed his plans for the cat tree. He took out his tape measure and confirmed the dimensions with Kathryn. Rachel watched Kathryn as she followed him around the post, checking the sturdiness of the platforms as she did.

"You want to feel?" Blas asked Rachel, pointing towards the post.

Not wanting to appear rude, she approached it, her hand reaching the coarse material just as Kathryn was removing hers, causing their hands to touch — a spark of electricity passed between them.

"Sorry," Rachel said, withdrawing her hand to her side. She met Kathryn's eyes and was convinced for the first time that she felt something too. The energy between the two women appeared unfelt by Blas, who was still busily inspecting the post. Kathryn stepped away abruptly and moved towards him.

"Ok," he said, "I think that is everything. Are you happy for us to continue?"

"Yes, what time would you like me to come back?"

"If you give us until the end of the day — maybe 4.30? It will be all finished by then."

"Fantastic, I look forward to seeing the end product," Kathryn said as they began walking towards the door.

"Great, I will get them to start it right away now."

"Actually, before we go," Rachel said, moving herself forward. "I have a few questions I'd like to ask, if that's okay?"

"Sure, fire away," he said.

\*\*\*

"That went well," Rachel said as they sat in the back of the chauffeur driven car.

"Yes, and a lot quicker than I thought. Maybe it would have been wiser to have trusted him at his word."

"I'm glad you didn't. It feels good to get away from London, even if it's for only one night but unfortunately we still can't escape the rain."

Kathryn gave a tight smile. She was still fighting with the emotion she had felt back at the factory — why did her stomach knot every time Rachel so much as looked at her? Even worse — she felt like her veins would explode every time they touched.

"So what do you want to do now?" Rachel said, interrupting her thoughts.

"I don't mind. What do you fancy?" Kathryn replied, opening the window. The cool air lowered her rising temperature.

"How about spending the rest of the morning sightseeing, then having lunch?"

"Yes, that sounds great — Aran," Kathryn said, leaning forward to speak to the capped driver. "Can you take us to the Little Mermaid, please."

"Yes, madam."

"We may as well start with the obvious," she said to Rachel as she leaned back in the seat.

\*\*\*

Having crammed in as much sightseeing they could, the women strolled along Stroge in central Copenhagen. Seeing a bench free as they approached Amager square, Rachel motioned towards it then collapsed into its wooden frame, her legs outstretched.

"Please explain to me what I was thinking when I put these shoes on this morning?"

Kathryn grinned, as she glanced down at the four-inch heels Rachel was wearing.

"I don't know how you wear them at the best of times. Let alone walking along Europe's longest pedestrian shopping area."

"I don't think my feet are ever going to be the same," Rachel said as she bent down, removing her shoes and flexing her toes. Feeling a brief respite from the pain, Rachel scanned the square, her attention drawn to the large fountain in the centre with three stone storks sat atop. "It's a beautiful place. I'd never thought of coming here for a holiday," she said, squeezing her aching feet back into her shoes.

"Isn't it? We're so lucky the rain has stopped."

Catching the fragrant aroma of freshly baked bread, Rachel's stomach growled. "Do you want to get something to eat? I'm starving."

"Sure, let's find somewhere nearby," Kathryn said, scanning the shop fronts for a restaurant. "The one over there looks nice," she said, helping Rachel to her feet by gently encircling her waist. Despite Kathryn's slight build, Rachel could feel the strength in her arms — she imagined what it would be like to feel those arms around her in a passionate embrace as they crossed the street.

They approached a three-story, tangerine-coloured building and climbed the three stone steps to the entrance. Before Kathryn could push open the door, it swung open and a young man with a heavy growth of bristle, wearing green pleated trousers with a gold belt, beckoned them in. "*Godeftermiddag*," he said, gesturing for them to take a seat at a table near the window. Above them, hams hung from the ceiling with small cups skewered underneath to catch the juices. A coffee machine splattered and spewed a few feet away on an aged oak bench, the spitting coffee causing the wood to stain.

"Hi," Kathryn replied. "I'm sorry we don't speak Danish."

"Ah, you are English. No problem, please sit," he said with a perfect accent.

Rachel hobbled over to the table and sat on a rustic wooden chair, closely followed by Kathryn. The waiter handed them both menus.

Scanning the room, Kathryn pointed to the artwork adorning the stark white walls. "You have some beautiful pictures here," she said to the waiter.

"Yes, we have a gallery across the courtyard. All our food is inspired by the current exhibition, either by the art itself or the artist. We change our menu monthly to coincide with our latest pieces."

"That's a fantastic concept," Kathryn said, turning to Rachel. "Shall we go and have a look after we have eaten?"

"I'd love to, yes."

Having ordered, they sat chatting about the day's events. The food arrived and the waiter refreshed both their glasses with wine. Rachel couldn't help but feel closer to Kathryn than she ever had before. She seemed so different from the Kathryn she had met in London — less reserved now and more at ease with herself. Familiar feelings of guilt and regret crept into her mind as the thought of how they first met resurfaced. What could she do? As much as she wanted to she couldn't change the past. If she told her the truth she would ruin everything. Not only the interview but the close relationship that had grown between them.

"Do you want to go back to the hotel and change your

shoes?" Kathryn asked.

"I'll be alright. There's always the option of going barefoot."

"You wouldn't?" Kathryn laughed.

"Sure I would, why not?"

"It's a good thing you're not married to my husband, he'd have a fit if I tried to do something so ... unconventional."

"I did notice that you wear very sensible shoes," Rachel said, leaning over to look under the table at Kathryn's flat-heeled boots. She deliberately ignored the unpleasant feeling that ripped through her when Kathryn had referred to her husband.

"I think that just about sums me up to a T."

"I wouldn't say that."

"No?"

"No, you know what they say, still rivers run deep."

"Not in my case, I'm afraid. What you see is what you get."

"I don't believe that for a minute, your reserves just haven't been tapped into ... yet," Rachel said, as she reclined back in her seat.

Kathryn lowered her eyes. "Let's eat up, I can't believe how quickly the time has gone," she said, checking her watch.

Having finished their meal, they made their way through the back of the restaurant and out to the courtyard. A quaint, stone building lay ahead of them and as they entered, Rachel was overwhelmed by the array of sculptures and paintings on display. As they wandered around the exhibition, Kathryn's hand brushed hers and Rachel wondered, just for a second, what it would be like to hold it.

After what seemed an age for Rachel's aching feet, the two returned to the courtyard.

"That was fantastic, I don't know why we don't have something like that in London," Kathryn gushed.

"I know, I loved the paintings, some of them were absolutely amazing."

"What would you like to do now?" Kathryn said, then glancing at Rachel's feet continued, "I think we'd better get you back to the hotel and you can give your feet a good soak."

"That sounds great. I think I've done all the walking I can for one day."

"Okay, let's go and find the car. I'll give Aran a call and see where he is."

Spotting a seat opposite them, Rachel said, "Would you mind if I wait here while you go and find him?"

"No of course not. Will you be alright?"

"Yes, I'll be fine," Rachel said, sitting on the chair and letting out a sigh of relief.

Kathryn laughed. "Okay, I shouldn't be too long."

Rachel watched as Kathryn disappeared out of view. "I think I will be just a little bit unconventional," she said, slipping her feet out of her shoes. She then stood up and walked back into the gallery.

## CHAPTER 18

As darkness fell over the vibrant city, Kathryn sat on the sofa by the window in Rachel's hotel room, a large glass of white wine in her hand.

She hadn't felt this relaxed in a long time. Every holiday she had been on with Gareth had been a strained one. She would want to go and explore nature, he would want to sit under a shade by the pool reading one of the many books he had taken with him. The evenings would be spent watching the international news channels. Not once had they spent any time together just relaxing like she had with Rachel.

Bringing the glass up to her lips, she watched as Rachel sat sprawled on the sofa — so comfortable in her own skin. It was one of the determining features that she felt so attracted by.

"I'm so relieved the tree house is sorted," Kathryn said, stretching her legs out in front of her.

"I bet you are, and it's nice it hasn't been all work since we got here. Work isn't everything, Kathryn. If you can't enjoy the benefits, what's the point of it all?"

"I know," Kathryn said, sighing. "Anyway, slight change of subject, what shall we do about dinner?"

"We could eat at the hotel tonight."

"Would you mind? I mean, I thought you might want to go out somewhere in town?"

"Of course not."

Kathryn was so relieved. If she was honest, she just didn't want anyone invading their time together — what little time they had left she wanted them to spend it alone. She didn't know when they'd have another opportunity once they returned to London. "Do you want to eat at the restaurant or room service?"

"Definitely room service," Rachel said, leaning over the chair to pick the menu up from the desk. "There's a good selection to choose from," she said, handing it over.

Kathryn studied the menu. "You're right, there's a lot on here."

A comfortable silence ensued as both women sipped on their drinks.

"This is so nice," Rachel said, breaking the silence.

"Yes it is," Kathryn said, looking at the red contents in her glass.

"I was talking about being here with you," Rachel ventured.

"Oh right, sorry," Kathryn said, slightly blushing.

"I didn't mean to make you uncomfortable. I just meant it's nice to spend time with you."

"Don't apologise. I feel the same way, it's nice to get away with a friend. I can't remember the last time I went away without Gareth."

"Must be quite stifling being married. I mean, most people lose contact with friends as they enter the world of coupledom," Rachel said, draining her glass and refilling it.

"Yes, I suppose so but I think in my case it's not so much about being married. I think work has been the stumbling block. Sometimes I just get so carried away on a project I totally forget there's a world that exists outside of it."

"Do you socialise much with your husband?"

Kathryn paused before she spoke — imagining him at home either watching TV or doing his crossword. That was what most of their lives consisted of recently — he would talk to her occasionally to ask her about a clue or sought her opinion on something to do with politics. She felt like an old maid just thinking about it.

"Not so much these days. I don't finish work until late, by the time I get home I'm just ready to crash." She held out her glass for more wine. "Do you go out much?"

Rachel averted her eyes. "A fair bit," she said. "Are you ready to eat?" she asked brightly, as she leaned over her shoulder and snapped the menu up from the desk.

"Yep, I'm famished."

\*\*\*

"Go on, try it," Kathryn said, raising the oyster towards Rachel's face.

Rachel leaned backwards, eyeing the slimy-looking thing in the grey casing dubiously. "I think I'll pass. The thought of that thing slipping down my throat makes me want to ...." She stopped. "Sorry, I don't want to put you off it."

"No chance of that, I love oysters," Kathryn said as she tilted her head back and in one go, tipped the shell, releasing the oyster into her open mouth.

Rachel pulled a face of disgust.

Kathryn laughed. "You surprise me, I thought you'd be up for anything," she said, raising her eyebrows.

"I am for most things, but a girl's got to draw the line

at something," Rachel said, digging her fork in to her penne pasta. "More wine?" she asked, glancing at Kathryn's empty glass.

"Why not?"

"Why not indeed," Rachel said, refilling both glasses.

"The food has been absolutely delicious," Kathryn said as she finished the remaining scraps on her plate. "As has the company."

Rachel grinned. "Thanks. So what do you fancy doing? Do you want to kick back and watch a film?" she said, desperately wanting Kathryn to stay longer. She didn't want to be alone in her room, thinking about this gorgeous woman in the room opposite her.

"Sounds good," Kathryn replied.

"Well, jump up on the bed and relax."

Kathryn looked at the bed warily, a look that wasn't lost on Rachel. "You don't have to worry," Rachel said softly. "I'm not going to try and seduce you."

"Sorry, it's just that ...."

"I'm a lesbian and you feel threatened, in the same way you would if I was a man and I suggested we watched a film together on a bed."

"Well, when you put it like that even I can see the absurdity of it, I'm sorry," Kathryn said, resting her arm on Rachel's shoulder.

"It's okay, really don't worry and stop apologising."

Kathryn let out a nervous laugh. "I seem to be doing that an awful lot around you, don't I."

"You can't help it, it's just being British," Rachel said, picking up the remote control and turning the TV on. "I'll arrange the chairs so you can enjoy the film without worrying about my roaming hands," she joked, pulling the back of the chair to turn it around. Kathryn put her hand over hers.

"No, it'll be more comfortable on the bed. I was just being stupid."

"I really don't mind, honestly."

Kathryn puffed up the pillows behind her back. "It's fine, come on, it will be like a sleep over," she said, slipping out of her shoes and jumping on the bed. "Bring the champers with you."

They settled on a slow-moving chick flick, of which they both bored quickly, but neither wanted the evening to end so they endured their suffering in silence. Tiredness overcame Kathryn in narcoleptic waves as she fought to keep her eyes open. She could feel the heat emanating from Rachel's body. She didn't know if it was the alcohol or just being in Rachel's company but as the night had gone on she had totally forgotten about Gareth, work, and just about every other thing that normally crowded her mind. All her thoughts consisted of Rachel. Giving in to the heaviness of her eyes, she closed them and sank into oblivion until she became aware of Rachel's face hovering tentatively above hers — the prolonged anticipation waiting for contact was almost unbearable. Finally she felt Rachel's mouth on hers, forcing her lips open with her thrusting tongue, softly caressing the inside of her mouth, sending currents of desire through her. She was shocked at her own eager response to the touch of her lips. She breathed heavily.

"Are you okay?" Rachel asked from a faraway place, breaking her fantasy. She sat up with a jolt — shocked by the intensity of how she felt.

"I'm ... I'm fine," she said, clearing her throat, confusion clouding her senses.

"You were breathing a bit heavy," Rachel said, staring at her with genuine concern.

"No, I'm fine honestly," Kathryn said, straining not to look at her, afraid of what her eyes would reveal. "I'd better go." She lifted herself of the bed. "It's a good thing you woke me. I would have ended up staying the night," she said, trying to make light of the situation.

"I wouldn't have minded," Rachel said.

Kathryn said nothing, not trusting herself to speak. She gathered her shoes from the floor and strode to the door, turning once she was at a safe distance. "Thanks for a lovely evening, Rachel. I'll see you in the morning," she said before opening the door and quickly disappearing through it.

"The pleasure was all mine," Rachel replied to the closing door, as she gathered the pillow Kathryn had laid upon, bringing it to her face and deeply inhaling her scent.

## CHAPTER 19

The following morning, Rachel selected a pair of faded blue jeans, black shirt and black knee-high boots from her case, before running herself a bath. Pulling her hair back into a ponytail, she turned to the mirror — her face devoid of make-up, she groaned. No amount of grease paint could conceal the puffy eyes and dark shadows beneath them. She had only managed a couple of hours sleep after Kathryn left and was feeling anxious to get home and get to bed — that was if Cody wasn't still there.

Before she had a chance to get in the bath, there was a gentle tap on the door. Slipping into the white cotton dressing gown hanging on the bathroom door, she opened it and was surprised to see Kathryn looking worse than she did.

"Bad night sleep?" she enquired.

Kathryn nodded.

"Me too, do you want to come in?"

"No, I just wanted to know if you want to get breakfast here or at the airport?"

"The airport would be better. I haven't got much of an appetite at the moment."

"Me neither."

"Okay, I'll be ready in half an hour."

"Great, I'll see you then."

The journey back to England was uneventful. The women slept on the flight and Kathryn had spent most of her time looking over paperwork on the trip back through London, leaving little time to talk. Rachel was grateful — she didn't know what to say. Something had shifted in their relationship and neither woman wanted to acknowledge what that something was.

Before she knew it, Rachel was unlocking the front door to her flat. She was relieved to hear silence. Heading straight to her bedroom, she quickly undressed — naked, she slid under her duvet, relishing the feeling of the soft cotton sheet beneath her. Although sleep deprived, she felt horny as she thought of Kathryn and slipped her hand between her legs. The sexual tension that had built between them fuelled her fantasy and she wasn't surprised to find herself already wet. She had been replaying the scene from the night before over and over in her mind — Kathryn lying beside her, breathing heavily and sensuously, as though she was in the throes of having hot sex. She gently caressed herself, letting out a slight groan as she imagined reaching out to Kathryn and touching her, feeling her, in her most intimate places.

"Is it safe to come in?" Zoe called from behind the door.

Rachel jumped, pulling her hand quickly above the quilt.

"Yes," she replied hoarsely, still in sex mode.

"So how did it go?" Zoe asked as she sat on the bottom of the bed.

"It was really nice."

"Is that it, just nice?"

"Yes, Zoe, what else could it have been?"

"I don't know, you tell me."

"Zoe, I'm not one of your clients, there's no hidden message behind what I'm saying. If you're asking if I slept with her, the answer is no. We had a meal, watched a film, then she went back to her own room."

"Oooh, you're a bit touchy, aren't you."

"No, just tired," Rachel said wearily.

"I'll let you sleep," Zoe said, getting up.

"Whoa, hang on a minute, sit back down and tell me what happened with you last night. Did Cody come round?"

Zoe sat back down, bowing her head. "Yes."

"And?" Rachel asked, smiling.

"And nothing. We shagged and she left. I felt like a prostitute — without being paid."

"I'm sorry, Zoe." And she really was. Zoe was so sensitive — she wasn't cut out for the rough and tough dating of the gay scene.

"Nah, don't be. I knew what I was letting myself in for."

"Are you going to see her again?"

Zoe shrugged her shoulders. "My libido is screaming yes but my mind is saying no."

"Sometimes you just have to go with the flow, stop letting your heart rule your head."

"I know what you're saying, but I'm really not into all this game playing. I don't know how you do it, it would drive me up the wall."

"The key is not to get emotionally involved — just take it for what it is. Your problem is that you see sex as emotional — I don't. The less emotional baggage the better things are," Rachel said, sleepily.

Zoe stood to leave. "It's not my way, Rach, it's just not my way," she said, sighing as she walked through the doorway.

## CHAPTER 20

"So how's fatherhood?" Kathryn asked Rob as they sat at her office desk for their first meeting since she had arrived back from Copenhagen.

"Great!" he replied, smiling proudly as he fished his mobile phone from his back pocket. "Eight pounds on the dot," he said, showing her the screensaver on his phone.

"Oh, Rob, he's adorable," she said, looking at the photo of his baby son. A mop of black hair like his father's, sleeping peacefully in his mother's arms.

"He is. I can't believe I held out so long on wanting a child. It really has been an amazing experience," he gushed, his features breaking out into a wide smile.

"I'm so happy for you, for you both."

"Thanks, Kath," he said. "I'm really sorry about letting you down at the last minute with Copenhagen."

"Hey, don't be silly. I wouldn't have expected you to leave your wife at a time like that, everything went fine."

He looked up, meeting her eyes. "I know, I just don't like letting you down."

"You haven't, not once in all the time we've worked together. So how is our other project coming along?" Kathryn asked, changing the subject.

"Great, it's been quite amusing for the lads. They've

been getting a lot of female attention, not to mention a bit of bottom pinching." They both laughed at the thought of it. "We should be finished by Friday and Ellie's early next week."

"Great. Are you sure you don't want some time off after that?"

Despite Kathryn's insistence that he take a few weeks off to bond with his child, he had been dead set against it.

"No, I'm glad of the distraction, if I'm honest with you. My mother-in-law ..." He shook his head. "Let's just say, the less time I spend in her company, the better it is for all of us."

"I see," she said. She often wondered if Gareth would have thought that way about her own mother if she had still been alive.

"If you change your mind, just say."

"Thanks, I appreciate it but with two projects on the go at once, I really need to be here."

Kathryn nodded. "And I'm eternally grateful," she said, briefly placing her hand over his.

"No problem. Well, I'd better get a move on." He stood up and walked to the door.

"Okay, Rob, again, congratulations."

"Thanks," he said, smiling boyishly as he left.

Kathryn leaned back in her chair. *God why can't my life be that simple?* She hadn't been able to concentrate on anything all morning. It had taken a lot of effort to engage in business talk with Rob and now she felt drained. She still hadn't been able to sleep properly since Tuesday. *Tuesday.* She closed her eyes. The dream she'd had felt so real. It had taken all of her might to get off the bed and get to her room. It would have been a matter of minutes before she fell into Rachel's arms and to hell with the consequences. The situation had now gone past the point of no return. She was falling in love with her — *that's if I haven't already*. What the hell was she going to do now? She was a married woman, albeit an unhappy one, but she was still tied to her husband. And what of Rachel? Had she not said on numerous occasions that she wasn't looking for a relationship — no matter who it was with? And therein lay another problem — was she really going to leave the security of her marriage to become Rachel's *friend with benefits*? She shook her head. That wasn't going to happen. There was no point jumping from the frying pan into the fire. But whatever she decided to do, she had better make a choice soon because she couldn't cope with these emotions anymore.

Feelings of guilt flooded her mind. Gareth would be devastated if he found out that she had feelings for another person, let alone another woman. She knew what she had to do — there was only one choice to be made. She just hoped it was the right one. Picking up the phone purposefully, she dialled and listened as the phone rang. After two rings, it was answered.

"What you said about getting away? I don't have as much work as I thought. How does this weekend sound?"

## CHAPTER 21

Rachel surfed the Internet, looking at nothing in particular. She couldn't get her mind in gear. She was meant to be coming up for new ideas for next month's edition of the magazine but all she could think about was Kathryn. *Is this what love feels like?* She realised that most of her waking hours now revolved around thinking about her. She looked down when she heard her mobile phone vibrating on her desk. Swooping it up, she peered onto the small screen — *Kathryn*. She smiled to herself as she opened the message. Kathryn was overjoyed with the interview and again invited her to the kittens' home coming.

Completely exhilarated by the fact that the piece was so well received, she brought up the interview on her computer and pressed the print button. She waited patiently whilst the machine chugged it out. She hadn't told Gloria she had finished it — she wanted the go ahead from Kathryn first. Pushing herself away from her desk, she swirled around in her seat before standing and strolling to Gloria's office, the papers wafting at her side. She tapped her knuckle against the door.

"Come in," Gloria called out.

Rachel pushed open the door and held the papers up in the air.

"Done and dusted you'll be pleased to know, and all done without incident, I may add."

A wide smile spread across Gloria's features. "I'm very glad to hear that," she said, taking the papers.

"I've just got to do the before and after section with the pictures but that'll only take me an hour," Rachel said. "I did tell you there was nothing to worry about."

"Yeah, well, we'll see," Gloria said as she began to read the piece in silence. Rachel took a seat in front of her, twisting a strand of her hair. After several minutes, Gloria pushed the papers to one side. It was several seconds before she spoke.

"Rachel, you have excelled yourself this time, you really have — you have captured the heart and soul of this woman without all that ...." She searched for the right word, "gushiness. I think she will love it."

"Um, I've already shown it to her."

"And?"

"Yes, she liked it."

"Just liked it, that I don't believe that for a second."

"Okay how about ..." Rachel said, thinking for a few seconds, "she was dazzled by my writing prowess and she can't wait for her adoring public to read all about her in our wonderful magazine. How about that?"

"Hmmm better. Well done, Rachel," Gloria said seriously.

"Thanks."

"So what are your plans now?"

"Plans?" Rachel asked, frowning.

"Yes, with Kathryn."

"I'll be attending the cats' welcome home party next week but beyond that there aren't any plans."

"That I find hard to believe, very hard."

"That may be, but it's true."

## CHAPTER 22

"Hello," Rachel said into the mouthpiece as she laid her tea cup on the coffee table. Her heart thumped against her chest. Was this the moment she had been waiting for — dreading?

"Hi, Rachel, before you worry — nothing's wrong with your mum, but I wondered if you could pop by today for a chat?" Helen, the manager at the Precious Moments care home said. Her shrill voice caused Rachel to hold the phone away from her ear whilst she spoke.

"Sure," she managed to reply, once the pounding resumed to its normal rhythm.

Before she could ask what it was about, Helen quickly said, "Great, see you about five-ish." Then the line went dead.

Looking at the clock and noting the time was just after ten, she let out a long groan. Her one day off and she was having to go to the most depressing place on earth.

As evening closed in, Rachel pressed the illuminated bell on the door of care home. As she had explained to Kathryn, it was the only dementia care home within a two-mile radius from where she lived — she hadn't wanted her mother to be further away than that. She waited patiently as a buxom figure appeared behind the frosted glass door.

"So glad you could come," Helen boomed, her ruddy complexion matching the red top she wore. Rachel was taken aback slightly — though never miserable, she had never seen this *happy* side of Helen before, though ecstatic would have been a more appropriate description.

Helen ushered her into a small enclosed area. As if programmed, Rachel did what she normally did when she entered the care home — focused her attention directly on Helen so she could block out the depressing surroundings. She was so focused on Helen, she didn't at once notice that the familiar smell of disinfectant and urine had been replaced by the smell of — fresh paint.

"Has someone been painting?" Rachel asked as she walked through the door into what looked like another reception room. She stopped in her tracks as though her feet were glued to the floor and looked around her in amazement. The walls, which had once been white but had yellowed over the years, had been repainted in light blue and were now home to modern abstract art prints. Patterned winged arm-chairs replaced the plastic moulded furniture that had been previously screwed down into the floor. Fresh lilies stood tall and proud in a large glass vase on the oak reception desk.

Rachel's mouth dropped open. "What on earth has happened here?" she asked, dumbfounded.

"There's more," Helen said, half dragging her to the lounge, her pink ankle-length skirt swishing and swaying as she moved hurriedly to their destination. Just like the reception area, the lounge had been transformed — all freshly painted with new furniture replacing the old. Sitting amongst four elderly women was a familiar figure — though she could only see the back of her, she would recognise Kathryn's hair anywhere. As though sensing she was there, Kathryn turned around — her face beaming.

"I can't believe you did this!" Rachel said, still in shock.

"Oh, it was nothing. It was Rob and the team who did all the hard work," she said modestly. "I just puffed up a few cushions here and there."

Rachel moved towards her and embraced her. "Kathryn, you will never know how much this means to me," she said, her voice breaking with emotion.

Kathryn rubbed her back affectionately. "It was a pleasure," she said, drawing her back to look at her. "I think you should go and have a look at your mum's room," she said gently, wiping away Rachel's tears.

Rachel gave Kathryn a quick smile and turned to walk the short distance to her mother's room. Tentatively pushing the heavy door open, she peeped in, unaware of what she was going to find. Her mum sat comfortably on a pea-mint arm chair by the window. The room had been painted a buttercup yellow. It was as if, just by changing the colours in the room, the energy had changed. Her mother's greying hair was loose about her shoulders, her face leaning on the wing of the chair. Reaching down, Rachel placed her hand over her mother's bony hand — she could feel the coolness of her skin. The blue blanket that had covered her had fallen to the floor. Picking it up, she covered her hands.

"I'm here, mum," Rachel said, choking back the tears. She gently stroked her long strands repetitively, speaking to her in soft tones, telling her how much she loved her and missed her. She watched her for a long while, thinking about all the suffering she must have gone through in silence. She imagined that each line etched in her mother's face told a story of its own. She couldn't shake the feeling that love was responsible for all of the heartache that her mother and father had been through. Lost in her thoughts, she only became aware that someone was in the room when she felt a hand on her shoulder

"Rachel," the nurse said softly. "We're about to serve dinner now."

"Okay." Rachel bent over her mother and kissed her forehead, before turning and returning to the day lounge. She was surprised to see Kathryn still there, helping one of the residents with a picture she was colouring in.

"Ahh, there's my friend now," Kathryn said, bending down to the elderly woman. "You keep up the good work, Mrs Alders, it's excellent."

The woman smiled at her, as Kathryn gave her shoulder a slight squeeze.

"How is she?" she asked as Rachel walked up beside her.

"The same as always—non-responsive. I sometimes wonder if she'd be better off …." She couldn't bring herself to finish the sentence.

Kathryn reached out to her and gently squeezed her arm. "Can I give you a lift home?"

"Yes, please," Rachel said as she blinked the tears away.

## CHAPTER 23

Endless rows of carbon copy shops filled the street, each looking as dilapidated as the next.

"It's just on your left," Rachel said as they neared her home in Kennington, a relatively disadvantaged area in South London.

Kathryn pulled the car up by the side of the road. The engine fading to a meaningless drone.

"Where do you live?" Kathryn asked, looking ahead of her.

"Above there," Rachel said, pointing towards a funeral parlour.

Kathryn craned her neck to follow Rachel's direction. "Are you kidding?"

Rachel laughed. "No, I really do."

"Is that not a bit ... creepy?" Kathryn asked, searching her face.

"Not really. When I first moved in, it took some getting used to, seeing them bringing in black body bags. My bedroom overlooks the back entrance, but I'm used to it now."

"It's a good thing you don't live alone."

"Do you want to come up for coffee?" Rachel asked as she turned to look at her.

Kathryn thought about it for a few seconds. "I'd love to but I've got a few things to tie up at the office."

"Okay," Rachel said as she opened the car door. She paused, then slammed the door shut and leaned towards Kathryn, enveloping her in her arms and pulling her towards her. Kathryn didn't resist. For several moments, they just held each other. Reluctantly Rachel released her, moving back so her face was only inches away from Kathryn's. "Thank you, Kathryn ... for everything." The raw emotion in her voice was unmistakable.

Kathryn reached up and gently stroked Rachel's cheek, no longer caring what Rachel saw in her eyes. Slowly, Rachel inched her face closer to hers, stopping just before their lips met. Kathryn turned away.

"I'm sorry," Rachel said, as she abruptly opened the door and exited the car.

Looking at the clock on the dashboard, Kathryn sighed heavily, trying her hardest not to think of the vulnerability she had seen in Rachel's eyes. She couldn't give in to the way she was feeling. She had desperately wanted *to kiss her, to touch her*. She gripped the steering wheel, watching her hands pale as she squeezed it tighter. She knew it was a dangerous game to give her thoughts a free rein — she had to control them, otherwise who knew what would happen. Through the windscreen she saw a light go on in Rachel's flat. *I can't, I just can't.* She fought with her inner demons. *Think of the consequences, think of Gareth and all that he's done for you think of ... Rachel.*

Instinctively she turned the engine off, grabbed her leather bag from the back seat and stepped out of the car.

*It's just coffee with a friend.* She walked up to the front door and paused before pressing the buzzer.

"Hello?" a tinny voice answered through the crackling reception.

"Is that offer of coffee still open?" Kathryn asked.

Immediately, she heard a buzz as the front door unlocked.

"Just give the door a good shove," Rachel called through the intercom.

Using more energy than she needed, Kathryn pushed the door open and walked into a dark small hallway. Stacks of newspapers lay on the floor, delivery leaflets on the sideboard. She heard footsteps coming down the stairs.

"I'm glad you changed your mind," Rachel said as she reached her, a hint of a smile on her lips.

"I realised I had more time."

They stood in darkness of the hall, a shard of light coming from an open doorway at the top of the stairs.

"I'm glad," Rachel said, reaching out to her and taking her hand. "You really don't know how much it means to me, what you did for my mum."

Kathryn smiled at her but didn't speak, fearing her voice would betray her nerves. In the limited space, she could feel the warmth of Rachel's body, causing her heart beat to ricochet against her chest. It flashed through her mind how easy it would be to reach out and touch Rachel, to pull her near, feel the thickness of her hair, the taste of her ....

"Come on up," Rachel said, breaking the moment — half twisting away, she led Kathryn up the flight of stairs.

"I hope you don't mind instant coffee," Rachel said as they reached the landing.

"Not at all," Kathryn said, exhaling.

"Mind your step," Rachel warned as she entered the

flat. Kathryn followed her, stepping over a thick raised block of wood, into a cramped but clean flat.

"I'll just put the kettle on, take a seat," Rachel said as she showed her into the lounge.

Kathryn eyed her surroundings and, spotting a chair by the window, walked over and sat down. Though the room was small, it had been decorated in a way that made the most of it by using light colours on the walls and furnishings. She watched Rachel in the small kitchenette, all traces of sadness now gone — the happy-go-lucky woman was back.

"I have a present for you," Rachel said as she stepped back into the lounge. "I was going to give it to you next week but since you're here now …."

"You needn't have done that," Kathryn protested.

"I wanted to. It's in my bedroom," Rachel said, gesturing for Kathryn to follow her. "I won't bite," she teased.

Kathryn stood up and followed Rachel to her bedroom.

"Now before you come in here," Rachel said, holding the door handle. "Don't get any ideas about transforming it. We should be moving out of here in a few weeks."

"Oh, where you planning on moving to?" Kathryn asked, hoping it was nearby.

"Battersea."

"Nice." Relief shot through her.

"My dad recently died, and he left his house to me," Rachel said in an emotionless voice.

"I'm so sorry — about your dad, not the house."

Rachel smiled. "Don't be, I hadn't seen him in a long time. The first I heard about him was when his solicitor contacted me about his will."

"That must have come as a shock."

"It was. I'd thought he'd forgotten all about me."

"Apparently not."

Rachel pushed open the bedroom door and switched on the light. The small room was neat and tidy — a double bed, single wardrobe and a desk were placed strategically around the room. An alcove containing rows and rows of shelves groaned under the weight of books and magazines.

Rachel reached down the side of her wardrobe and extracted a large canvas wrapped in white paper. Lifting it up, she stood it on the bed.

"Here you go, it's nothing much. It's just a thank you gift, you know for the interview and everything," Rachel said.

"Thank you," Kathryn said as she gently unwrapped the sheet of tissue, revealing an abstract painting of two women entwined. "Oh, Rachel," she said, covering her mouth with her hand. "How did you buy this without me knowing?!"

"I went back to the gallery when you went to find the car. I had it sent to me."

"Thank you so much — I love it," Kathryn said, leaning towards her and kissing her cheek. "Do you mind if I sit?" She motioned towards the bed.

"Not at all. I'll go and get the coffees."

"Thanks, I could use paintings like these in my projects," she said, holding the canvas in the air, admiring its design.

"I'm sure Ellie's husband would be more than happy to have one in his bedroom," Rachel remarked as she left the room.

All that worrying about nothing. Kathryn scorned herself.

Several minutes later, the door burst open, startling Kathryn.

"The kitchen tap just burst for the second time this month," Rachel explained as she quickly removed her soaking wet top. "It was only replaced a few weeks ago."

"Oh no, did you manage to turn the water off?"

"Yes, I'm an expert at it now," Rachel replied, reaching into her wardrobe and retrieving a towel, then slowly dabbing at the water from her chest.

Kathryn couldn't help but stare at her. The sight of Rachel half naked was loosening her defences, which she normally held steadfast. Rachel reached back into the wardrobe and pulled out a T-shirt before slowly turning towards Kathryn. *Does she know I've been staring at her? Wanting her?* Kathryn tried to avert her gaze to anything but Rachel. As if sensing her thoughts, Rachel threw the T-shirt onto the bed and walked towards her. Stopping just inches from her, she reached down and took her hand in hers and brought it to her mouth.

"Rachel, I ...." Kathryn began.

"Shhh, it's alright," Rachel said reassuringly, as she pulled her up from the bed, took her in her arms and very gently kissed her. The touch of her lips sent her reeling. She had never realised how a simple kiss could reach so far into her soul. This feeling was what she had read about in magazines but had never experienced herself. All too soon it was replaced by spasms of guilt. *I have a husband.* With all the mental force she could muster, Kathryn turned her head and rested the side of her face against Rachel's shoulder.

They stood silently, holding each other, until Kathryn

said with a sigh, "I can't do this, Rachel." She lifted her head and took a step back.

"I can't help the way I feel about you, Kathryn."

Before another word could be spoken, Kathryn's mobile began to ring. Relieved, she withdrew it from her pocket. "Sorry," she mouthed to Rachel. "Hi, yes I'm just on my way home now — yes, I've just got to throw a few things together. Okay see you." She disconnected her phone.

"Going somewhere?"

"Yes ... away for the weekend with my ..." the words caught in her throat, "husband."

"That's nice," Rachel replied as she walked back to the bed and scooped up her top, pulling it over her head. "I'm sorry for just now, I thought ...."

I ... I," Kathryn stammered, not knowing what to say out loud but inside, her heart was pounding. She wanted to tell Rachel that it was what she wanted as well, but she could never do that to Gareth, not as long as they were married. "I really care about you, Rachel."

"But?"

"But nothing can come of this, I'm sorry," Kathryn said as she hurried from the room. Reaching the front door, she nearly collided with a tall woman who was closely followed by Cody. Kathryn gasped as she looked into Cody's eyes before fleeing past her and down the stairs.

## CHAPTER 24

"I can't bloody believe it." Cody shook her head, laughing. "I would never have believed it."

"I would," Zoe said, unzipping her black biker jacket and carelessly throwing it on the sofa.

"I am here, you know," Rachel interrupted by waving her hand in the air. "You're both talking as though I'm invisible."

"I'm aware that you're not, you sly cow. What happened to not muddying the line?" Zoe said.

"I didn't sleep with her, if that's what you think."

"Well, you did something to her. She looked like a deer caught in the headlights. That's exactly how I felt after I was deflowered by my first lover." Cody grinned.

"I find that hard to believe," Zoe said, rolling her eyes.

"It's true," Cody replied. "I haven't always been this experienced, you know, it took a lot of practice," she said, encircling Zoe's waist, "but I've never been so in lust before."

Cody began nuzzling Zoe's neck but Zoe squirmed awkwardly and she released her. "And what happens when the fire has gone?"

"Who says it has to?" Cody asked, smirking.

"Okay," Rachel said, interrupting as she pushed

herself onto her feet, "as much as I'd love to hear you two having a domestic. I think I'll go to my room."

"No, don't go," Cody said quickly, grabbing Rachel's arm as she passed her. "I want to know what happened."

Shaking free of her grip, Rachel turned to face her. "Like I said, nothing happened. She came up for coffee and that was *all*."

Cody looked at her suspiciously. "Nah, I don't believe you, if I hadn't have seen that look in her eye, I may have believed you, but," she shook her head, "something physical happened, I would bet my house on it."

"I didn't take you for a loser, Cody, but this is one bet you'll definitely not win," Rachel said.

"Don't worry if you think I'm going to say anything, she's still my boss, as far as I'm concerned I didn't see her here."

"Why don't you go wait in my room?" Zoe said, sensing Rachel was at the end of her tether.

"Okay, but hurry though. I've only got a couple of hours to spare."

"That's nothing new," Zoe said under her breath, but smiled sweetly at her. "I'll be five minutes."

"Okay." Cody reluctantly walked to the door. "You need to give me some of your tips, Rachel, I'm obviously falling short somewhere." She grinned broadly as she left the room.

"Are you okay?" Zoe asked.

"Yep, great." Rachel flashed a smile. "Never better."

"Do you want to talk?"

"No thanks, counsellor. I think you have more pressing issues that need attending to," Rachel said, jerking her head towards the door.

"She can wait, it might do her good," Zoe said glumly.

"Don't take her too seriously, Zoe. She's just messing with you."

"That's the problem, everything is like a joke to her. Anyway ... did something happen?"

Rachel shook her head. "I kissed her but she pulled away — she seems to take her marriage vows very seriously."

"That's good, I'm glad to hear it. So I take it that means there isn't any talk of a future rendezvous outside business hours?"

"No, but it does leave me in an awkward position. I have to see her, not once but twice, at the kittens' home coming then the party," Rachel said with a sigh as she collapsed onto the sofa.

"No doubt Mr Kassel will be accompanying her."

"Without a doubt. Oh God what a bloody mess," Rachel said, burying her face in her hands.

Cody put her head around the door, wearing Zoe's pink dressing gown. "Can you girls gossip later? I'm kind of lonely in here." She pouted.

Rachel smiled at Zoe. "Go on, I'll speak to you tomorrow. I'm going to bed to read, then have an early night."

"Okay," Zoe said, squeezing her shoulder before walking into Cody's eager arms.

## CHAPTER 25

"Are you sure you don't want me to call the doctor?" Gareth asked, concern etched in his face.

"No," Kathryn said. *Is there a cure for guilt?* Another wave of nausea hit her.

"Is there anything I can get you?"

*Rachel.* "No I think I just need to sleep."

"Okay, call me if you need anything."

"Thank you ... and Gareth?"

"Yes?"

He turned to her at the door.

"I'm sorry we had to cancel this weekend."

"So am I, but it can't be helped. You weren't to know you'd be ill all night."

She smiled weakly. "Thanks for being so understanding," she said, rolling onto her back.

"Sleep now, I'll bring you some chicken broth in a while."

She waited until she heard his footsteps receding down the hallway, then let out a long sigh.

In her state of confusion, there was no way that she could have gone along with their plans to go away for the weekend. The thought of being in a hotel room with Gareth with no distractions sent a chill down her spine. Had he been capable of making her body feel as though it was going to explode into a million pieces, she may well have been tempted, but she doubted anyone, other than Rachel, could make her feel like that. She was still reeling from the shock of her emotions during their brief encounter. The guilt of her enjoyment still overwhelmed her as she thought of what the future now held for her and Gareth.

Feeling restless, she tossed the quilt away from her and sat upright. Glancing at her phone on the bedside table, she was tempted to call Rachel or at least text her to apologise for the way she left. There had been too many conflicting emotions going on inside her and she had needed to get away. Bumping into Cody was the icing on the cake. She was the last person she expected to see there. Was she dating the tall woman who must have been Rachel's flat mate? She wouldn't have blamed her if she was, as the woman was gorgeous.

Reaching over, she clasped the phone in her hand and held it up to her mouth for several seconds whilst she mulled over her options. She was going to have to see Rachel again the following week and if she didn't make some kind of contact, things were going to be pretty awkward between them. She flipped open the phone and typed in a message apologising for the previous night and asking if they could discuss it after Ellie's next week. She quickly pressed send before she changed her mind. Within seconds her phone bleeped.

She leaned back against the headboard, tilting her head upwards as the nausea slowly subsidised now she knew Rachel didn't harbour any hard feelings towards her. She was tempted to text back and ask if Cody had mentioned anything, but she knew that would be a stupid question. She knew she would have. She'd had guilt written all over her face when she had seen both women. Things were going to be tricky at work with her, she thought dismally. She had fought for so long to keep her personal and work life separate, now they both seemed to be colliding.

CHAPTER 26

Rachel couldn't believe the room she was standing in was the same one from weeks earlier. It had been transformed from a blank canvas into a cats' dream home. All of the many guests had been in awe of Kathryn's design and a tad jealous of the felines who were going to inhabit it. Rachel bent down to stroke the small leopard looking kittens that were circling around her ankles. She'd heard that cats didn't have expressions but these two were definitely in seventh heaven as they moved away from her to chase each other up the scratching post, finally delighting in the walkways high in the air.

"Can you all just stand a bit closer? Lovely, just one more and we're done," Mike, the photographer said, addressing Kathryn and Ellie as they posed for pictures for the magazine.

"Kathryn, darling, you've excelled yourself," Ellie said, patting her on the shoulder.

"Thanks, Ellie, that means a lot to me to hear you say that."

"I only give credit where it's due, my dear."

Kathryn smiled gratefully.

"But tell me, dear, have you been burning the candle at both ends? You're looking rather tired and thin, if you don't mind me saying so."

So I'm not the only one that's noticed. Rachel walked over to join them.

It had been five days since Rachel had last seen Kathryn and she was shocked by her appearance. Though still beautiful, the gloss seemed to have disappeared from her features. She looked as if she hadn't slept or eaten for days.

"I'm fine, I've had a tummy bug, nothing serious."

"I'm glad to hear it. Now the photography is finished, you get yourself home and into bed."

"I will," Kathryn said, bending down to give the old woman a kiss on the cheek.

Rachel shook Ellie's hand. "I can't thank you enough for letting us cover this project. I will send you a copy of the magazine as soon as it is printed."

"Thank you, dear, I appreciate it."

\*\*\*

Once outside, Mike, tall and gangly with blond cropped hair, caught up with Rachel before she got back into Kathryn's car.

"Hey, Rachel, I don't need a lift back to the office. I'm going to have a look round Harrods."

"Ooh the last of the big spenders," she teased him.

"I wish! No, I'll just be hanging around like the sad git I am, watching other people spend money I haven't got."

"One day, Mikey, your photography will take off and you'll be the one doing all the spending in Harrods."

"Yeah right, one day, anyway." He leaned into the open door. "Bye, Kathryn," he said before turning back to Rachel. "I'll see you later, and please don't tell Gloria where I've gone. She'll have my balls on a plate if she thinks I'm skiving."

Rachel laughed. "I won't."

"Are you okay?" Rachel asked once they were seated in the privacy of Kathryn's car.

"Do you want the truth?" Kathryn's grip tightened on the wheel.

"Yes."

"No I'm not okay, in fact I'm about as far away from okay as I ever imagined," Kathryn said, clenching her jaw until it hurt. She kept her gaze focused on the Rolls Royce parked in front.

"Because of the other night?"

"Yes, because of the other night," Kathryn said as Rachel reached over and gently turned Kathryn's face to hers.

"I'm sorry."

"This might be old hat to you but this has never happened to me before," Kathryn said, removing Rachel's hand from her face but still holding it.

"Is there anything I can do to make things better?"

Kathryn held her gaze as she fought the urge to lean over and kiss her, instead she said, "Apart from disappearing, no?"

"Is that what you want?" Rachel asked, the hurt evident in her tone.

"No, of course not," Kathryn said, unable to deny what she felt for her any longer. "I'm not going to lie, I do have feelings for you, feelings that I shouldn't have but it's just not that simple."

Kathryn turned away from her. The thought of what it might feel like to be in her arms again was proving too much for her to bear — she needed space and she needed it urgently.

"Do you want to come back to my place to talk?"

Kathryn hesitated a moment. "No."

"So what do you suggest we do?"

"I don't know, I really don't," Kathryn whispered tentatively. "I mean, I don't even know if I can stay married to a man knowing that I have stronger feelings for someone else." She paused. "I don't love him, at least not in the way a wife should love her husband." She would never have imagined saying these words out loud to anybody — not in a million years, but here she was, spilling her heart out to the woman she truly wanted to be with.

"I'm not going to put any demands on you, Kathryn, whatever you do has to be your choice," Rachel said, resting her hand on her knee.

Every part of Kathryn's body tightened at her touch. She tried to ignore the sensual impact the feel of her hand had on her. She shut her eyes, trying to banish the image of Rachel's body pressed against hers, feeling the nakedness of her skin. "I know," she finally managed to say.

"We can't leave things like this."

Kathryn shrugged. "I have nothing to offer you at the moment. You're just going to have to give me some time to work things out in my head."

"Will you still be coming on Friday?" Rachel asked.

"Yes, and to make matters worse, Gareth is coming to the party with me."

"Kathryn, I would never say anything to him," she said quickly.

"No, I know you wouldn't, but he knows me. If anything's out of kilter he will pick up on it like a shark sensing blood."

"I can always give the party a miss if that will help."

"No."

Kathryn turned the key in the ignition and started the car. "Let's just get Friday over with," she said, edging the car out onto the road. "Are you going back to work?" she asked, her attention focused directly on the road ahead.

"Yes ... unless, like I said, you want to come back to mine?"

Kathryn's face broke into a faint smile. "No, I'll drop you at work. I don't trust myself being alone with you at the moment."

## CHAPTER 27

Kathryn applied the last of her makeup with a generous coating of the lip gloss she always wore. Her stomach was in knots as she walked into the bedroom.

Gareth whistled as he looked at her appreciatively. "I am one lucky son-of-a-gun," he said, admiring the black cocktail dress she wore with ankle strap stilettos. "You look mouth-wateringly delicious."

"Thank you," she said with a small curtsy. "You look quite dapper yourself."

And he did. Dressed in a black Armani suit and crisp white shirt, he looked as if he had just stepped out of a glossy magazine. The earthy scent of his aftershave hung in the air, overpowering her more subtle Chanel No 5. *Why can't I just love him? Life would be so much easier.* She took her coat from the hanger on the back of the door and put her arm through, as Gareth held it for her. Closing in behind her, he pulled her to him. "I love you, Kathryn," he said close to her ear.

"I know," she replied, stroking his smooth cheek. "We'd better get a move on, the guest of honour can't be late," she said, disentangling herself from his embrace.

\*\*\*

Gloria had hired an exclusive venue located in the heart of

London. The elegant hall was filled to its capacity. Each of the thirty round tables, covered in pristine white table cloths, had an array of the best wine money could buy, as well as waiters walking around with trays of champagne for those unseated. Rachel was impressed with her efforts — Gloria had pulled out all the stops to make sure that the evening would be a successful one. She watched from afar as Gloria glided through the aisles, stopping to speak to someone for a few seconds before leaving a trail of laughter behind her as she moved on to the next person. *This is what Gloria excels at.* Rachel smiled to herself.

"It's her," a petite woman called out excitedly, as a black Mercedes pulled up outside the venue.

Most, if not all, the guests had already arrived and were busy mingling. Hearing the commotion at the door, Rachel looked over to see Kathryn and Gareth make their grand entrance. Watching them took her breath away. They looked perfect together and complemented each other in a way that she thought near enough impossible. They were both smiling in unison as people rushed to greet them. The respect and admiration from their peers was evident.

"Come on, girl, let's get this show on the road," Gloria said in her ear. She hadn't even realised she was standing there.

"I don't think I can."

"What do you mean?" Gloria asked impatiently. "What's happened between you two?"

"Nothing, I just —" It was one thing seeing them together in a photo but seeing him with his arm around Kathryn tore at her heart.

"Rachel," Gloria said in a low voice. "You promised me you wouldn't get involved with her."

"I didn't. I'm just a bit nervous — I'll be fine," Rachel said, regaining her composure.

"Good, now let's go."

Heart in her mouth, Rachel walked with Gloria to join the queue of people waiting to greet the couple. Eventually a space became available and Gloria gently pushed Rachel into it.

"Rachel, lovely to see you," Kathryn said, as if she were one of her acquaintances. "I'd like you to meet my husband Gareth," she said, turning towards him.

"I've heard great things about you, the interview was classy," he said.

"Well, that's what we're aiming for. I'm Gloria." She thrust her hand to Kathryn. "I'm so pleased that you could attend tonight."

"It's my pleasure."

"Your table is up front, I'll have drinks brought to you right away."

"Thank you," Gareth said as he laid claim to his wife, holding her around the waist as he guided her to their seats.

"Oh my God," Gloria said when they were out of hearing range. "She really is more beautiful in person — oh my, if I was gay."

"If you were gay what?" a voice asked from behind them. Gloria spun around, smiling to the owner. "Tony darling, I was just saying if I was gay I'd never had met you," she lied, closing in to kiss him.

"I believe you," he said, smiling at Rachel before embracing her. "How are you, darling?" he said, his voice deep and manly.

"Good, and you?"

"Oh, I can't complain. So..." he said, looking around,

"where is she? The one who is going to stop us going bankrupt."

Rachel nodded towards Kathryn. "With her husband at the table at the front."

Gloria encircled her husband's waist. "Look at all these people, Tony. Can you believe Kathryn has this much clout? Normally I couldn't even speak to these people on the phone, let alone get them to come to a party."

Tony planted a kiss on the top off her head. "Don't worry darling, your time will come soon, then they'll be begging for you."

Gloria beamed. "Let's hope so."

"So am I going to be introduced to Ms Kassel any time soon tonight?" Tony asked, looking from one woman to the other.

"Of course — Rachel, would you do the honours please?"

"Sure," Rachel said, waiting while Tony gracefully took a glass of champagne from one of the waiter's trays.

"Follow me," Rachel said, looping his free arm and leading the way through the crowds to Kathryn's table.

Kathryn was seated next to a stocky, balding man wearing an expensive dark blue suit, his arm casually resting on the back of her chair, their heads inclined, engrossed in conversation. Rachel's eyes searched the room for Gareth and, realising he was nowhere to be seen, stood beside Kathryn's chair, waiting until there was a natural break in her conversation before placing a hand on her shoulder. Kathryn excused herself and rose.

"Kathryn, I'd like to introduce you to Tony, co-owner of the magazine."

"Kathryn, I must say due to your appearance on this

month's cover we have been inundated with calls." He leaned forward to kiss her on her cheek.

"I'm glad to hear it but I think the success is more to do with the great writers you have working for you," Kathryn said, glancing at Rachel.

"Well, yes, without a doubt but it didn't do us any harm running your first interview in years," he continued, stroking his chin. "We're all very grateful at the magazine that you chose us."

"I'm glad I did, I really enjoyed working with Rachel," Kathryn said, looking at her, their eyes meeting and holding for the first time.

Rachel felt as though she would melt under her gaze.

"Would you mind awfully having some photos taken?" Tony asked.

"No, of course not," Kathryn said, reluctantly tearing her eyes away from Rachel.

"Rachel, can you make sure everyone is well taken care of?" Tony said, before whisking Kathryn off into the crowd.

"So Pandora," a raspy whisper sounded behind her. He stood so close she could smell the sour odour of whiskey on his breath. She whirled around to look up at him and froze. His presence overpowering her. This interaction wasn't in the safety of her own home, behind her computer screen — it was in the real world and she felt a little more than intimidated by him.

"Have you been fucking my wife?" he spoke as innocently as you would talking about the weather.

At first she wasn't sure if she had heard him correctly but when she looked into his steely green eyes, she knew she'd heard right the first time.

"Um, no, no I haven't. As I explained to you in my email, nothing happened then or now," she said, her voice shaking.

"But you wished it had," he said.

Outraged by his comment, she felt a renewed confidence rise within her.

"You know something, I really felt sorry for you, I thought you were a decent man, evidently I was wrong. If you'll excuse me I've got guests to attend to."

His hand clamped her shoulder gently as she went to walk away. "After tonight I want you to stay away from my wife."

"Is that what your wife wants?"

"Don't get ahead of yourself, you don't know who you're dealing with."

"Oh, but I think I do," she said, looking him in the eye defiantly.

"There you are Rachel," Gloria said coming into view. "Is everything alright?" she asked, suspiciously eyeing Gareth.

"Yes it's fine," Rachel replied, relief coursed through every inch of her body.

"If you'll excuse us," Gloria said, "there are a few people who I want Rachel to meet."

\*\*\*

Kathryn scanned the crowd of party goers, hoping to catch a glimpse of Rachel — she had barely seen her all night. On the one hand, she was thankful as there was less chance for Gareth to suspect anything between them, but at the same time she longed to be near her.

"Enjoying yourself, darling?" Gareth asked.

She nodded her head. "Yes, tired though. If it's okay

with you, I'd like to call it a night soon."

"No problem," he said, downing the remains of his drink. "You haven't seen much of the journalist, what's her name again?"

"Rachel."

"Ah yes, Rachel, I thought you two had become close, what with you baring your soul to her."

"I don't think it was that extreme," she said, smiling as a passer-by waved at her.

"Shall we go then?" he said, standing.

"Gareth," boomed a merry voice coming from the throng of people directly in front of them.

He squinted his eyes, then widened them as he recognised the owner of the voice. "Lilly! My God it's been years, it's so good to see you," he said, hugging her tightly. "You look wonderful."

"Yeah right, I look like a baby whale, I still haven't managed to lose the baby weight," Lilly said as she brushed a cloud of copper red hair out of her eyes.

"No, you don't," Gareth said, laughing. "A bit of weight suits you."

"It's done wonders for my chest," Lilly said confidently. "I do actually prefer the way I look now." She swirled around, showing off her buxom figure squeezed into strapless chiffon gown, revealing her high-perched breasts.

"So how long have you been back in London?" he said, looking at her up and down appreciatively.

"A few months — I finally left Marcus and now I'm home for good," Lilly said with dramatic flair.

As if finally coming to his senses, he turned towards Kathryn. "Where are my manners? Kathryn," he said, "you remember my old University friend Lilly?"

"Less of the old," Lilly said, playfully punching his shoulder, before spinning around and looking down at Kathryn in her chair. "Good to see you again, Kathryn, quite a bash they're having here, isn't it?"

"Yes it is," Kathryn said politely. There was no love lost between the two women. When they had met many years ago, Lilly had made it quite obvious that she thought Gareth was making a mistake marrying Kathryn — believing he should have married her instead. In a way, Kathryn wished he had.

"You don't mind if I whisk your husband off for a quick dance, do you? All the men here move like robots." Lilly laughed loudly.

"Not at all," Kathryn said, looking up at her.

Gareth looked past Lilly. "Are you sure?"

Kathryn nodded her head. "Positive."

"This will only take a minute, then we'll leave, I promise," he said as Lilly propelled him onto the makeshift dance floor.

"Alone at last," Rachel said, slipping into the seat beside her.

"Have you been spying on me?"

"No, just admiring you from afar."

Their eyes met with growing intensity.

"Tonight has been a great success. Gloria is over the moon," Rachel said.

"And you?"

"Is that a professional question or personal?" Rachel asked with a weak smile.

"Personal."

"It's harder than I thought, watching you with him,"

Rachel said, as she turned her attention to the dance floor to watch Gareth.

"I'm sorry," Kathryn said as she slid her hand under the table and put it over hers.

"So what happens now? Am I going to see you again?"

"I don't know, Rachel, this situation we're in isn't that easy."

"Anything worth having never is."

"Is that what you really believe?"

"Don't you?"

The music faded and Rachel saw Gareth making his way back to the table, Lilly hanging onto his arm, both laughing like a young couple in love. She stood up ready to walk away, when Kathryn caught her by her arm and pulled her down towards her.

"Yes, I think I do," she said, quickly cupping the side of her face, before Rachel pivoted on the spot and disappeared into the crowd.

CHAPTER 28

Even the fresh sunny day could not raise Rachel's dampened spirits. For the first time in her life she knew what it felt like to be heartbroken. Even the sorrow she had felt when circumstances had forced her to put her mum in a care home couldn't compete with this.

"Staring at the phone isn't going to make it ring," Zoe said, snapping Rachel out of her trance.

Rachel smiled faintly, looking away from the phone on the worktop. "No, it's not," she said as she resumed washing the dishes.

"How long has it been since you heard from her?" Zoe asked, squeezing herself beside Rachel, then drying the dishes as she passed them to her.

"Two weeks."

"Oh well, that's not too long," Zoe said, inspecting the plate. "You've missed a bit." She pointed at the mark and returned it to her.

"What?" Rachel asked distracted.

"I said you haven't washed it properly."

"Oh sorry," Rachel said, putting the dish under hot running water before giving it a thorough clean with the dish cloth.

"There was never going to be any winners in this, you

know," Zoe said, taking a sideward glance at Rachel.

"Yeah, I know. At least Gloria has come out of this happy. Sales of the magazine have skyrocketed and there have been so many companies wanting to advertise she's had to hire more sales staff just to cope."

"That's brilliant. I'm really pleased for her — for you both. At least you get to keep your job."

"And a pay rise."

"You're lucky being in a job that you love."

"Don't I know it," Rachel said, washing the last remaining dish then drying her hands on some kitchen roll.

"I wish I could work for myself, instead of working for people who care more about money than our clients. The government is making cutbacks and guess who got the biggest cut — outsourced counselling for the NHS," Zoe said, following Rachel into the living room. She stood by the window, looking below. "Ahh another one bites the dust," she said, referring to a grieving family being led towards the funeral parlour's door. "I swear this has been *the* month of death," she said before clamping her mouth with her hand. "Sorry, that was a bit insensitive."

"Zoe, I wish you would stop it."

"Sorry."

"And stop bloody apologising," Rachel said, throwing a cushion at her. Zoe ducked in time and it went straight through the open window.

They heard a shout from below before breaking into laughter. "Oh shit," Rachel said.

They waited a few tense minutes, and when no knock came at the door they fell back on the sofa and put their feet up on the table.

"You know," Rachel said, putting her hand on Zoe's

shoulder. "I don't know why you don't you work for yourself. What's stopping you?"

"How would I be able to afford to rent a property? Rob a bank?" Zoe asked, raising her brows.

"Nothing so drastic, Zoe. You can use one of the downstairs rooms as your office. Loads of therapists work from their own home."

"Are you serious? You wouldn't mind?" Zoe said, jerking forward, swinging her body around to face her.

"Of course not." Rachel laughed. "It's as much your home as it is mine," she said, picking up several sheets of paper from the table. "All you have to do is let your clients know that you're moving on, I'm sure some of them will follow you." She still couldn't believe the house was theirs.

"That's a bit unethical," Zoe said, frowning.

"No, it's not. They're free to see who they want. All you'll be doing is giving them a choice. Isn't that what counselling is all about?" She leafed through the particulars before returning them to the table.

"Yeah, I s'pose you're right," Zoe said, rubbing her hands together. "Do you really think I could do it?"

"Zoe, I know you can. If you ever needed convincing, look at the good job you've done with me," Rachel said, fluttering her eye lashes.

"I don't think using you as an example would give me much creditability, Rach," Zoe said, smiling fondly at her.

"No, I s'pose not, but if it wasn't for your presence in my life, I could have been a lot worse."

"I doubt it," Zoe said, laughing.

Despite her low mood, Rachel joined in with her laughter.

"So ... are you going to give it a go?"

Zoe paused for several seconds, before a big smile formed on her face. "You know what, I think I will. What have I got to lose? I can start by doing weekend appointments while I still work, until I get the business on its feet."

"Exactly."

"That's why I love living with you, I never know what's around the corner."

"That's the beauty of life."

"So what are you going to do about Kathryn then?"

Rachel shrugged. "Dunno. My head is telling me to let her go and move on, but my instincts are saying otherwise."

"And what do you think will win over?"

Rachel fell back against the sofa, letting out a deep sigh. "My instincts, obviously. The last time I saw her, she said she'd be in touch, so I'm just waiting for her to make the next move."

"Talking of moving, have you finished packing yet? I've still got loads to do," Zoe said, pushing herself up from the sofa.

"Yep, I'm almost done. I've just got to pack my books and stuff."

"I can't believe that this time tomorrow we will be in a new place," Zoe said, placing a hand on her hip as she looked around the room wistfully.

"I know, I'll miss this place in a funny way."

"I know what you mean. We've had some good times here."

"Well, it's up to us to make sure we have even better ones where we're going next," Rachel said as Zoe helped her up from the sofa.

"Amen to that." Zoe gave her a high five.

"Are you inviting Cody over?"

"Yes, she said she'd help us unpack tomorrow."

"As well as other things?"

Zoe put her face in her hands. "She just drives me crazy, I just can't make her out. I never thought I would ever be attracted to someone who was so ..." She paused to search for the right word. "Erratic — I like order and she's one big mess."

"Come on, Zoe, she's not that bad."

"Says you. Considering you're so much alike, I'm surprised you two didn't hit it off."

"She wasn't my type. It would be like going out with my twin sister."

Zoe grinned. "Yeah, I s'pose it would."

CHAPTER 29

The three bedroom mews house was situated close to Battersea Park. The ground floor alone was bigger than their previous flat. A large reception room with bay windows led onto a small well-maintained garden at the back of the house. The open-plan kitchen had several skylights, letting in a stream of natural light onto the modern appliances including, most importantly, a built-in dishwasher.

"This house is impressive," Cody said as the three women sat amongst large brown boxes and suitcases, which they had dumped in the front room. "Much better than your old place."

"There's no comparison," Rachel said, taking in her spacious surroundings. The two-storey house was in pristine condition and had obviously been maintained to a high standard.

"How did you manage to get your hands on a place like this?"

"Inheritance," Rachel said, omitting from who.

"Blimey, I wish someone would leave me a place like this. Whose was it? A long lost aunt or someone?"

"No, my dad."

"Oh, I'm sorry, I didn't realise."

"Don't worry about it."

"Cody, why don't we start unpacking?" Zoe said, sliding a box over to her.

Cody looked over at her and gave a puzzled look as Zoe frantically shook her head.

"What?" Cody asked innocently.

Zoe rolled her eyes. "Jesus," she hissed under her breath.

Seeing their exchange, Rachel laughed. "It's okay, Zoe. I'm not that fragile. I won't break if someone asks about him."

Zoe gripped a large box in her arms. "Alright, enough with the talking. How about we get these boxes sorted then I'll go out and get us an Indian for dinner?"

"Good idea," Rachel said.

Hours later, the three women sat on the wooden floor eating Indian out of foil containers and drinking beer out of bottles. The atmosphere was calm after a hectic day spent trying to arrange their new home. It was surprising how the big the house was — even with all of their belongings in place, it still looked half empty.

"Well, that was an easy move," Cody commented, putting the last remains of food in her mouth.

"Only because we didn't have that much stuff. Most of what was in the flat belonged to the landlord."

"At least now we get to buy what we actually want," Rachel said.

"That's what I love about working for Kathryn —"

The very mention of her name gave Rachel butterflies. It was so unexpected it took her by surprise. *Am I ever going to see her again?*

"— she doesn't set a budget on anything I buy."

"How is she?" Rachel asked, trying to keep her voice neutral. As hard as it was, she had made a promise to herself — she was not going to call Kathryn under any circumstances. Contact, if any, had to come from her, as she was the one with the most to lose. She had a whole life set in place and Rachel knew she couldn't just walk away from it for a life of uncertainty with a woman she hardly knew.

Cody shrugged her shoulders. "Fine as far as I know. She's been really busy and not in the office much."

Rachel finished the rest of her beer in one long gulp. She had suddenly lost her appetite for food. From what Cody had said, it was obvious Kathryn had moved on and it was about time she did the same. She sprang up, dusting off the seat of her jeans.

"Hey, where you going?" Zoe asked.

"Going to get ready."

Cody raised her eyebrows. "Going to meet someone, are we?"

"Who knows, a girl can only try."

"I thought we were going to watch a movie tonight?" Zoe asked.

"I'm not in the mood. I haven't been out in ages — I need to clear the cobwebs."

"Do you fancy some company? I wouldn't mind getting out myself," Cody asked, jumping up from the floor.

"Not tonight, I fancy going solo. Anyway, I'm sure you two will have a better night here alone."

"If you want to go out, I'm not standing in your way," Zoe said, her eyes narrow as she glanced up at Cody.

Cody threw her hands in the air. "Chill out, babe, it was only a suggestion."

"I'll see you both later," Rachel said.

"Or in the morning." A coy smile spread across Cody's lips.

"There's only one bed I spend the night in and that's my own," Rachel replied before heading up the stairs to her bedroom.

Zoe opened a bottle of beer, not bothering to offer Cody one. Though she never spoke, her body language was tense.

"There's no need for you to stay here if you think you can have a better time going out with Rachel," Zoe said.

"What did I say? I only thought it would be nice for the three of us to go out instead of staying in *again*."

Zoe took a bite of an onion bhaji, as she looked down at the floor. "I don't recall holding a gun to your head. If you want to go out and do whatever you want to do, by all means go ahead."

Cody turned to her and cupped her face in her hands. "Jesus, sweetheart, I didn't mean anything by it."

Batting away her hand, Zoe raised her eyes to meet Cody's. "Your constant innuendoes are also getting a bit boring."

Cody rose to her feet. "Babe — I was only kidding with her."

"Did you see me laughing?"

"Yeah, well maybe I'm no longer finding *this* fun anymore," Cody said, standing up and grabbing her jacket from the door knob. "This is exactly why I stay single — too much bloody drama!"

∗∗∗

Mojo's was the latest lesbian bar to hit the gay scene. Dimly lit and low ceilinged, it was known for its reputation of being the place for anonymous liaisons. Rachel had decided to try her luck there as the Internet hadn't been connected in their new home yet. She drifted through the hordes of sweaty women dancing on the small dance floor and headed straight to the bar, getting served immediately.

"JD and Coke," she said as she briefly surveyed the crowd before turning back around. She slipped a note onto the counter and was surprised when a hand covered hers.

"This is on me," a woman dressed in a black biker jacket and skin-tight trousers said, leering at her. The deep-seated lines on her tanned skin gave the appearance of an old piece of leather.

"Why thanks," Rachel said, turning towards her and instantly deciding that she was not her type, "but I'll pay for my own drink," she said politely, withdrawing her hand.

"What? My money not good enough for you?" the woman said, a vein on her forehead becoming engorged.

"I didn't say that, I just prefer buying my own drinks. If that's alright with you," Rachel said, staring back into her protruding eyes.

"And what if it's not?" She roughly gripped her wrist.

"You really don't want to know the answer to that question," a voice came from behind her. A woman came into view, a black cap covering her head — at first glance she could have been mistaken for a young man. Her complexion was a rich espresso brown and at five foot eight inches tall, with a broad frame, she towered over Rachel's antagonist by at least four inches. "Do you?" the stranger asked as she leaned in closer to the woman's face.

"Hey, sorry, I thought she was alone," she stammered as she slowly backed away.

"Well, she's not, okay?" Rachel's protector said menacingly.

"Okay okay, I get the message," the woman replied, disappearing into the darkness.

"Are you alright?" the stranger asked Rachel.

"Thanks, but I could have handled her myself, you know."

The woman raised her hands in surrender. "I'm sorry, I didn't mean to step on anyone's toes," she said, turning to walk away.

Rachel reached out, placing her hand on the other woman's forearm. "You're forgiven."

"Thanks." Her face split into a girlish grin, revealing pearly white teeth.

"Can I get you a drink …?" Rachel asked, probing for her name.

"DJ."

"DJ, I'm Rachel, nice to meet you."

DJ nodded at her. "I've got a drink, thanks," she said, revealing the bottle of beer in her hand. "Can I ask you something?" She slid onto a wooden stool beside her.

"Fire away."

"What are you doing in a place like this?"

"Having a drink," Rachel said innocently.

DJ rolled her eyes. "You know what I'm talking about. This isn't the sort of place a woman like you should be hanging out."

"Thanks, Mum, any more advice before you send me home to bed?"

"I don't mean to be intrusive, what I mean is, this place isn't safe for someone like you."

"Oh yeah and what am I?"

"Young and by the looks of it, very naive. That pretty face of yours is going to cause you big problems in a place like this."

"Things are going okay so far." Rachel smirked.

"I wouldn't be so sure of that," DJ said, quickly putting her drink on the bar. "I think it's time we left," she said, grabbing Rachel by the arm.

"Hey ... what the —" Rachel began to say before she noticed the biker woman was heading towards them with a group of aggressive-looking women.

"You're right," Rachel said, quickly draining her drink and fleeing the bar with DJ.

Upon leaving, DJ removed her jacket and placed it over Rachel's bare shoulders. "Do you want to come back to my place?" she said, as they took off down the road, still looking back towards the bar to see if they were being followed.

"I don't know ..." Rachel said as images of Kathryn flashed through her mind.

"I thought you were single and fancy free?"

"I was ... I am." *Who am I kidding? Kathryn doesn't want me. Who am I saving myself for?*

"Is that a yes then?"

"Sure why not," Rachel said, her resolve crumbling as she banished thoughts of Kathryn.

DJ suddenly leapt out into the road and waved frantically at a cab that was driving past on the other side. She let out a loud whistle, at which the cab driver noticed her and did a U-turn in the middle of the street. As the cab drew up beside them, DJ opened the door for Rachel then climbed in behind her.

"Camden town, mate," DJ said as they settled back into the taxi's cold leather seat.

\*\*\*

Rachel followed DJ into a three story block of flats. As soon as they were through the front door of her flat, DJ unzipped her jacket and threw it to the floor before grabbing hold of Rachel, pulling her roughly towards her. In one swift movement, DJ's hand slid up Rachel's top, her cold skin making contact with her breast.

"I want you so bad," DJ said as she crushed her mouth against Rachel's, using her tongue to prise her lips apart.

Rachel had no choice but to respond — she wrapped her arms around DJ's hips, pressing hard against her as the familiar stirrings of sexual desire began to rise within her. She opened her eyes and in an instant felt as if someone had thrown a bucket of ice cold water on her. She couldn't go through with it. She didn't want to have sex with this stranger. The only person she wanted was Kathryn.

Seemingly unaware of Rachel's change of heart, DJ's hand moved to Rachel's waist, tugging at the button on her jeans.

Rachel put her hand firmly over DJ's, stopping her eager hands in their track. "I'm sorry," she whispered. "I can't"

DJ took a small step back and quizzically regarded her with a slight smile. "Whoever's on your mind is a lucky lady."

"There's no one —"

"Save it, babe, you can tell a mile off that you've got your heart set on someone."

"It's that obvious, huh?"

"Yes, come on, follow me to the kitchen. I'll make you a coffee and you can tell me all about her. There's no point wasting the whole evening."

## CHAPTER 30

As if on autopilot, Kathryn cracked two eggs into the pan of boiling water and put a slice of wholemeal bread into the toaster. "Aren't you getting dressed today?" Gareth asked as he walked into the kitchen, noticing she was still in her white dressing gown.

"Later, I thought I'd make your breakfast before I go and have a long soak in the bath."

"Is anything wrong? You look tired."

"No, I've got a lot on my plate at the moment," she said.

"Well, you have been burning the candle at both ends for the past few weeks," he said, admonishing her rather than showing any concern.

Kathryn shrugged her shoulders wearily. "Well, there's only one of me. I can't be at ten places at once."

Gareth said nothing. Instead, he walked over to the worktop and poured two cups of coffee from the pot and sat down at the table.

The toast popped out of the toaster, giving Kathryn a fright. She picked it out quickly; burning the tips of her fingers in the process and laying it on the plate, deliberately taking her time. She used the utensil to scoop out both eggs and laid them by the bread.

"If I remember clearly, it was you who said I should take on more clients," she said, placing the plate on the table and sitting down heavily on the chair opposite him.

"I thought it would be good for you. You seemed down — depressed even."

"Maybe I am," she said quietly, bringing the hot coffee mug to her mouth and blowing it before taking a sip.

Gareth ignored her comment and began to eat. "Aren't you eating?" he asked between mouthfuls of toast.

"Nope, not hungry," she said. The very thought of food made her stomach constrict.

She pushed her hair back into a ponytail and tied it with a band from her wrist. "I think I'll go and have that bath," she said, picking up the coffee to take with her. She was in no mood to sit through ten minutes of questioning from Gareth that morning.

\*\*\*

Cody smiled as Kathryn walked into her office and shut the door softly behind her.

Kathryn looked at her almost shyly. "Am I disturbing you?"

Cody rose from her desk. "No."

"How was your trip?"

"Very good, I was just writing up a report on it. I found some great stuff, as well as getting a great tan but I take it that isn't what you wanted to talk to me about."

Kathryn shifted uncomfortably on her feet, her eyes cast downwards. "No, actually. It's about when I bumped into you a few weeks ago."

"At Rachel's, you mean?"

Kathryn looked up and met her gaze. "Yes. I haven't had the courage to mention it till now."

"What about it?"

"I was a bit rude, not saying hello or anything."

"Kathryn, take a seat," Cody said, "please."

Kathryn walked the short distance to the swivel chair and sat down as Cody resumed her place behind her desk.

"Look, tell me if I'm out of order here," Cody began awkwardly, "but I know what you're going through."

Kathryn looked at her, puzzled. "I don't know what you mean."

Cody let out a deep breath. "Okay here goes, I just hope you don't fire me for saying this ... I know about you and Rachel."

Kathryn began to rise from her chair. "I don't know what you're talking about."

"Please sit down. I know what you're going through because I've been there myself."

Kathryn lowered herself back onto the chair.

"I hate talking about this," Cody said, putting her head in both hands. "Eight years ago, I was married to a man I thought could make me *normal*," she said, using her fingers as quotations. "I wanted, more than anything, to fit in with society. Hell, I even wanted to have a kid or two," she said, smiling at the long distant memory. "I could have carried on living like that if I hadn't met Vanessa."

She finally looked at Kathryn and seeing her interest, carried on, "She was a client I met through my old agency. She was a very outspoken lesbian activist who had no qualms about her sexuality and who knew about it. Well, just what I can see happening between you and Rachel happened between us. After a lot of toing and froing we eventually ..." she paused, trying to find the right words, "you know — slept together. I'm not proud I cheated on my husband, but the attraction was so strong, I felt like I was possessed. Anyway," she continued, "she wanted me to leave Mike, my ex-husband, but I couldn't. I couldn't leave the security that marriage enabled me have. The end shot of it was that she was not willing to wait it out — she walked out of my life and it's my biggest regret. I take it you see where I'm going with this."

Kathryn nodded.

"Every day, I wish I could turn the clock back and follow my heart instead of my head, but ...." She clasped her hands together.

Kathryn placed her hand over Cody's before standing. "Thank you, Cody."

\*\*\*

Later that evening at home, Kathryn threw the pencil she was holding on the desk. The last thing she wanted to think about was materials and colour schemes, when she just couldn't get Rachel out of her mind. She felt guilty about not contacting her since the party but she couldn't risk seeing her again before she'd decided what to do about Gareth.

*I need to just deal with it!*

There was a soft tap on her office door, then it was pushed open.

"Can I get you some tea?" Gareth asked, seeming to notice the look of frustration on her face but saying nothing.

"Yes, tea will be great, thanks."

"How's it going?" he said, nodding towards the blank piece of paper in front of her.

"It's not," she replied.

"What's the matter?"

"I'm just not in the mood for it, if I'm honest."

"Why don't you go out for a bit of fresh air, clear your head?"

She glanced out of the window, then looked at him. "It's pissing down."

"Oh, so it is," he said ruefully, easing himself into the chair next to her. "Do you want to talk, Kathryn?" He watched her face closely.

She dropped her eyes to the floor — in part out of guilt, in part because she knew she was about to break his heart. She spoke quietly, playing with the gold band he had placed on her finger all those years ago. "I think we need to, Gareth."

"This doesn't sound good."

A tear formed at the corner of her eye. "I don't know where to begin."

"At the beginning usually helps," he said, rubbing her arm.

"I think ... I think I'm going to move out for a while."

His mouth fell open. "This is a bit out of the blue, isn't it?"

"Not really, not to me anyway. I've been feeling like this for quite a while. I thought it would pass but ...."

"But what?"

She looked up at him as the tears began to fall freely. "If I'm brutally honest, I'm just not happy."

"Have you met someone else? Is this what this is about?"

"In a way yes — I haven't cheated on you, I never would ... but that's not why I'm leaving. I'm trying to find me — can you understand that?"

He shook his head. "I'm such a fool, this is all my own

doing."

She stroked his cheek with her hand. "Don't say that, Gareth, you haven't done anything to cause this. I've just changed, I've realised I need more from life — more than you can give me."

Grabbing her hand in sudden desperation, he spluttered, "We can fix this, whatever it is, you don't have to leave, we can work through it together."

"I'm sorry, Gareth, not this time we can't," she said, wiping away the tears.

"So what are we talking about here ... divorce?"

"I don't know. All I know is that I need to get away for a bit to try and sort my head out. I'll go and stay with Jo for a while," she said, turning away from him. She couldn't bring herself to look at him for a second longer — his eyes bright with unshed tears, the guilt was too much to bear.

He stood gracefully, holding his chin high, seemingly mustering all the dignity he could gather. "I'm going out, I take it you'll be gone before I get back?"

She nodded mutely.

"So be it," he said, closing the door softly behind him

## CHAPTER 31

Rachel walked into the kitchen, shaking her head. "That's the tenth time Cody's called now. She said she isn't going to stop until you speak to her."

"Well, she'll be wasting her time because whatever *it* was, is over," Zoe said, washing back the last dregs of coffee and placing the white mug in the sink.

"It's alright for you, I'm the one who has to answer the phone to her," Rachel said, opening the fridge and grabbing a small bottle of water.

"Unplug it!" Zoe replied, moving towards the table, tightening the grey cord around her tracksuit bottoms as she did.

"Why are you being so bloody pigheaded? Is this all because she wanted a night out?" Rachel asked, unscrewing the cap and drinking straight from the bottle.

"It's not just about that," Zoe sighed.

"Then what is it?"

Zoe sank onto the kitchen chair and tilted her head back at a forty-five degree angle. "I want more than what she's offering."

"Like?" Rachel urged as she joined her at the table, placing the bottle on a coaster.

"Like ... a relationship," Zoe said, snapping her head

back down. "Alright, there I said it, I want a relationship with her. One to one and all the sloppy crap that goes with it."

Rachel tried to suppress the smile that was fighting its way to her mouth. "So what's the problem?"

"Isn't it obvious? She doesn't want one," Zoe said, scratching the back of her head before rubbing her hand over it.

"Is that what she said?"

"Not exactly, no but —"

"So how do you know?" Rachel asked, drawing her feet up on to the chair.

"I just do."

"Come on, Zoe, you can't go around making statements like that without having anything to back it up."

"Alright then how about this." Zoe paused. Then, using her index finger to emphasise each point, she said, "She has never invited me to her place! We've never done anything but have sex and a take away! Every time I talk about the future she changes the subject! Need I go on?"

"Okay, if I'm honest that doesn't sound too good, but —" Rachel pondered for a moment.

Zoe inclined her head. "But what?" she said, her voice flat.

"Maybe she's just a slow mover."

"Don't make me laugh. We slept together the first night we met," Zoe spat, her head jerking up.

"Yes, I remember it well," Rachel said, clearing her throat. "Anyway, I'm not talking about in that department, I meant emotionally. For Pete's sake, Zoe, you're a therapist, surely you should have firsthand knowledge when it comes to people's emotions and how they express them."

"I do when it comes to clients, it's more difficult when I'm so close to the action."

"Take it from me, the fact that she keeps calling you tells me that she feels more for you than she's letting on."

"Do you think so?"

"Yes I do — look, why don't you just talk to her, get it all out in the open? Then at least you'll know where you stand."

"No way! I know exactly what will happen, she'll start fluttering those eyelashes at me and before I know it we'll end up in bed and back to square one."

"Hiding from her isn't going to help matters."

"I just don't understand what she wants."

Rachel started to answer but the sound of the doorbell ringing interrupted their conversation.

Rachel shot her a confident look. "I think you're about to find out."

"Don't tell me that's her," Zoe said frantically as Rachel slid back her chair. "Don't open it, I look a mess!"

"Don't be silly, you look beautiful."

"I'm going to kill you for this," Zoe said, standing and tucking her vest into her tracksuit bottoms.

"No you won't, you'll thank me later," Rachel replied as she stepped towards the door.

## CHAPTER 32

Though Kathryn was on her fourth glass of wine of the night, the alcohol had failed miserably in numbing her emotions. As she sat in Jo's living room, she could feel the tears start to form in her eyes.

"It's okay to cry," Jo said, sitting down next to her and pulling Kathryn into her arms. "It's going to be okay."

"No, it's not," Kathryn snivelled. "I've ruined a decent man's life, and for what?"

"I don't know, Kath, but I know you wouldn't have left unless you needed to."

"Has my whole life been a lie?"

"Of course it hasn't — you loved him once, you've just fallen out of love with him. It happens unfortunately."

"Oh God, I must look such a mess," Kathryn said, rising to her feet and inspecting her mascara-stained face in the living room mirror.

"You resemble Rudolph," Jo playfully tapped the tip of Kathryn's red nose, "but the rest of you is fine, your life is fine."

"How can you say that? I've just left my husband."

"Who you don't love," Jo pointed out.

"That's beside the point."

"Is it?"

"Yes, look at all he's done for me."

Jo pulled Kathryn towards her, holding her at arm's length. "Right, so just because someone has done things for you, you're obliged to live the rest of your life in misery. Is that it?"

Kathryn raised her eyes to meet Jo's. "I would hardly call my life miserable. I just wasn't happy."

Jo began to pace the room, her growing frustration obvious. "Kathryn, I'm sorry to have to be the one to tell you this, but Gareth really isn't the knight in shining armour you like to make him out. Jesus, Kath, you were eighteen when he met you. He took advantage of a young innocent girl."

"No," Kathryn said, blowing her nose.

"Yes," Jo said more forcefully, as she turned to face her. "He knew you were lacking security and he groomed you. He knew exactly how to draw you in and you fell for it hook, line and sinker."

"But he loves me, and I've let him down."

"I've no doubt that he loves you in some strange fashion, but the only person you've let down is yourself," Jo said, sitting back down and taking her face in her hands. "Listen to me, Kathryn, you get one shot at this life, just one, and you've got to live it to the max. Remember what we use to say when we were younger?"

Kathryn nodded. "No regrets," she said softly, barely audible.

"That's right, live your life for you — nobody else. Do you want to go back?"

Kathryn shook her head.

"Then don't, you can stay here as long as you want."

"No, I don't want to infringe on your space."

"You wouldn't be, we'd love having you here."

Kathryn managed a faint smile. "Thanks, but I need to stand on my own two feet. I'm going to rent a place for a few months until I find something I want to buy."

"And what are you going to do about Gareth?"

"I don't know, I really don't," she said as she burst into tears again.

## CHAPTER 33

Gareth had finally given in and reached out to his brother. As much as he hated having to lean on anybody, there was no choice — he felt as though he was on the verge of a breakdown. Looking around the home he had shared with his wife for the past ten years, he felt a sharp twinge in his chest. *This is all my own fault!* The pain vanished as quickly as it had appeared. Wasn't he the one responsible for putting the temptation in front of her in the first place? It was equivalent to putting a mouse in front of a cat and expecting the cat to ignore it. Attraction was all about instincts and the woman he had used had unleashed Kathryn's.

The bell chimed, causing him to momentarily put all thoughts aside as he rushed to the door. When he pulled it open, his brother stood there with Porsche by his side, his face wracked with worry.

"What's the urgency?" Bill asked Gareth as he rushed past him and into the hallway. "Is Kathryn alright?"

"No ... yes," Gareth said running his hand through his hair.

"Well, what is it?" Porsche asked him impatiently. "I hate the way neither of you can ever get straight to the point."

"Let me pour you both a drink then I'll explain."

Bill and Porsche followed Gareth into the living room and waited whilst he poured brandy from the crystal decanter. Handing them their glasses, he said, "I think you'd both better sit down."

"No, I'll stand. Now tell us what the hell's going on," Porsche said.

For a few moments, words failed Gareth, until finally he whispered, "Kathryn's left me."

Bill gave him a blank stare, as though he couldn't quite grasp the statement he had just heard.

"What!" Porsche squealed, as her eyes widened in disbelief.

Gareth sighed. "She said she wasn't happy. Things haven't been that great for some time now." His throat ached as though the words he spoke had themselves caused him physical pain. He cast his eyes downwards. A moment of shame pulsed through him. His wife had left him for another woman. An echo of humiliation sounded through his mind. A woman who could give her something that he clearly couldn't, despite trying his hardest to fill that void in her life.

"I need to sit down," Porsche said as she marched across the room and sank into the sofa. Gareth took the decanter and refilled his brother's now empty glass.

"Is she seeing someone else?" Bill asked, finding his voice.

The question stabbed at his heart. Forcing himself to meet his brother's eyes, he said with an air of resignation, "Yes."

"I would never have thought she had it in her," Porsche said, more to herself than to anyone else in the room. "Give me a refill, will you, Gareth?" She held out her empty glass.

Gareth refilled it, then said, "Well that's something we can both agree on." Placing the decanter down on the table, he dropped down heavily into the arm chair. An overwhelming feeling of grief overcame him and he wished the ground would just swallow him up.

"I just can't believe it," Bill said, shaking his head as he lowered himself on to the sofa next to his wife. "I mean, you don't have any idea who he is?"

Gareth's could feel the blood rushing to his face. "Yes. I found a woman on a dating website who said she would try and flirt with her to see if she was a lesbian." Just hearing himself saying these words aloud made him realise what a fool he'd been.

"What!?" Porsche asked, spraying the contents of her glass over her white top. Ignoring the stains, she continued in disbelief, "You asked a woman to seduce Kathryn? Did I hear you right?"

"Flirt, Porsche, not seduce!"

She glanced at him. "And you're surprised she left you?"

He looked up from his drink and looked at her. "Yes, well no ... I don't know."

"How long have you had your suspicions she batted for the same team," Porsche asked, flicking her hair and staring at him in cold triumph.

Gareth frowned. "Quite a while, but I just thought it was some sort of phase she was going through."

"I'm sorry to have to tell you this, but Kathryn has never struck me as the sort of woman who goes through phases of any kind."

Time stood still as Porsche's words stewed in his mind. Could Kathryn have been a lesbian from the beginning? Surely these things didn't just happen overnight — there would have been signs.

"So what are you going to do now?" Bill asked.

Letting out a heavy sigh, Gareth said, "Pray to God that she comes to her senses."

"I don't think that's very likely considering she actually walked out on you," Porsche said.

Gareth slumped down onto his seat and held his face in his hands. "As much as it kills me to admit it, Porsche, I think you're right!"

\*\*\*

Kathryn hovered the cursor over the send button before finally pressing down on it. She had just emailed an invoice to her latest client — an eccentric multi-millionaire who had wanted a futuristic-looking home. He had been ecstatic with the end result, which looked like something out of *Star Trek*. It had been her toughest project yet — not because of the design itself, but because of the emotional turmoil she had been going through. Leaving Gareth had been the hardest thing she had ever done, but it was also the kindest. She knew Gareth didn't see it that way, but there was no future for them. She was in love with Rachel and there was no denying it anymore. So many times over the last few weeks she had been on the brink of calling her to let her know how she felt but had stopped herself. Uncertainty over the response she would receive and feelings of guilt clouded her mind. But she couldn't wait any longer — she needed to hear her voice. She picked up the phone and dialled the number she knew by heart.

"Kathryn?"

"Hello, Rachel."

"It's good to hear from you. How have you been?"

"Busy sorting my life out."

"And have you?"

"What?"

"Sorted you're life out?"

"A little ...." Kathryn said hesitantly.

"I've missed you."

Kathryn remained silent as Rachel's words caused her heart to flutter.

"Kathryn, are you still there?"

"Yes ... I've missed you too," she said softly.

"Can I see you?"

"That's why I'm calling. I was wondering if you wanted to get together for dinner or something?"

"Something?" Rachel teased.

"Drinks?" Kathryn said, flustered.

"I was only teasing. Yes, I would love to meet up. When were you thinking?"

"Tonight? We can go out or you could come over to mine?"

"Um ... have dinner at yours?" Rachel said in an uncertain tone. "Are you sure that's wise?"

"Yes, I've got my own place."

"You have? What happened to —"

"It's a long story, I'll explain when I see you. I'll text you my address."

"Okay, do you want me to bring anything?"

"No ... So are you up for trying some oysters tonight?"

"Hmmm, sounds tempting but I think I'll pass," Rachel said lightly.

Kathryn laughed. "I'll cover them in tempura batter

before grilling them. That way you won't have to see them."

"In that case, I'll try one."

"Good, so I'll see you around eight?"

"Perfect, see you then."

Kathryn replaced the handset onto the cradle. Was it even humanly possible for one's heart to sing? Because hers felt as if it was. She opened her desk drawer, withdrew a pad and pen and began writing the ingredients for the evening meal. *I hope she'll try other shellfish*. Finishing, she looked around her and smiled — for the first time in years she felt whole.

## CHAPTER 34

The full moon shone down, casting a silver shadow across the rooftops, the stars a boundless sea of twinkling lights. Kathryn watched from her window as Rachel exited the cab and made her way up the pathway that led to her two-story town house. Kathryn rushed to the front door and just as Rachel was reaching forward with her index finger to press the bell, she swung the door open with a broad smile on her face. "Come in," she said, feeling all the excitement of being given a precious gift.

Kathryn's heart raced as Rachel stepped over the threshold and closed the door behind her. The two women stood in the hallway, staring at each other — unable to look away. The need to touch Rachel was so great that she wasn't even thinking as she stepped forward closing the gap between them in one quick movement. She embraced her, holding her tightly, losing herself in her soft curves as she moulded to her body. The heat Rachel radiated was intoxicating.

"I've missed you so much," Kathryn whispered, burying her head against Rachel's neck, inhaling the freshness of her scent.

Rachel let out a contented sigh as she held Kathryn tighter. "If someone would've told me I would be holding you in my arms tonight I would've thought they were insane."

After a few moments, Kathryn reluctantly moved back. "You look so good," she said, taking in Rachel's chic print shirt and the black jeans she wore beneath a black knee length coat.

"So do you." Rachel said, her eyes not leaving Kathryn's mouth.

Kathryn smiled as she led Rachel the short distance to the living room door. "Come through," she said.

Rachel followed her into a sparsely furnished living area with a large grey sofa and jade-coloured cushions just feet away from a roaring fire, crackling and hissing underneath a large gold glinted mirror. A glass dining table sat beneath a bay window.

"Wow, a real fire, did you make it yourself?" Rachel joked.

"Yes, I'm a woman of many talents," Kathryn laughed easily.

"I bet you are," Rachel said, as she stood only inches away.

Kathryn's initial confidence began to wane as her nerves got the better of her. She quickly said, "Can I take your coat?"

"Thanks," Rachel replied, acknowledging her apprehension with a smile. She slipped it off before handing it to her then veered towards the fire as Kathryn placed her coat on the back of a chair.

"This fireplace is absolutely amazing," Rachel said, warming her hands.

Seeing Rachel in her home looked so natural to Kathryn. She had wondered over the last few weeks about the reality of sharing her life with another woman and whether she could actually do it. But looking at Rachel now, she knew in her heart that it was something she wanted more than life itself. She only hoped Rachel wanted the same thing.

"So have you moved into your new place yet?" Kathryn asked watching as Rachel leaned further towards the fire.

"Yes, it's like heaven."

"I'm glad to hear it. And how are things at work?"

"Brilliant" Rachel said turning away towards her. "Things have improved drastically since your interview, so much so that Gloria has taken on new staff."

"I'm so pleased." Kathryn suddenly felt tongue tied. She had been waiting for this moment for so long and now that it was here she didn't know what to do. Maybe what she needed was a glass of wine to take the edge off. "What can I get you to drink? I've got white or red wine and beer?"

"Red would be lovely please."

"Make yourself comfortable," Kathryn called out as she entered the adjoining kitchen. Her hands trembled as she picked up the wine bottle. *What the hell is wrong with me? It's only dinner.* She wished she could physically shake some sense into herself for blowing everything out of proportion. She couldn't believe the state she was getting herself into. Not for the first time did she wish she had the confidence that Rachel possessed. Though she was more than confident in her business life, when it came to matters of the heart she reverted to an inexperienced teenager. Taking a deep breath, she quickly poured two generous glasses of wine before making her way back into the living room.

"This is some place," Rachel said as Kathryn approached her.

"Thanks, here you go," Kathryn said, handing her a glass. "Cheers."

"Cheers … mmm it's beautiful it feels like velvet coating my mouth," Rachel said as she swallowed the wine.

"It's a 2005 Château Pétrus. I took a few bottles from our wine collection," Kathryn said, settling onto the sofa next to her.

"Won't Gareth mind?"

Kathryn shook her head slightly. Gareth was the last person she wanted to be reminded off this evening. "No," she finally said. "It was a collection we'd both built up over the years," Kathryn said, smiling.

"I'm glad you did … So, how come you're here and he's not?" Rachel asked, her eyes dropping to Kathryn's bare wedding finger.

Kathryn shrugged her shoulders and let out a heavy sigh. "It just wasn't working for obvious reasons."

"I'm sorry."

"Are you?"

A faint smile touched Rachel's lips. "Yes, for him, I am."

They sat in an awkward silence for a few moments before Kathryn pushed herself up from the sofa. "Right, are you ready for oysters?"

Rachel hesitated. "Not really, but if they're cooked I'm sure they can't be that bad."

"They're not. I won't be long," Kathryn said, disappearing into the kitchen before returning ten minutes later, carrying a platter of oysters grilled with lime, herb and garlic breadcrumbs accompanied by a red chilli sauce. She laid the tray on the glass dining table as Rachel took a seat.

"Okay, this is chilli sauce," Kathryn said pointing at a small pot of red sauce.

"Home made?"

"Of course, dip in and enjoy," Kathryn said, taking one herself.

Rachel picked one of the shells up and, using her fingers, plucked out the oyster before popping it into her mouth and slowly chewing. "Hey, that tastes really good," she said.

"I told you."

"So where did you learn to make these?" Rachel asked, taking another from the plate.

Kathryn smiled sheepishly. "I have to confess I took cookery lessons".

"I'm glad to see it wasn't wasted. I take it that our main is shellfish too?"

"Baked Lobster in garlic butter with homemade chips."

Rachel leaned back in her chair. "Wow, I could get use to this."

"And if you have room for dessert — crème brulee."

Rachel licked her lips. "I can't wait."

"Hopefully by the end of this evening I will have converted you into a shellfish lover."

"Let's hope that's not all," Rachel said, as she smiled at her mischievously.

\*\*\*

Two hours later, as Kathryn sat on the sofa in front of the crackling fire, the last thing she should have felt was cold. But cold she was, her blood like ice in her veins as she listened to the noises emanating from her kitchen. Rachel seemed to be taking her time clearing away the dishes, something she had insisted upon, and Kathryn wasn't certain whether she felt grateful for the temporary reprieve or simply anxious about the night ahead. She pinched a lock of her hair between her thumb and forefinger and rubbed the strands over one another as she sat with her legs curled beneath her.

The silence that fell from the kitchen came all too soon, and Kathryn swallowed her nerves as Rachel entered the living room. Kathryn's heart ached as he took in how beautiful Rachel looked as she joined her on the sofa, leaving several inches of space between them, and flashed her a smile.

"That meal was amazing, thank you," Rachel said.

"You're welcome." The words died in Kathryn's throat as Rachel leaned over and laid her slender hand on her thigh. Kathryn felt her knees quiver as their eyes locked momentarily until she broke the gaze and looked down to Rachel's hand. She lowered her own hand over it — not to remove it but to slowly raise it gently to her lips. As she pressed a lingering kiss on each of Rachel's finger tips Kathryn could smell a citrus scent.

"Your hands are so soft," she whispered, bringing Rachel's hand to rest against her cheek. The unmistakable arousal in Rachel's eyes hit her like a thunder bolt, reminding her of the sweet taste of her mouth when they had first kissed. Rachel's reassuring smile gave Kathryn all the confidence she needed as she leaned over towards her, reaching around the back of her neck and drawing her closer.

This was it. There was no turning back now — this is what she wanted more than anything. To make love to

Rachel with no feelings of guilt or self-doubt.

"Kathryn, you know we don't have to do anything if you don't want to," Rachel said, resting her free hand gently against Kathryn's cheek. Kathryn's eyes widened and she bit her lip as she lifted her gaze to meet Rachel's comforting one. Smoothing back a loose lock of hair away from Kathryn's face she continued, "It's fine if you don't feel ready. We can just sit and talk ...."

Kathryn slowly shook her head. Just Rachel's touch sent shivers of a different kind racing through her body. If she wasn't ready now, with her, after such a perfect night, she would never be. Kathryn returned her smile, suddenly feeling much bolder than she ever remembered.

"I ... I'm ready, Rachel," she whispered. Rachel smiled sensuously as she closed the space between them. Kathryn leaned into Rachel's embrace, her heart fluttering wildly with every tender kiss Rachel planted on her lips. Kathryn's hands took on a life of their own and began to roam under Rachel's clothes. She trembled with excitement as she felt at last the perfect body she'd spent so many nights fantasising about.

The sudden sound of a door slamming outside caused Kathryn to momentarily jump back. Quickly glancing towards the window then back to Rachel, she bowed her head, a shadow of doubt touching her features. "I'm sorry."

"Just relax," Rachel said softly, tilting Kathryn's face upwards and gently stroking her cheek with the back of her hand. To Kathryn, her touch felt like a feather, so soft and tantalising and utterly arousing. She leaned in towards her, hovering for just a moment before letting out a soft sigh as she moved her mouth over Rachel's in a sensuous exploration, her tongue slipping between her lips. She could taste the sweetness of wine as she cupped Rachel's face, pressing her lips hard against her own.

Kathryn's mouth soon left Rachel's to explore the feminine curve of her silky smooth neck, her red lipstick leaving behind sweet reminders of her touch. The feel of Rachel's skin against her lips made her want to explore much more. She breathed in dizzily, longing for Rachel to take charge and show her the way.

As if reading her mind, Rachel's confident fingers began to unbutton Kathryn's shirt and remove her bra. Kathryn's breath came in short, sharp gasps as Rachel took her nipples between her lips, one after the other. Her tongue swirled around her sensitive orbs, pausing only for a brief moment as she stopped to shuck Kathryn from her now superfluous clothing. Kathryn lay back on the sofa, at last entirely vulnerable to her ministrations, and whimpered with need as Rachel peeled off her own top.

Expertly, Rachel reached around her back and single handily unclipped her own bra, leaving her naked except for the jeans she wore. Kathryn felt every drop of her blood in her veins surge to her face as she took in the beautiful female form before her. How long had she been waiting for this moment? She knew that this was where she was meant to be and nothing else mattered in the universe except Rachel.

She heard Rachel's breath catch above the crackling of the burning wood as Rachel stared at her with desire — the glare of the flames glowing in Rachel's eyes.

The feel of Rachel's beating heart against her chest exalted her as she drew her into a tight embrace, Rachel's tongue searching her own with great ferocity.

Swallowing hard past a lump in her throat, Kathryn

reached out and took one of Rachel's pert breasts in her hand, her thumb gently caressing her nipple, causing it to tighten into a hard ball.

The first teasing tingles of desire were just beginning to build in her burning core when Rachel moved slightly away from her before gently pulling her down to join her on the shag pile carpet. No longer self-conscious of her nakedness, Kathryn slid willingly into Rachel's opened arms. Her fingers laced through Rachel's hair as she caressed the outline of her mouth with the tip of her tongue, before kissing her deeply, savouring every moment. A quick moan escaped Rachel's mouth as Kathryn grazed her neck with her tongue, her hot breath against her skin. Kathryn pushed her gently down onto her back. Slowly, she began to unbutton Rachel's jeans, all the while holding her gaze, a lazy smile on her face until she undid the last button and eased them down. She drew in a quick breath as she noticed Rachel wasn't wearing any underwear.

Slowly and seductively, Kathryn's gaze slid over Rachel's body. "You are so beautiful," Kathryn said hoarsely as she outlined Rachel's breasts with the tip of her finger. She slowly moved downwards, over her flat stomach, taking pleasure in feeling the softness of her skin. Rachel's stomach rose and fell quickly, her chest expanding with every breath she took. As Rachel pulled Kathryn onto to her, Kathryn's world spun and careened on its axis as they lay skin to skin as though they were one, finding the tempo that bound their bodies together. With each caress, Kathryn was dimly aware of the differences between Rachel's body and her soon to be ex-husband's. Everything about Rachel — from the curve of her shoulders, to the softness of her skin, and her feminine scent — was different, and different was so thrilling. From out of nowhere, memories of her wedding day and the vows she took, swearing to love, honour and obey, to forsake all others, flooded her mind only to melt away like sugar over an open flame as Rachel's hands caressed her body.

Kathryn's eyes swung between open and shut as Rachel filled both her senses and her thoughts. Rachel's movements were slow and patient, and it felt like she knew just when and where to touch her. Kathryn's eyes brimmed with joyful tears as Rachel whispered soft, sweet endearments against her neck; it was exactly as she'd always imagined, and infinitely better.

"I want to feel *you* inside me," Rachel cried, guiding Kathryn's hand between her thighs, and letting out a moan of delight as Kathryn's fingers glided easily into her. With Rachel's hand covering Kathryn's, Rachel encouraged her to thrust harder with each breath she took, pulling Kathryn closer and kissing her deeply. Kathryn clung to her and buried her face into Rachel's hair as she sank herself into her, inch by tantalizing inch. Rachel's muffled moans filled the room and urged Kathryn on.

"I want to taste you," Kathryn whispered into Rachel's ear. She lay on her back, her body quivering in anticipation as Rachel moved along the length of Kathryn's body on her knees until she reached Kathryn's mouth. Kathryn raised her chin, rolled back her head and reached up with the tip of her tongue to make contact with Rachel's epicentre. Her stomach flittered when Rachel moaned in ecstasy as she lowered herself firmly onto Kathryn's tongue, slowly moving rhythmically against it. With a throbbing sensation mounting between her own legs, Kathryn reached down and began to stroke herself, the pace of her finger matching the flickering of her tongue against Rachel's clit, savouring her taste. She quickened the motion of her finger as Rachel's hip's began to move faster, pressing down on her tongue so hard she could barely breathe. Kathryn was too caught up in the ecstasy of the moment to care as she matched her urgency by probing and licking Rachel's pleasure point until Rachel let out a long cry before slumping forward on all fours. Rachel's chest rose and fell under her laboured breathing. It was several moments before she moved to lay opposite Kathryn.

Rachel dropped her chin on her chest with a sigh of pleasure. "Are you sure you haven't done this before?"

"Positive."

"Well, I give you ten out of ten for being a quick learner," Rachel said with a flicker of amusement in her expression.

Kathryn smiled before she realised that she still had her hand between her legs. She attempted to move it before Rachel clasped her hand.

"Don't move — I want to watch you."

Kathryn glanced up with shyness as an unwelcomed blush crept into her cheeks. "I —" Kathryn was about to protest until she saw the smouldering flame in Rachel's eyes. All feelings of embarrassment vanished as the desire to please Rachel overwhelmed her.

Closing her eyes, she resumed stoking herself. Knowing Rachel was watching her made the experience all the more sensual. She arched her back as she felt Rachel caress her breast, tugging gently on her hardened nipples before trailing her finger down her stomach and replacing Kathryn's hand with her own — stimulating her clitoris with her finger and thumb.

With every stroke, her heart beat faster, each barely audible groan that escaped Rachel's lips made the blood pound through Kathryn's veins. As Rachel lowered her head and teasingly licked her stomach in circular motions, Kathryn suppressed the urge to laugh as her abdomen tensed in response to the sensation.

"Are you ticklish?" Rachel asked between movements.

"A little, but don't stop, I like it."

"I wasn't going to," Rachel said, as she traced a path of kisses downward until her face disappeared between Kathryn's legs. Within moments, Rachel's skilful tongue sent Kathryn careening toward heights of pleasure she'd never even suspected. Her every touch drew forth notes of delight from the instrument of her body and she hoped she would never stop playing her.

Kathryn stifled a cry, biting down on her bottom lip as she felt Rachel's tongue ease deep into her, then withdraw and tease her with soft stokes. She brought her to the edge with a fast flicker, before retreating to drop butterfly kisses along her inner thigh. Kathryn didn't know how much longer she could last before exploding — it was too much to bear.

As Rachel brought her tongue to her centre again, Kathryn arched her back, gripping Rachel's slender shoulders, pressing her nails in deep as Rachel's tongue moved over her engorged clit with strong impelling strokes. Kathryn's hands slid off the perspiration on Rachel's back. Kathryn squirmed and writhed with aching need, desperate for Rachel's touch to bring her the rest of the way.

She closed her eyes, face contorted and teeth clenched. Kathryn held Rachel's head in place fiercely as the last delicious, shuddering moments came upon her.

Lost in a moment of euphoria, Kathryn smiled to herself as Rachel sidled up beside her, showering her with little kisses along the way until she finally reached her face.

Kathryn turned her head to look at her. "I feel like I've died and gone to heaven."

Rachel smiled broadly. "That was just the beginning," she said, tenderly stroking her arm. "I've got a lot more to teach you."

"I can't wait." Everything was perfect. She had finally filled that gaping hole that had been there all of her life.

Their bodies naked and still moist from their lovemaking, they lay in each other's arms, caressing each other gently.

"I never knew," Kathryn murmured after a while, "I never dreamt it could be so sweet."

"Believe it or not, it only gets sweeter," Rachel answered with a grin and planted a kiss on the top of her head, before snuggling down into the crook of Kathryn's arm.

Kathryn softly stroked Rachel's hair until she fell asleep, then leaning in, she whispered into her ear, "I love you."

\*\*\*

The birds chirping in the morning sky weren't the only ones that were happy. Rachel smiled a long lazy smile as Kathryn opened her eyes.

"Good morning," Rachel said, gently touching Kathryn's cheek.

"How long have you been up?" Kathryn asked as she shielded the light from her eyes.

"A while."

"You should have woken me."

"I didn't want to disturb you, besides, I was enjoying watching you sleep."

Kathryn pulled a face then tugged the quilt she had retrieved from the bedroom the previous night over her head. "I bet I look a right mess."

"No, you look beautiful," Rachel said, pulling back the quilt and planting a kiss on Kathryn's lips. "Are you okay?"

Kathryn nodded. "It just feels a bit —"

"Strange sleeping with a woman?" Rachel finished for her.

"Yes, you could say that."

"Do you have any regrets?"

"None whatsoever. It's not so much about you being a woman, I think I'd have felt this way even if you were a man. Gareth is the only partner I've ever had."

Rachel's mouth dropped open. "You're kidding?"

"No it's true, he was the first and only person I've ever slept with, apart from you."

"Wow," Rachel said.

"I feel a bit guilty if I'm honest. I feel as if I'm still married to him even though we are separated."

"You have nothing to feel guilty about, he's a grown man and can look after himself."

"Yes, I know, but when you've been in a relationship for so long it's strange not being with them. Can you understand?"

Rachel shifted uncomfortably and shrugged her shoulders. "Well seeing as I haven't been in a relationship before, I can't really say I do," she said unapologetically as she let out a long sigh. "As far as I'm concerned relationships are more hassle than their worth."

"Oh," Kathryn said, pulling the quilt closer to her

chest. "So what we did was just like a one night stand for you?"

Rachel smiled. "No, at least I hope not," she replied, gently tugging at the quilt.

Kathryn clamped her hand over Rachel's stopping her from going any further. "So what is it? You obviously aren't looking for a relationship."

Rachel threw her hands up in an open gesture. "Why does it have to be anything? Why can't we just enjoy each other until —"

"Until what? You tire of me? Christ, what was I thinking?" Kathryn asked herself as she sat up abruptly and grabbed her clothes from the floor next to her.

Rachel frowned. "Kathryn. What is it you want from me?"

"What do I want?" Kathryn spun around to face her. "Absolutely nothing. You're right, anything more than a casual fling isn't worth the hassle. In fact, do you know what — I don't even think a casual fling is worth it," she said, the words choking in her throat.

Rachel attempted to reach out to her. "I'm sorry if I've upset you."

"You haven't. I'm glad we both know where we stand before it went any further."

"Do you want me to leave?"

"Yes, I think it's for the best, don't you?"

Kathryn waited for an answer — receiving none, she strode into the bathroom, slamming the door behind her.

Hearing the lock turn, Rachel gathered her clothes and quickly dressed. Standing outside the bathroom, she waited for a few moments before gently tapping the door. "Kathryn," she said quietly, leaning her forehead against the door. Hearing muffled sobs, she felt sick to her stomach. "I'm sorry," she said as she wondered how her voice could sound so normal when her insides were in turmoil. She ran her hand over her face, feeling as if Kathryn's sadness had somehow managed to transfer itself into her soul.

"So am I ... please just go."

## CHAPTER 35

"You are well out of order this time. When are you going to quit fucking with people's emotions?"

Rachel was shocked to see the anger in Zoe's normally placid face. "But —"

Zoe held her hand up in mid-air. "Do you know what — I don't want to hear it. I warned you about getting involved, but, oh no, you have to be the big player. Getting what you want, regardless of the consequences. Preying on a woman who didn't ask you to come into her life and turn it upside down. You chose to do that, with that sick fuck of a husband of hers. Everything is such a game to you, isn't it? Well, it's time you realised that you are dealing with real people here. Yeah, so your dad fucked your mum over. Does that give you the right to do the same to others?"

Rachel stood still, shocked by Zoe's outburst. "If you would just hear me out for a minute, I've tried ringing her to explain but she won't answer my calls."

"You know what? Neither would I. I bet she's as fed up with your bullshit as I am. I need to get out of here. I can't bear to be in the same space as you at the moment."

As Zoe stormed out, Rachel sat at the bottom of the stairs feeling numb, recalling the previous evening's events. She couldn't understand how things had taken such a drastic turn, after what had been a wonderful evening. *What's wrong with me? Why do I always have to fuck things up?* She was damned if she knew. All her life it had been the same — whenever she felt any resemblance of a normal emotion she clammed up, almost suffocating on a feeling of dread. *Am I going to live the rest of my life in the shadow of my father's destructive legacy?* When he'd disappeared out of her life, she had always believed he would come back, despite her mother telling her he wouldn't. All traces of him were removed overnight and it was as if he never existed in the first place. Her mother forbade her from talking about him, only stating that he had ruined their once happy lives by running off with another woman. *What did it really matter?* She wiped the tears from her eyes. *I'm not a child anymore, and he's dead, so what does it all matter? I don't need anyone.* She stood up defiantly and headed up to her bedroom, flopping down on her bed, her mind filled with thoughts of Kathryn.

Half an hour later Rachel looked up as her bedroom door opened.

Zoe's hand shook a white hanky through the crack of the door. "Is it safe to come in?"

"Yes," Rachel laughed.

"I'm sorry I lost it," Zoe said as she sat on the edge of the bed. "I just can't bear to see you keep hurting yourself."

Rachel remained silent.

"I think you need to read whatever is in this, Rachel," she said, withdrawing a large envelope from behind her back.

"I thought I'd thrown that away?" Rachel said, recognising the handwriting as her father's.

"Yeah well, you're too impulsive for your own good

sometimes. That's why I took it back out of the bin. Maybe it will contain the answers you've been looking for, then you can move on."

"I doubt it. He left us, that's all there is to it."

"There's always two sides to a story, Rachel. Why don't you read what he has to say?" Zoe stood and walked to the door, pausing before she walked through. "I'll be downstairs if you need to talk."

Rachel stared at the envelope for a long time before tentatively picking it up and unsealing the flap at the back. She dipped her hand in and withdrew the letter. As she did, pieces of newspaper clippings fluttered carelessly down to the floor. She bent down, scooping them up, her face a sea of confusion. Why would her father send her clippings? She opened the white sheet of folded paper, and her eyes travelled down the page as she read.

*My dearest Rachel*

*Where do I begin after so long? I have so much to say but so little time left. What I need you to know is how much I love you. Not a day has passed that I have not thought about you and wondered if you have grown into the beautiful woman that I always dreamt you would. I hope your life has turned out well despite having a father like me.*

Rachel closed her eyes. She didn't want to read anymore, didn't want to hear his excuses. What could possibly justify him leaving her, when she had needed her daddy so badly? Taking a deep breath, she resumed reading.

*I don't know what your mother told you about me leaving but you need to hear my side of the story and why I did what I did. I'm not proud of myself for the way I dealt with things but it was the only way I knew how at the time. Looking back now, I wish I had let the proper authorities deal with it, as that would have meant I would have still been able to remain a father to you. But walking in and finding that animal in your bed, trying to touch you, like a man would his wife, was more than I could bear.*

Rachel's blood ran cold — *what the fuck was he talking about?* She frantically read the clippings.

*Local man Max Lexington, 36, has been charged today with the unlawful killing of his brother-in-law Michael Thompson, 34, of Hackney, north London. Mr Lexington allegedly walked in as Mr Thompson was attempting to sexually abuse his nine-year-old daughter, who cannot be named for legal reasons. Mr Lexington pleaded guilty at the crown court today. He was denied bail and remanded in custody. The case continues.*

Rachel just barely reached the bathroom before she began retching into the toilet bowl. *No, no, it couldn't be true — it was a lie. Why would he say things like that? Surely she would remember. Wouldn't she?* She couldn't even remember her mum's brother. Surely her mother wouldn't have lied to her for all these years, letting her believe that her father had abandoned her. *Could she be that cruel?*

"Rachel, are you alright?" Zoe's concerned voice called from the other side of the door.

Gathering all the strength she could, she pulled herself up out of her slump and opened the door.

"What the hell happened to you?" Zoe asked, shocked at Rachel's pale appearance.

"The paper," she said faintly.

"What paper?"

"In there."

"What are you talking about?" Zoe said, taking her by the arm and coaxing her out of the bathroom and back into the bedroom.

Zoe looked at the scattered paper clippings on the floor. "What are they about?"

"They're ... about ... my ... father, read them."

Zoe picked them up, reading each piece in silence, her expression changing as the painful words hit home. She held her hand to her mouth. "Oh my God, Rachel." Her voice sank to a whisper as tears welled in her eyes. "Oh, Rachel," she repeated, stepping forward to take her in her arms. "Oh, baby," she said rocking her. "I'm so sorry." Her voice choked.

"Why wouldn't my mum have told me?"

"I don't know. It's no excuse, but maybe she wanted to protect you, and thought she was doing the right thing."

"Do you think she did the right thing?" Rachel asked.

"It's not about being right or wrong, I don't know what the answer is," Zoe said, easing Rachel onto the bed and sitting beside her, her arm around her shoulder. "But she should have got you counselling, even if she couldn't have dealt with it herself, she should have gotten help for you."

"But why wouldn't she have told me the truth about my father? Why did she let me grow up hating him?"

"Rachel, people do the strangest things. She may be your mother but she obviously had her own issues and to think that her own flesh and blood had ..." She couldn't bring herself to say the words. Anger boiled within her as she fought to maintain a neutral voice. "Tried to hurt you," she said instead.

"Can you read the rest of the letter for me?"

"Of course I will. Where did you get up to?"

"The bit where ... where he walked in and ..."

"It's alright, I've found it," Rachel said then cleared her voice. "I just wanted him to get away from you, you were screaming but he wouldn't go. He didn't realise I had come home early from work. He thought nobody was home. I only had the knife in my hand because I was chopping up vegetables in the kitchen when I heard you scream. I thought you had hurt yourself, nothing could have prepared me for what I saw — then I lost it. I don't regret killing him, what I do regret is what happened to you. I have been released from prison on compassionate leave because I'm dying," Zoe's voice stuttered, before continuing. "I would have so loved to have seen you just one last time — hold on a second," she said, trying to regain her composure. "But it's not meant to be. Please forgive me, Rachel, and know that I will always be with you. I love you. Your loving father." Zoe sobbed, unable to contain herself any longer. The women embraced, both incapable of stemming the flow of tears.

"All these years I've hated him, when he didn't leave me at all."

"No, he didn't. I'm sorry you found out this way, Rach."

"You weren't to know. What am I going to do?"

Wiping the tears from her eyes, Zoe brought her emotions under control. "Well, the first thing is to talk to someone about all this. I'm too close to you for me to be able to help you in a professional capacity, but I will refer you to my friend and colleague Gillian. Then I think you should call your uncle and find out where your dad's buried. Then go and make peace with him."

## CHAPTER 36

Kathryn sat by the large window of a French cafe with Jo, unconsciously drawing sad faces onto the steamy window. She still wore her jacket as the air was chilly and only slightly warmer than the bleak weather outside. Not that Kathryn cared about her surroundings; she had more important things on her mind.

"My life's a bloody mess!" Kathryn said, rubbing out the face with the palm of her hand.

"Hey, what's happened?" Jo asked. "Are you regretting leaving Gareth?"

She shook her head and she dried her hand with a napkin. "No."

"Then what is it? If you don't tell me I can't help you."

Kathryn toyed with her wine glass before eventually answering. "I've slept with somebody."

Jo's face beamed. "I knew it! Why didn't you tell me before?"

"Because I didn't think anything was going to happen."

"So tell all. Who is he?" Jo said, the excitement evident on her face.

Kathryn looked at her friend. She was apprehensive. *Should I tell her?* Taking a sip of her wine, she knew she had to confide in someone. Jo wouldn't judge her — that she was sure of. Mustering all the courage she had, she replied confidently, "It's not a he ... it's a she."

"What!" Jo spurted out the wine she had just sipped, then dabbed at her mouth, trying to compose herself.

"It's a woman," Kathryn said in a hushed voice, her confidence slightly knocked by Jo's reaction.

"What do you mean it's a woman?"

"I'm in love with a woman," Kathryn said, dropping her gaze with something like relief. She had been going insane having no one to talk to about what had happened.

Jo grinned. "Well, I'm speechless," she said, obviously trying to get her head around the bombshell her friend had just landed on her. "You are the last person on this earth I would have expected to hear something like that from."

Kathryn raised her eyes to meet her friend's then laughed. "Am I that bad?"

"Far from it, you're that good! Mother Theresa had nothing on you," Jo teased. "Anyway how did it happen and more to the point where did you meet her?"

"Well, it just so happens you've seen a picture of her."

"I have?" Jo asked, raising her eyebrows.

Kathryn nodded her head. "Yep, you remember Rachel, the journalist."

"Are you kidding me?" Jo gasped, "You slept with her?" she almost shouted.

"Shhh," Kathryn said as other diners turned to stare at the commotion.

"But ... but I mean when did it go from having an interview with her, to ending up in bed together?" Jo said in a more hushed voice.

"A few nights ago and it wasn't in bed, it was on the

sofa, then ...."

"Alright show off, no need to brag," Jo said, laughing. "I can't believe it. So how did it, you know, happen?"

"She came by for dinner, we got talking and then it sort of just happened," Kathryn told her matter-of-factly.

"Whoa, hold it there. How can having an encounter with a woman just sort of happen?"

"I don't know but it did."

"And?"

"And what?"

"What was is bloody like?" Jo laughed, reached across the table and squeezed Kathryn's hand, offering her reassurance.

"It was ..." Kathryn stopped and looked up whilst she tried to find an appropriate word. "Amazing."

"I have to say I'm really shocked."

"You can't be any more shocked than me, I still can't believe it. I feel so guilty, even though I'm no longer with Gareth, I still feel like I've been unfaithful."

"Oh come on, honey, you're separated. It's not the same as cheating on him when you're still together," Jo said, reassuringly.

"Say it enough times and I might start to believe it," Kathryn said sadly.

"Anyway," Jo said, perking up. "That's one feather in your cap for being daring and adventurous. Hell, I've had my own fantasies about women. I wish a stunner like Rachel would make a move on me."

Kathryn looked at her, shocked.

"I don't tell you everything, you know. A girl has to have some secrets." Jo drank her wine. "Have you ever been attracted to women before?"

"Yes, from as far back as I can remember," Kathryn said truthfully. "After my mum died, my sexuality just wasn't a priority anymore, just being loved by someone was." *And that person just happened to be Gareth.* "From the moment I laid eyes on Rachel, I just felt it — you know, how you always used to go on about how you felt when you met Ben, that you just knew he was the one. Well, that's how I felt about Rachel but I just couldn't admit it."

"Until now," Jo said.

"Yes, until now." Rachel's touch had burnt into her and left a scorched mark that only she could extinguish — there was no going back.

"But if you knew you were attracted to women, how could you have coped with …" Jo didn't need to continue, Kathryn caught her drift.

"We've always had a brother-sister type relationship. Sex wasn't a regular occurrence, and I didn't think I was missing anything until last week."

"So what are you going to do? Are you going to tell him about her?" Jo asked.

"I don't know, I really don't. The next morning didn't go down too well. I think I came on too strong."

"How so?"

"I just stupidly thought that once we, you know — did it, we'd just automatically be a couple."

"And I take it that wasn't what she wanted."

Kathryn shook her head and stared down into her glass. She had been so upset when Rachel had been blasé about everything. The whole encounter had been a big deal for her, and she thought Rachel felt the same way but the look on her face when they talked about relationships, soon had her thinking otherwise.

"Don't be too hard on yourself. You've been out of the dating game a long time. Look at it from her perspective — you're still married, at least on paper. Why should she invest all her emotions in you, when she doesn't know how things are going to pan out with you and Gareth?"

"So do you think I should try again?"

"Yes, I do, but just take things slow. What's meant to be will be. Can I ask you something?"

"Anything."

"Why didn't you tell me Kath, I thought we didn't keep secrets from each other?"

"I don't know I really don't. Once I married Gareth it just didn't seem important anymore."

"It would have mattered to me. I could have at least tried to talk some sense into you about marrying him."

Kathryn reached over and squeezed Jo's hand. "If I'm honest I don't think I was ready to face it at that time. I truly believe there's a time for everything and that just wasn't mine."

The waitress appeared at their table to take their order. "Can I get you ladies some more drinks?"

"Yes, please, a dry white wine — a large one!" Jo said. "I think I need it

!

## CHAPTER 37

Rachel glanced over at her uncle as the grey pick-up truck snaked its way through the narrow cemetery roads, passing both old and new tombstones. She was again taken aback with the uncanny resemblance to her father, "I'm really sorry about the way I treated you when you came to see me."

"Don't worry about it. I would have reacted the same."

"I just don't understand why I wasn't told."

"We couldn't find you and believe me we searched. Once your mum changed your surnames, you sort of disappeared off the radar."

He brought the truck to a halt at a copious mound of freshly dug mud, clumped together so it rose inches from the ground. A solitary wooden cross sat at the top end, bearing the name of her father on a brass plate.

"Here he is," he said, nodding towards it.

He opened his side of the car, the scent of freshly cut grass breezed in, replacing the odour of stale cigarettes. She bit on her bottom lip, her sweaty hands gripping each other. Feeling the tingling at the back of her eyes, she slowly closed them. She felt the cool breeze as her door was opened and her uncle held out his hand to her.

"I know if there's an afterlife, he'll be happy that you're here," he said.

She looked up at him, a quivering smile on her lips, before hesitantly taking his hand and allowing herself to be edged towards her father's final resting place. Hovering for a few moments, she kowtowed to the mound of fresh earth.

"I'm here, Dad," she choked, her vision blurred by the tears. "I'm so sorry, I'm so sorry," she repeated over and over as she skimmed her hands across the dirt.

"Why didn't you tell me?" Rachel asked the mound as if it held the answers. "Why didn't you tell me?"

Her uncle looked away, searching for a cigarette in his pocket and lighting it, then taking a deep inhale of smoke. After a short while, he bent down beside her, putting a strong hand on her shoulder. "You were the one thing that got him through the day. Knowing you were safe — you were his life."

"But I grew up hating him," she said, turning to him. She knew she must have looked a pitiful sight, with traces of dirt intermingling with her tears. "He died thinking I hated him."

"Come on now, he never thought any such thing. He knew if you knew the truth, you wouldn't have hated him. Life just panned out the way it did — it's no one's fault."

"It is," she said, wiping her face with the back of her hand. "My mum should have told me the truth, she should have let me see him."

He took a deep breath and flicked his cigarette onto the road. "I think she just went into denial. She didn't want to believe that her own flesh and blood could have tried to … well, you know," he said awkwardly.

"But I don't remember any of it."

"You've blocked it out, Rach, it was a traumatic experience for you."

"Why didn't he just call the police?"

"I've asked myself that a thousand times. But your dad was always impulsive about everything — seeing that monster in your bed just made him snap."

"What a mess," she said more to herself. All of those years, wasted on anger and resentment. Why didn't she try to find her father and hear his side of the story instead of just taking what her mum had told her as the truth? She knew the way the world worked — the lies and deceit people were capable of. Why hadn't she applied the same rule to her mother? Instead, for years she had gone on unquestioning every lie she ever told her and now it was too late.

Her uncle struggled to his feet. "I'll leave you alone to have a few words — take all the time you need," he said, giving her shoulder a quick rub before going back to the truck.

\*\*\*

"Do you feel better now you've been to the cemetery?" Zoe asked Rachel as they both sat on the window seat in their living room.

"Definitely, I feel like I've reclaimed a part of my life." Rachel looked out of the window at the traffic buzzing past, each of the occupants with their own dramas.

"Good, I'm glad," Zoe said, watching her as she stared out of the window. "I really love you, you know."

"I know you do and I love you too," Rachel said, looking at her briefly with a weak smile.

"Do you fancy hanging out with me and Cody tonight?"

"As much as I'd love to," Rachel said as she closed the curtain. "I can't, I've got plans. How are things between you both now?"

"They're good. She finally admitted she wanted a relationship so I can see a future for us."

"I'm so glad Zoe, you two are good together."

"Thanks," she replied, glancing across at Rachel as she put her boots on. "Oh no, please don't tell me you're going bar hopping."

Rachel laughed. "Nope, I think those days are well and truly over."

"Boy, am I glad to hear that," Zoe said, pretending to wipe sweat from her brow. "Then where are you off to?"

"To see if I can salvage anything with Kathryn," Rachel said, swooping down to pick her mobile phone from the seat.

"Do you think you're ready?"

"As I'll ever be," Rachel said, smiling as she stood and left the room.

## CHAPTER 38

"It's a nice place," Gareth said, glancing around Kathryn's living room. "Very compact."

"It serves its purpose," Kathryn said, ignoring the sarcasm in his voice. *It may not be a penthouse, but it's mine and you don't live here.*

"I've brought your mail," he said, removing several envelopes from the inside of his dark blue blazer and handing them to her.

"Thank you."

"So how have you been?" he asked, remaining close by her side, his familiar scent now feeling like a distant memory.

"Good."

"You look tired."

"I am a bit, we've had an influx of orders from cat owners," she said, smiling as she flicked through her mail, wishing he would back off and stop invading her space.

"And you're actually pleased about that?"

"Yes, I am," she said in a steady, low pitched voice. She was damned if he was going to make her feel like she was doing something wrong. He had done that for most of their marriage and she wasn't going to let him do it anymore.

"I don't think you've come this far in your career to

end up designing cat pads."

"It's not *all* I do, but it makes a change at the moment," she said, leaning back slightly to create some space between them.

"You seem to be making a lot of changes."

"That's a bit below the belt, Gareth," she said, carelessly throwing her mail on the dining table, unable to move away from him despite the discomfort she felt.

"Is it? Is it really? You think just deciding one day that you no longer want to be married is something that should just be swept underneath the carpet?"

"I'm not saying that."

"Then what are you saying? Because from where I'm standing, you're not saying very much."

"I told you I just need time to sort my head out." she said, raking her hand through her hair.

"And have you?"

Kathryn nodded her head and stared down at her hands.

"And?" he asked, slightly raising his voice. "It seems I'm the last to know about anything that's going on in that head of yours."

"What's that supposed to mean?" she asked, looking up at him, her eyes widening.

"That Jo has been making the rounds, telling people we've separated."

"I'm sorry, she had no right to do that."

"So what have you decided? Are you serious about getting a divorce or do you want to come home?" he asked, crossing his arms over his chest.

Kathryn shook her head. "I can't come back, Gareth."

"And why not?" he asked with a fixed stare.

"Because ... I don't love you." She could feel her stomach tightening as the words left her mouth.

"I see."

She noticed him flinch as if she had delivered him a physical blow. "I'm sorry, Gareth, I don't want to hurt you."

"So what do you think you're doing?" he asked, his voice hardening.

"Setting you free, so you can find someone you truly deserve."

He let out a dismissive laugh. "What a load of old tosh. Do you think we're in the middle of a tacky romance novel, where we break up and we both find love again and live happily ever after? Don't be so bloody naïve, Kathryn — this is real life, crap like that only happens in fiction."

"That may well be, but I just don't think it's fair on either of us to live unhappily," she said, finally finding the strength to move across the room.

"Who said I was unhappy?" he asked, squinting his eyes as they followed her.

"Aren't you, Gareth? Things haven't been right between us for a long time." She threw her hands up in the air, suddenly feeling very tired, just wanting to diffuse the friction. "Look, why don't I make us a coffee?"

He stared at her for a long time, his face revealing nothing, until it visibly softened and he let out a sigh. "Okay, can you make it a tea instead? Coffee is giving me the jitters lately."

"Tea it is then," she said, laying her hand on his arm as she walked past him.

At the sound of the doorbell, Kathryn called out from the kitchen. "Can you answer that for me, Gareth? I'm expecting a delivery."

"Okay," he called back.

Opening the front door, he blinked several times before focusing his eyes on the woman that stood there.

"You!" he said

Rachel said nothing, she just looked down at her feet.

"Jesus Christ. I don't believe this, what are you doing coming to where my wife lives?"

"I —"

"Listen to me very carefully, I don't know what your game is but it had better not include my wife."

"Look —"

"I haven't finished. If you don't back off from her, I'm going to have to tell her about our little — what shall we say? — pre-planned event that we staged. Believe me, if she ever found out the truth about you and what you're really like, let's just say the likelihood of there being a friendship is nil."

"You wouldn't tell her," Rachel blurted out in disbelief.

"Wouldn't I? Do you really want to test me? I thought not, now go back to the stone you crawled from underneath. Your kind is not the sort Kathryn needs around her."

With that, he shut the door in her face, hoping that would be the last he ever saw of her. The truth was, the threat he made had been an idle one. Not only would Kathryn not be able to forgive Rachel, she wouldn't forgive him, which would scupper any chance of the reunion he so badly craved.

"It was just a charity collection," he said as he sat down on the sofa, gracefully accepting the tea Kathryn handed him.

"Oh, which one?"

"Um ... er ... Cancer research, I slipped them a few quid."

"Good."

"So where were we?"

Kathryn sighed. "There's no point us keep going over it, Gareth, we both just need to move on."

"Just like that?"

"There isn't ever going to an easy way to end it. Believe me, I've thought about it."

"Just know one thing, Kathryn," he said, putting his cup on the table. "I think one day you're going to realise that you've made a mistake and when you do I will be waiting ... I'll never stop fighting for you," he said.

"Please don't waste your time thinking that there's going to be another chance — there's not."

"Somehow, I think you're wrong." As far as he was concerned, now that Rachel was no longer in the picture, there wouldn't be any reason for her wanting out of their marriage.

## CHAPTER 39

"Do you think he really meant it, that he'd actually tell her that he set the whole of your meeting up?" Zoe asked.

"Yes I do, what has he got to lose, she's already left him," Rachel said, nursing her wine.

"What a bastard," Zoe said, as she caught the bartender's attention with her hand. "Another round please."

"I don't blame him in a way. I don't think his wife leaving him was part of the plan when he asked me to meet her."

"Yeah, well it's his own bloody fault, that's what happens when you play with fire," Zoe said, pouring her beer into a frosted glass.

"Have a heart, Zoe, no one's come out of this smelling of roses," Rachel said, leaning her elbows on the bar, her face disappearing into her hands.

"Apart from the innocent victim in this — Kathryn. So what are you going to do now?"

"There's nothing I can do. I can't risk her finding out the truth. She'd never forgive me. Looking back, I can't believe I ever agreed to do it in the first place — what on earth was I thinking?" She let out a small sound of displeasure.

"You weren't, Rachel, that's the problem," Zoe said sadly. "I think you're running on auto pilot has a lot to do with your childhood. Emotions have a way of playing out in the most unexpected of ways."

"That's no excuse for the way I behaved. Like you said at the start of all this, it would have been different if it was consensual but to do it behind her back is inexcusable," Rachel said, lifting her face up, a pained expression crossing her features.

"Don't beat yourself up about it. There's not been that much harm done. I think in the end she would have left him whether she would have met you or not. You were just the catalyst to their undoing."

"What a joke though, the first time I fall in love this happens."

"Whoa, lets back up for a minute. Did you just mention the word love?" Zoe's mouth dropped.

"I think ... I think I did." Rachel sat erect in her chair.

"Oh my God, I never thought I'd live to see the day when you muttered that word out of your mouth."

"I think I fell in love with her the first time I met her," Rachel said, her body suddenly slouching.

"These last couple of months really have been a learning curve for you, haven't they?"

"In more ways than one." Rachel sighed. "It's just going to take time to not feel angry at my mum. I still can't believe the way she dealt with things."

"I think she coped with it by falling into a depression where she wouldn't have to deal with reality. I think she was traumatised as well by the whole event."

"It's understandable, I suppose," Rachel said, linking her arm around Zoe's shoulders and pulling her in for a hug.

*** 

In only a few ticks of time, Rachel's life had crumbled. What could have been the start of something great was marred by lies and deceit and it was all of her own doing. She sat looking at the blank screen in front of her, having told Gloria she would be working from home for a while. She'd been staring at it for well over an hour, hoping some kind of inspiration would take a hold of her but it continued to elude her. The chime of the doorbell alerted Rachel to the fact that a world existed outside her own. Reluctantly pushing herself away from the desk, she went to the window, opening the blinds with a tentative finger to peer down beneath her.

"Shit," she hissed between clenched teeth, as she saw Kathryn standing patiently at her door. Her first instinct was to ignore her and pretend she wasn't in. She stood as still as a mannequin, barely breathing, afraid that Kathryn would be able to hear her. She jerked back suddenly as Kathryn looked up at the window as if sensing her there, banging her head on the wall behind her in the process and biting down on her hand in order to stop herself from yelling 'ouch'. Tenderly she rubbed the small bump that was already forming on the back of her head. *Can things get any worse?* The doorbell chimed again.

"Just go away," Rachel said under her breath. She pressed her back up against the wall as if she was in a firing line. The sound of Kathryn's muffled voice on the phone, moving away from the house, gave her a sense of relief as she pressed her face close to the blind, seeing her retreating figure walking back towards to her car. Just as she thought she was home free, she heard the rattling sound of Zoe's keys in the door and saw Kathryn turn back towards the house. Peering through the blind, she saw Kathryn shaking Zoe's hand and then glancing up at the window, their voices muffled. To Rachel's shock, the two of them walked up the path and after a few seconds entered the house.

"Rachel," Zoe called out. "Rachel," she tried a second time.

*Is she for real?* Rachel thought angrily. Wasn't it obvious to Zoe that she hadn't answered the door because she didn't want to see Kathryn?

She backed away from the window as she heard Zoe taking the stairs two at a time and then briskly pushing open her door.

"Didn't you hear the door?" Zoe asked her.

"Yes, I did, but I'm trying to work, as you can see," Rachel said, pointing at the blank screen.

"Yeah, great work," Zoe said sarcastically. "Anyway, Kathryn is downstairs."

"Are you kidding me? You know I can't see her again."

"Sorry, but I'm not going to lie for you," Zoe said, walking away.

Rachel paced her room for a few minutes before building enough courage to go downstairs.

"You're the last person I expected to see, I thought you were still angry at me," Rachel said, jumping off the last two steps.

"I'm not angry with you, Rachel, I'm angry at myself. I had no right to have any kind of expectations from you, I've been trying to call you and you haven't returned my calls."

"This isn't a good time for me."

"Shall I come back later?"

Rachel shook her head. "No."

"Is this all because I came on a bit strong? If it is, that's why I'm here, to apologise."

"You didn't do anything wrong."

"Then what is it?" Kathryn ventured nervously.

Rachel winced. "Just some stuff that's come up."

"Oh."

"It's kind of personal." When Rachel felt her emotions threatening to overwhelm her, she took a few seconds to compose herself by busying herself, tidying the room.

"So it has nothing to do with us?" Kathryn's curiosity was heightened, as her eyes followed her.

"Not directly, no."

"Okay I'm really confused now."

"It's nothing really."

"It doesn't sound like nothing, Rachel. I thought … even before this happened, that we were friends, we could talk to each other."

Rachel turned to look at her. "We could, we can."

Stepping towards her and taking her hands, Kathryn said, "So why are you blocking me out?"

Unable to look into her eyes, Rachel turned her head. "Because, it's not that easy."

"Okay, I'm not going to pressure you into telling me what it is, just know that I'm there if you ever need me."

Releasing her hands, Kathryn walked towards the front door.

"Kathryn, wait!"

She stopped, her hand hovering above the handle.

"It's best you see for yourself."

Kathryn followed Rachel into a small box room, which was used as an office. On top of the metallic desk lay a cream folder. Scooping it up, Rachel handed it to her, then leaned against the edge of the desk and watched as Kathryn opened the folder and began to read. She guessed she had gotten the gist of the story when she looked up at her, eyes wide and her face ghost white.

"Oh my God, Rachel, I'm so sorry," she said, the words stumbling from her mouth "When ... how did you find out?"

"A few days ago."

Unable to speak, Kathryn moved towards her but Rachel stood, wrapping her arms around her chest, creating an invisible barrier between them, stopping Kathryn in her tracks.

"It's no biggie, really, I don't remember any of it."

"But ... it still must have come as a big shock." Kathryn's voice caught with emotion.

"Yeah, well, I'm a big girl, I can take care of myself."

"Cos that's the way it's always been, huh? Never letting anyone in, always being the strong one."

Rachel shrugged her shoulders noncommittally, her eyes leaving Kathryn's face.

Kathryn held out the folder. "If you won't let me in, there's nothing I can do."

"There isn't anything anyone can do, it's in the past — it's over, nothing will bring my dad back. What happened can't be undone." Rachel took the folder from Kathryn and dropped it on the desk.

Kathryn shook her head. "I wish there was something I could say."

"There isn't." Rachel knew every word she spoke was a lie, but what choice did she have? She would rather Kathryn be angry at her for pushing her away, then hate her for deceiving her. She could see the bewilderment in her eyes as Kathryn turned, stopping halfway, as if she had something to say then changing her mind. Silently, she walked out of the office and to the front door, closing it quietly behind her.

Rachel stood rooted to the spot for several minutes before dragging a chair out from underneath her desk and collapsing into it. "Can this get any worse?" she said out loud as she leaned her forehead against the palms of her hands. "What am I going to do?"

"What you're going to do," Zoe said from the doorway, making Rachel nearly jump out of skin. "Is go to her, and tell her the truth, the real truth!"

"I can't, Zoe, I just can't."

"Rachel, she loves you. It takes a strong woman to do what she did today, she came to you with her heart on her sleeve and you rejected her, but she still wanted to be there for you. I think if you explain to her what happened, she'll forgive you ... in time."

"Do you think so?" Rachel looked at her.

"Yes, I do, but you need to do it sooner rather than later. If the truth is going to come out, it's better it comes from your mouth rather than Gareth's."

Rachel took a deep breath as she contemplated Zoe's words. She had never been so scared in her life.

"Ok," she said as she stood, "I'll tell her."

"Good." Zoe put her hand out to stop her before she left. "Just remember she's going to be angry with you, and rightly so, but I think when she comes to terms with it, she'll understand."

"I hope so," Rachel said.

***

Rachel's finger trembled as she pressed the sliver button, her heart skipping a beat when she heard Kathryn's voice from behind the door.

"Hello."

"It's Rachel."

After a few moments, the door flew open and Kathryn stood there.

"I'm sorry," Rachel said, moving in to embrace her. They held each other, Kathryn planting kisses on her head.

"It's okay, we'll get through this, I promise," Kathryn said, leaning back to look into her eyes. "Come on, come in. We'll freeze to death out here," she said, taking her by the hand, holding her close by.

They stood in the hallway as Rachel removed her jacket, Kathryn leaned in towards her, dropping a soft lingering kiss on her mouth.

"Hmmm," Rachel groaned, wrapping her arms around her waist, pulling her in for a deeper kiss.

Kathryn laughed, pulling away. "Later."

"No," Rachel pouted. "Now."

"We can't," Kathryn whispered, holding her at bay with her hands against her chest.

"Why are we whispering?" Rachel asked in a hushed voice, smiling at their little game.

"Because," Kathryn said, kissing her once more before nodding towards the front room door. "Gareth's here."

Rachel's mouth fell open.

"Don't worry, I was just in the process of telling him about you. Not that I thought there was going to be an us but I was going to tell him I couldn't go back to him because ..." She paused, looking into her eyes as if gauging if it was safe to tell her. "Because I was in love with someone else."

Rachel remained unresponsive, still shocked to the core by this unexpected situation.

"Has the cat got your tongue?"

Finding her voice, Rachel finally spoke, "There's something I have to tell you first."

"I'm not expecting you to say you love me too, I —"

"No, it's not that. I mean I do ... love you, that is." Rachel stopped talking — she had said it without even realising — she loved her, with every fibre of her body, but their love could never be pure if she didn't tell her the truth.

"You do!"

"Yes, very much."

"Well, aren't you two quite the love birds," Gareth said as he leaned against the door frame, watching them.

"Gareth, how long have you been standing there?" Kathryn asked, spinning round to face him.

"Long enough," he said.

"I'm sorry, Gareth, I was going to tell you all about it."

"And what's *it*? This is what you left me for?" he said, nodding at Rachel, who was leaning flat up against the wall.

"Not exactly. I left because our marriage wasn't working anymore and, if the truth be known, it never had."

"The truth," he said, looking up in the air, letting out a harsh laugh. "We've all got some home truths to tell, haven't we?" He lowered his gaze to look directly at Rachel. "*Pandora!*"

Kathryn looked between them both. "What are you talking about?" she asked, confused.

"Do you want to tell her or shall I?" Gareth asked.

"Look, Gareth, it doesn't have to be like this," Rachel urged.

"Doesn't it? Do you really think I'm going to let you end up with my wife?"

"Please don't tell her like this," Rachel begged, tears rimming her eyes.

"Tell me what?" Kathryn asked. "Gareth, Rachel — what's going on?"

Rachel turned to her. "Nothing, nothing's going on."

"Isn't there?" he growled.

"Tell me what? What's going on here?" Kathryn asked again, looking at them both for answers.

"I'm sorry, Kathryn," Rachel said.

"Sorry for what? Will someone please tell me!" Kathryn pleaded, her eyes darting from one to the other.

"Go on, Rachel, tell her. Tell how you accidently met her in the bar that first night, tell her why you befriended her. How you searched the Internet looking for horny women to fuck."

Kathryn looked towards Rachel, who lowered her head in shame. "What's he talking about, is it true?"

"Yes, it's true." His voice echoed throughout the hallway. "It was so you could get your lesbian lust satisfied by this slut, who shags anything that moves. You were just another one on a long list."

Kathryn stood still, stunned.

"That's not true, Kathryn. You've got to believe me. I was just going to flirt with you, but I fell in love."

Kathryn turned to Gareth. "How do you know about all of this?"

"Because I set the whole thing up."

"You set me up?"

"Yes, I knew you wanted sex with a woman, so I gave you *that*." He pointed at Rachel.

Kathryn blinked as the enormity of the situation sank in. "You both toyed with my life, and you," she said to Rachel, "how could you do this to me?"

"I'm sorry ...."

"I want you to leave," Kathryn said.

"Please just let me explain"

"I said I want you to leave now!"

Obediently Rachel opened the door and walked through it. She turned to say something as the tears streamed down her cheeks.

"Just go," Kathryn shouted at her before slamming the door behind her. "I can't believe that you could have done something like that to me," she said, turning to face Gareth, her voice shaking in disbelief.

"Oh, you're a fine one to talk. You didn't exactly fight her off, did you?" Gareth said squaring up to her.

"But why? Why would you do this to me?"

"Because you were unhappy, that's why. Because I knew I couldn't give you what you wanted, what you *needed*. I'm not stupid, Kathryn. I knew you married me for security and not for love and that was enough for me but it wasn't enough for you in the end." His voice faltered, and he tilted his head upwards, tears rolling down either side of his face.

He looked pitiful, and her heart went out to him. The anger she felt for him diminished. She went to his side and wrapped her arms around him, letting him rest his head on her shoulder. She thought of all the years they had wasted in a loveless marriage, Gareth as much as her. Neither of them had been happy, but they had both soldiered on regardless and she had inadvertently reduced this wonderful, caring man to going on websites looking for another woman to make her happy. She didn't know whether to laugh or cry at the absurdity of the situation.

"I'm sorry, Gareth, I really am," she said, taking responsibility for her own part of this mess. If only she had just left him when she realised there was no hope for their relationship. Didn't that make her just as bad as him? Wasn't she just as deceitful?

"Do you forgive me?" he asked boyishly, hope in his eyes.

"If you can forgive me," she said, releasing him from their embrace and standing back to look at him.

"Of course I can, I'd forgive anything of you. I really did do it because I love you."

"I know you believe you do, Gareth."

"So can we go back to how things were and put her behind us?"

Kathryn walked into the living room, closely followed by Gareth, and sat on the edge of the sofa. The place where she had rediscovered a part of herself. "I'm sorry, but there's no going back."

"But you said —" A look of confusion spread across his features.

"I know what I said and it's the truth. It's because of the lies I told myself that I created this whole sordid mess."

"You need me, Kathryn, you always have and you always will. Do you think a woman can offer you the security I give you?"

She could hear the desperation in his voice but nothing could make her return to him now. Despite the revelations, she now knew what love was. Even if she wasn't going to be with Rachel, she would no longer settle for less.

"You told me that story for so long I grew to believe

it." She shook her head sadly. "And we both suffered for believing that lie."

"How did things come to this?"

"Some things are just meant to be," she said sadly as she watched him lower his head like a broken man, the fight knocked out of him. "Are you going to be okay?"

He looked up at her, pride in his eyes. "Yes, I'll have to be. Lilly has invited me to spend the holidays with her and the kids in the South of France."

"You do know she's in love with you." Kathryn smiled.

"Can you blame her?" he half joked.

"No, I don't. Whoever you fall in love with is going to be a very lucky woman."

"You don't have to say that."

"I mean it. None of this had anything to do with you as a person, you are one of the kindest sweetest men I've ever known."

"Enough, I won't be able to get my head out the door if you carry on."

"I just want you to be happy."

"So where do we go from here?"

Kathryn lowered her gaze. She didn't want to see his eyes when she delivered the final blow. "Start divorce proceedings."

He walked to the door and turned. She could see by the way he looked at her that he had accepted it was over. "So that's it, you're going to be with ... her."

"I didn't say that, I can understand your motives but I can't understand hers." And she couldn't. Rachel had ample opportunity to tell her the truth. Hell, if she had told her the first night they met, she might have even been able to laugh it off — but to know that she'd shared so much of herself with Rachel, in and out of bed, and she still didn't tell her, well, that was unforgiveable.

CHAPTER 40

Sunlight permeated through the dense tangled branches of the oak trees that lined the street, patches of golden light hitting the ground. What had started out as a twenty-minute walk had soon turned into an hour, as Kathryn struggled to find an answer to the question that had refused to go away — what was she going to do? She was no closer to an answer now than she had been the previous night. Had everything that she had with Rachel been a lie? She couldn't bring herself to believe that but the facts did seem to speak for themselves. She turned onto her street, glancing at her watch, before quickening her pace — if she didn't get a move on she would be late for her first appointment of the day, and she needed the distraction more than anything. Minutes later, she was at her front door, withdrawing her keys from her pocket. As she inserted her key into the lock, she froze when she felt a hand on her shoulder.

"Kathryn."

Kathryn's heart stopped as she recognised the voice. She forced herself to turn around, immediately noting Rachel's eyes welling up, her bottom lip quivering.

"You scared me," Kathryn said, letting out a deep breath, trying to keep her voice even.

"I'm sorry ... can we talk?" Rachel asked, rubbing her

hands together.

"I have nothing to say to you." Kathryn turned back to the door, her hand pressing against it.

"Kathryn, please wait, just let me explain."

"What on earth could you tell me that could make what you did alright?" Kathryn shook her head, holding the door open ajar with her foot.

"This might sound pathetic, but this had nothing to do with you."

Kathryn mulled over it for a few seconds. "You're right, it does sound pathetic."

"But it's true."

"Are you serious? I was played for a fool yet this has nothing to do with me?" Kathryn felt her cheeks flush with anger.

Rachel met her eyes with regret. "I swear, the plan was off as soon as I met you, and I told Gareth. I made a mistake and I'm sorry. What would you have done in my position?"

Kathryn shrugged her shoulders. "I wouldn't have been in your position in the first place. Nothing you say is going to make a difference."

"So that's it?"

"Yes, that's it."

"Please don't end things like this, I love you." Rachel reached out and touched her.

Kathryn almost laughed as she felt her stomach tense. "I don't need your type of love. I'm sure you will easily find someone else on the website you frequent."

Rachel winced. "I don't do that anymore. I haven't been on that site since I met you."

"Well, maybe you should, you seem to be very good

at it." Kathryn pushed the door open and stepped inside. As she heard Rachel's footsteps retreating from her door, the tears began to tumble down her cheeks.

## CHAPTER 41

Everyone had left the office for the day except for Kathryn and Carol. Carol picked up her phone and buzzed Kathryn's office. She spoke briefly to tell her Rachel's flatmate Zoe wanted to see her.

"Kathryn will see you now," Carol said. "Down the hall, it's the first door on the left."

Kathryn looked up at the door as it opened.

"I thought you wouldn't see me?"

Kathryn frowned slightly. "Why not? You're not the one who betrayed me."

Zoe gave a sad shake of her head. "Rachel was right then, she said you wouldn't ever forgive her," Zoe said, walking over to her desk. "Do you mind if I sit down?"

"Feel free." Kathryn waited until she was seated. "Did she send you here?"

"No, she didn't, I came of my own accord."

"There's nothing you can tell me that will change my mind."

"I'm not here to change your mind, I'm just here to tell you the truth. What you choose to do with it is your decision."

Kathryn leaned back in her chair, taking the time to study Zoe — she could understand why Rachel was close friends with her, she seemed like a genuine person.

"First of all, let me be clear that I am not making excuses for her. What she did with your husband was despicable, there's no way around that." Zoe's neutral expression softened. "But you have to understand where Rachel was coming from — her whole life, until a few years ago, was all about caring for her mother. She didn't have a normal life in the sense that she never did the normal things young people do. She never dated, it was all about her mum. Knowing Rachel, if she had the choice to do it all again she would, because that's the kind of person she is."

"I can believe that," Kathryn said softly.

Encouraged, Zoe continued, "When her mum went into the home, it was like letting a bird free from a cage," she said, smiling. "Yes, she was a bit of a player but the people she got involved with were willing participants. She never made any promises and she never broke any, which brings me to you."

Kathryn shifted in her seat, crossing her arms as she did.

"At first she thought she was just going to be helping out someone in need —"

"But —"

Zoe held up her hand. "I'm not saying that was the only reason she went through with it, but it was one of them. But after meeting you, her feelings changed."

"So why didn't she tell me the truth?"

"That's something I can't answer — embarrassed, ashamed, I don't know."

"Why are you telling me all this? Why does it that matter now?"

"Because she loves you and she needs you. I might be

just guessing, but I think you love her too."

"What do you expect me to do?"

"I don't expect you to do anything. I just thought you would appreciate hearing it from a third party."

"And now you've told me, what do you think I should do?"

"If you're asking me if I think you should forgive her, I would say yes. If you're lucky enough to find genuine love, I would grab it with both hands and never let go."

"Is that your professional opinion?"

"Yes," Zoe smiled, "and you just got it for free."

\*\*\*

When Kathryn closed her eyes she could picture Rachel's face etched in pain as she demanded to hear her side of the story. She surmised the sorrow in Rachel's eyes would have been hard to fake. Could she be telling the truth? That what had started off as a meaningless act had turned into something they both hadn't expected. *They had fallen in love.*

Kathryn rubbed her forehead with the tips of her fingers, as if doing so could rid her of the pain, that ache that seemed to be a constant companion. She had only seen an honesty in Rachel that was so rare. She didn't hide her true self. What you saw was what you got. The combined sense of hurt and betrayal began to ebb away as she recalled the touching moments of her interview when she had laid herself open to Rachel without any fear.

She was going to trust her gut instinct which told her Rachel was telling her the truth. Kathryn went over the scenario of their first meeting in her head. Rachel had not made any advances towards her. In fact she had just been friendly, and Kathryn was completely unaware at that point that Rachel was even gay. She hadn't probed her for information outside the scope of her work life. In a moment of weakness she couldn't help but wonder what the future held for her if she turned her back on Rachel and never gave their relationship a chance. *Rachel had said she loved her*. She had said it from her own free will. She stood resolutely. She wasn't going to make the same mistake again and travel down the road of restraint. It was time to throw caution to the wind and follow her heart. The nagging doubt that it might be too late to make things right with Rachel was short lived when her mobile began to ring.

She flipped open her phone. "Hello," she said.

"It's me," Rachel said. "Please, I need to talk to you. I need to explain everything. We can't leave things like this — I don't want to lose you."

"Where are you?"

"I'm outside your office."

Several moments later, Kathryn opened the street door to her office. Rachel stood there with her hands stuffed in her pockets.

Kathryn stepped back and remained silent as Rachel entered and closed the door behind her. Rachel tugged her hand through her hair, her eyes downcast and sad. "Thank you for seeing me," she said, slouching against the door.

Kathryn wanted to go to her, to hold her in her arms and banish the look of sadness from her eyes. But she remained rooted to the floor. She had to hear Rachel's side of things before she gave herself to her completely. The air had to be cleared once and for all. She didn't want what had happened to remain the focus of their relationship.

"What happened was not how your husband made it out to be Kathryn."

"Soon to be ex-husband you mean," Kathryn

interrupted.

A slight smile reached Rachel's lips before she carried on. "Yes, I went on dating sites and yes, I may have been a little flirtatious."

At this Kathryn cocked her head and raised her eyebrows

"Okay, okay, I wasn't a saint."

Rachel held up her hands. "But I had no reason to be. I was single and relationships were the last thing on my mind. When ...." She smiled. "... Your soon to be ex contacted me, there is no way in this world I could have imagined that this would have happened. I was meant to do a little flirting with you then report back. As simple as that. I wasn't supposed to seduce you and take you to bed like he said. He just wanted to know if his suspicions were right."

"But why didn't you just tell me the truth?"

"Because I didn't want to lose you. The night we met, I went home and emailed Gareth straight away. I told him nothing happened. I then deleted my account from the site. I wanted nothing more to do with it. If I could turn back the clock I would but I can't, so all you have is my word that I love you and I would never lie to you again."

"If that's all you've got that will have to do," Kathryn said, stepping towards her and raising her hand to smooth back Rachel's hair.

Rachel's eyes widened. "Does this mean what I think it means?"

Kathryn nodded as she drew Rachel's face near as a burning desire swept through her. Within seconds, their lips found their way instinctively to each other. The kiss sealed what she knew her heart had been telling her all along.

"So where do we go from here?" Rachel asked softly.

Kathryn looked her over seductively, then took her by the hand and led her up the stairs. "I've always wanted to try out the sofa in my office," she said to the woman who had unlocked her heart and soul.

Rachel laughed. "You're crazy."

"Only about you Rachel."

Printed in Great
Britain
by Amazon